THE LOYAL STAR

A JACK SAGE WESTERN

DONALD L. ROBERTSON

Edited by
PAULINE NOLET

Illustrated by
DAMONZA.COM

COPYRIGHT

The Loyal Star

Copyright © 2025 Donald L. Robertson
CM Publishing, LLC

All rights reserved. No part of this publication may be reproduced, distributed or transmitted in any form or by any means, including photocopying, recording, or other electronic or mechanical methods, without the prior written permission of the publisher, except in the case of brief quotations embodied in critical reviews and certain other noncommercial uses permitted by copyright law.

Publisher's Note: This is a work of fiction. Names, characters, and incidents are a product of the author's imagination. Locales and public names are sometimes used for atmospheric purposes. Any resemblance to actual people, living or dead, or to businesses, companies, or events, is completely coincidental. For information contact:

Books@DonaldLRobertson.com

ISBN: 979-8-9912601-3-8

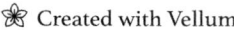 Created with Vellum

1

October 12, 1875

Civilization's not far ahead, Jack Sage thought. His mind drifted to the wagon master he had spoken with at Fort Gibson. He was leading a late train of wagons headed for Denver, where they'd winter before pushing across the mountains.

He pulled his slicker tighter around him. Cold raindrops fell from the brim of his gray Stetson. Dark clouds brushed the skeleton-like tops of the leafless black walnut trees. Larger drops accumulated on the thick limbs above him until, swollen and heavy, they tore from the rough bark to fall and splatter on the slicker across his thick shoulders. Shattering into smaller droplets, they smashed against his exposed neck between bandanna and hat, some striking the old rope scar and causing forever-damaged nerves to tingle in revolt.

Silence followed him along the forested river, broken only by the patter of the falling rain and the soft clump of horses' hooves on the soaked, leaf-covered ground. The musty smell of soaked trees and the rotting carpet of leaves along the riverbed drifted up, through the falling raindrops, to offend Jack's senses. He patted his big grulla's neck and smoothed the long black mane lying soaked against its soft gray coat. He checked the other three, two horses and a mule, trailing along on their leads. The animals, tired from the long trail from Wyoming, plodded along the forested river bottom. Their heads hung low, bobbing slowly as they followed Jack and Smokey on lead ropes dripping water like the limbs above. Like him, they were used to open rangeland, hills and mountains, not the tight, suffocating feel of the thick forest.

"It won't be long, boys, and you'll be able to rest up in a dry stable."

Only Stonewall the mule, which had been with Jack and his grulla, Smokey, since Mexico, tilted his head and shot a quick glance at the big man. His stare was broken when the big head jerked up and stared in the direction they were traveling, ears forward and twitching. All three horses followed suit.

Jack had heard it too. Using his right hand, he unbuttoned the lower three buttons of his slicker, reached beneath it, and slipped the loops from both of his .44-caliber Smith & Wesson Americans. Out of habit, he moved the revolver in his right holster just enough to make sure it rested easy and loose and continued walking the horses forward.

Voices could be heard down the trail. He couldn't make out what was being said, but he recognized they came from several men. Two sounded sharp and demanding. There was another speaking in low persuasive tones.

Though all of the leaves were gone except for the deep green of a few loblolly pines, the birches and thick trunks of the black walnuts obscured the trail ahead.

If there was an argument going on, Jack didn't want to surprise the men and face a hail of bullets. In this country, some men shot first and asked questions after the gun smoke cleared. He started whistling "Silver Threads Among the Gold." He wasn't the best whistler in the world, since he couldn't abide music. At the first note, the voices ceased, and a heavy silence met his off-key ballad. He continued along the winding trail. Trees thrust high to his right and left. The Arkansas River softly murmured beyond the trees to his right.

Suddenly the trail swung around a thicket of redbud and a wide-trunked black walnut, and he was confronted by four husky wet mules pulling a prairie schooner. It was driven by a wide-shouldered younger man. A handsome woman of similar age sat alongside him, holding tight to a heavily wrapped baby, while two little boys gawked from under the wagon's bonnet. The cold gleam of a rifle muzzle poked above the man's leg between the seat and the side of the wagon. Almost totally blocked from view, on the narrow trail, Jack could see two additional wagons behind the first.

Four heavily bearded mounted men, horses facing the wagons, were turned in their saddles, eyes focused on Jack from under dripping slouch hats. Grubby coats were pulled tight around them. Jack had dealt with riffraff, thieves, and killers for what seemed like his entire life, and he instantly recognized the type. He didn't know the skill level of these vermin, but he knew they were thieves and were in the process of attempting to rob these honest folks and possibly worse. He didn't like the idea of gunfire with the families so close, but in this case, it appeared inevitable.

The oldest of the robbers placed both hands on his saddle horn, leaned to the side of his horse facing Jack, moved a chew around in his overfilled cheek, and fired a stream of brown tobacco juice. It flew straight, striking an armadillo that, in his search for grubs, had wandered out of the brush onto the well-traveled road. The spittle struck the little grub hunter between its shell and right ear. It released a frightened grunt, leaped into the air, and raced across the trail, disappearing into the brush on the opposite side.

The tobacco chewer's partner, on the opposite side of the first wagon, burst out in a loud barking laugh. When he stopped, his grin exposed blackened and broken teeth. "You were dead on, Milo. Dang, brother, you don't ever miss." He paused for a moment, his beady eyes staring at Jack. "Not with that there tobaccy juice or lead."

A pleased smirk on his face, the man wiped his tobacco-stained sleeve across thick lips. "Mighty sour day for a feller to be ridin', mister. Where you headed with those fine-lookin' horses?"

Jack could see two other riders, each at the second and third wagon, ease their horses away from their respective wagons so they could get a better look at him. *Good,* he thought, *at least I have these four in sight, though two of them are partially blocked by this spitter. If I have to shoot though, their location might work in my favor, giving me a few more seconds to get to them.*

He spoke to the wagon driver and the woman, his voice conversational. "Morning, folks, I'm U.S. Marshal Jack Sage. Hope your day is going well, though I imagine this rain is a bit unpleasant. You stopped here for any special reason? Seems a mite early in the day to be contemplating pitching camp."

At Jack's mention of being a U.S. marshal, the woman's eyes lit with hope, and a slight smile tugged at her tense lips. He also noticed the two men partially blocked by Milo gave an involuntary jerk and stared at the tobacco chewer. The laugher across from his leader kept his beady eyes locked on Jack.

Milo was scowling, his thick eyebrows pulled together, forming a long dark hedge across his forehead. "I asked you a question, big man. Marshal or no marshal, it ain't proper not to answer."

Jack maintained his focus on the wagon driver though he was keeping a sharp watch on the four robbers. He gave a slight nod toward the man, prompting him to answer his question. "Sir?"

Jack could tell the fella was concerned for his family, but he spoke up.

"Marshal, we are the Franklins. I'm Jarrod, and this is my wife, Charlotte."

The woman gave Jack a small nod under her soaked blue bonnet.

"We are not planning on camping here. One of our group has been ill, and we elected to stay with him and his family until his health improved. That put us on a late start from Fort Smith. We were trying to catch up with the rest of our train when these four men accosted us. They have threatened us with bodily harm if we would not turn over all of our possessions."

When Jarrod finished speaking, Jack turned his cold gray eyes on Milo. "What do you have to say for yourself?" Jack assessed his situation. Milo was the leader, but not necessarily because he was fastest with a gun. He was big, with wide shoulders, a thick chest, and a big belly. The man across from him, whose eyes had not left Jack, had called Milo brother. This entire bunch could be related.

The other two robbers were partially hidden from Jack by the bulk of Milo and his horse, but the man across from Milo, on the opposite side of the wagon, was in the clear. His eyes hadn't left Jack since he rode up. The man's left hand hung loose to his side, hidden by the bulk of his horse, while his right gripped his reins. Jack could see no bulge of a holster under his coat on his right side. *He's left-handed and has a gun in his hand. He's also lean, unlike Milo. Odds are he'll be the fastest, and he's got the look of a gunfighter. I'll take him first.*

The slim outlaw gave Jack a broken-toothed grin, as if he could read his thoughts.

Milo pressed his hands onto the saddle horn, stretching forward over his horse's neck, and stared at the trail behind the marshal. Next, he leaned back, acting as if he were trying to look around Jack for other riders. "Don't look like you have any help, Marshal. You planning on arresting all of us?"

Jack laid an icy grin on Milo. "Only need one marshal for one pack of coyotes."

Milo's face turned red. "No man talks to me or my kin like that. Drop yore gun, and do it now."

Jack laughed at the big outlaw, the laugh ominous in the wet forest. A lone squirrel jumped in the trees, causing a blast of showers to pummel the ground. He didn't move. His grin, cold and threatening, remained on his face. "You're using my line, Milo. So let me show you how to handle a command like that." The grin disappeared, and a grim stare replaced it. "I'm United States Marshal Jack Sage, and I order you, under threat of death, to drop your guns." He raised his voice. "And that goes for you two in the back. You'll only get this one chance."

The smaller man still had his eyes locked on Jack. "Milo, you want I should kill him?"

Jack could see the beginning of fear in the big man's eyes. "Maybe we should talk about it, Joey. Why don't you holster up yore shooter."

Jack said nothing. He knew Joey was going to swing his gun up and try to kill him. His muscles felt loose, his mind clear. He must shoot straight, going first to the gunfighter, then swing across to Milo. He didn't like swinging the muzzle across the family. He'd lift it as it crossed. That would slow him a bit, but he didn't think Milo would be overly fast. *No more than two bullets for each,* he thought, *preferably one. I still have the other two behind Milo. There might not be time to draw my remaining revolver. Not a good time to be wearing my slicker.*

"I ain't holsterin' nothin'," Joey shouted. His left arm jerked.

Milo yelled, "Don't do it, Joey. I know him!"

Jack moved. Leaning hard to his left, his right hand disappeared under his slicker, emerging instantly filled with a big Smith & Wesson. Joey, probably feeling Jack would take forever drawing his revolver from under the coat, slowly and deliberately brought the Colt into view from behind his left side. His confident grin melted into wide-eyed shock when Jack's revolver appeared. Joey jerked the weapon up, striving to beat the lawman.

Too confident, Jack thought. He pulled the trigger as the muzzle, still moving up, covered the outlaw's chest. The roar of his Smith preceded the gunman's only by a fraction of a second. Smoke billowed in the clearing from the blast of the two handguns. Jack felt the whip of the bullet as it flew past his right ear. He had a momentary thought, *Good thing I leaned left.* He saw a red blotch appear at the junction of the outlaw's neck and chest. There was no second shot from the gunman. His spine severed just below the base of his skull, he collapsed from his saddle.

Jack no longer watched the dead man. The muzzle of his Smith lifted as it passed the Franklins and dropped to settle on the thick chest of the leader, but the man hadn't drawn. His hands were stretched to the sky as if he were trying to grab the heavy clouds above the treetops. The other two outlaws had thrown their hands skyward, imitating their leader. Jack relaxed the pressure on the trigger. Milo Clagg would never know how close he had come to dying. Jack, his voice still calm and commanding, punctuated the returned silence of the forest. "Like I said, drop your guns."

This time, the response was immediate. Hands carefully eased down to belt buckles, and holsters fell to the ground.

"Now keep those hands high, boys." Jack glanced to Jarrod. "You and a couple of men from the other wagons collect all their weapons. Make sure you have everything. Check behind their belts, front and back. Also check their boots."

Jarrod nodded to Jack, looped the reins around the brake handle, grabbed his Spencer, and jumped to the ground. "Yes, sir, Marshal. We'll be glad to."

Jack could see other men appearing from the wagons behind Jarrod's. Also armed with rifles, they waved and headed for the outlaws.

Milo was staring through the mules' traces at the body of his brother. He muttered in a low, disbelieving voice, "You killed him. He was one of the fastest men I've ever seen with a sixgun. But I told him not to draw. I've heard of you. There cain't be two marshals your size."

Jack glanced at the dead man. "He picked the wrong day to take his time." He turned back to Milo. "Tell me your full name and the name of your gang members."

"It's Milo Clagg. You done killed Joey Clagg. Man, he was known all over the Indian Territory."

Jack nodded toward the two mounted men beyond Clagg. "Who are they?"

"Brothers. The first one is Bo, and the big one is Flint."

Milo grunted when Jarrod ran his hand under the man's coat and pulled first a sixgun from his front and then one from behind his back. Then Jarrod pulled up one pants leg and felt around inside the boot. He pulled out a long Arkansas Toothpick, along with the sheath. Eyebrows raised, he looked across the back of Clagg's horse at Jack and dropped it into the pile. "Seems he's well armed, Marshal."

"Don't forget his rifle."

Jack watched while the family man pulled Clagg's Winchester from the scabbard, then nodded to the men disarming Bo and Flint. "Mr. Franklin, do you have a gunnysack you and your friends can drop those weapons into?"

"We sure do, Marshal. Once I get these picked up, I'll get the dead man's weapons."

"I'd be obliged."

Jarrod called to his friends, "Sack those weapons, and bring them here when you're finished."

The wagon men and several strapping boys waved back.

The older of the two Franklin boys whipped around, disappeared inside the wagon, and reemerged with an empty sack. He leaned around the side of the wagon and handed it down to Jarrod, who took it with a nod. "Thank you, son."

Jack's attention was drawn to Charlotte, who sat white-faced, trying to comfort the baby, who was still screaming from the blasts of the guns. After getting the sack, the two boys tried to climb onto the seat next to her so they could see better what was going on, but Charlotte shooed them back. Now they were in their original position, eyes wide and switching back and forth between their pa and the big marshal sitting on the grulla.

"Ma'am, I'm mighty sorry this had to happen in front of you and your children."

She raised her eyes to Jack. They were pretty brown eyes, still wide from the shock of the sudden action and death in front of her. "Marshal Sage, please don't apologize." She turned and glared at Milo Clagg. "He should be the one apologizing, frightening my children like he did."

The older boy, who had gotten the sack, spoke up from behind her. "I wasn't scared, Ma. If'n I had a gun, I woulda shot that feller myself."

Charlotte's head snapped around. "Hush your mouth, Elijah Robert Franklin. You'll take no human life. Talk like that will get your mouth washed out with lye soap. Is that what you want?"

The boy looked down at the wagon floor, shook his head, and muttered softly, "No, ma'am."

Charlotte turned back to Jack. "I'm sorry, Marshal. Elijah is sometimes a bit precocious."

Jack had been having a difficult time keeping a straight face. He had also been surprised at the rapid and sharp response from Mrs. Franklin. She must be older than she looked. "Yes, ma'am, I understand. Though it might be hard to imagine, I was a boy once myself."

Jack could see the woman's expression momentarily change to disgust. It was quickly replaced with sadness as she glanced at the younger gunfighter on the ground. He could almost read the mother's thoughts, and it brought him a somber feeling. *The thought gives her fear her son might grow up like me.* He nodded to himself. *I don't blame her. It would scare any mother.*

Jarrod and the two other men carrying sacks walked forward. The boys followed, with the rifles, and Jarrod Franklin spoke up. "We've got all of their guns and knives, Marshal. Every one of them had a knife in his boot. One of them had a knife and a derringer. These must really be bad men."

Jack kept his eyes on the now disarmed outlaws. He had reloaded and holstered his revolver and pulled his Winchester from its scabbard. His left hand held Smokey's reins and the rifle at the small of the stock, with the butt resting on his thigh, muzzle up. "You're right, Mr. Franklin, I believe they are very bad men. That's why I'm taking them on to Fort Smith. How far do I have to go?"

Jarrod jerked his head toward their back trail. "Not far, Marshal. No more than two, maybe three miles down the road. I imagine if it wasn't raining, they would have heard the shooting in town, and we'd have riders coming up soon. You need some help taking them in?"

Jack shook his head. "No, but thanks. If you'll tie those sacks on my horses and mule and tie the rifles behind me, you folks can be on your way."

Jarrod Franklin turned and nodded at the dead gunman. "What about him?"

"You checked him closely for weapons?"

"Yes, sir, I sure did."

"Then leave him. You've got quite a ways to go. I talked to the wagon master of your train this morning. They were preparing to pull out of Fort Gibson, so it'll probably take you several days to catch up to them, and you're traveling through Indian territory."

"Thanks, Marshal," Franklin said, tying his sack on Stonewall. The other men tied their sacks and, with their boys, hurried back to their wagons. Jarrod secured the three rifles behind Jack and turned for his. He stopped and swung around. "They would have killed us, wouldn't they?"

Grim faced, Jack stared down at the man and thought, *He needs to know the truth. Too many of these folks are used to civilized law enforcement where they don't have to worry about someone killing them and their family for no more than a dollar.* "I can't say for sure, but I've been doing this many a year. These men fill the bill. Yeah, I believe they would have killed every one of you and raped your womenfolk, young and old, before killing them. They would have also killed all of the kids so they wouldn't grow up and come after them. The war bred hard men, and some of them turned to the outlaw trail. Many have yet to be caught."

Jack wasn't surprised at the stunned look on Jarrod Franklin's face. "Mr. Franklin, you've got to be prepared. I saw your rifle up there, but it does no good sitting at your side. Have it ready. All of your family should be able to shoot, and you should have more weapons, handguns, shotguns, or smaller rifles your wife and even your sons can use." He nodded to the west. "There's some great country out there but with few lawmen. Until civilization moves west, folks have to provide their own law. Don't let strangers approach you without you being armed and ready. Now, you best get moving. You've got a long way to go."

Jarrod Franklin nodded solemnly. "Thanks again, Marshal. I reckon you saved our lives. We owe you." He turned and strode back to the wagon, stepping around the fallen outlaw. He swung up and handed the rifle to his wife. She looked at it, then to Jack, and laid it across her lap. Her husband picked up the reins, snapped them, and clucked to the mules.

The wagon jerked and started forward. As it passed, Mrs. Franklin looked into Jack's eyes and quietly said, "Thank you."

He touched his hat to her and to each of the wives in the following two wagons. Once they were past, he turned to the outlaws and lowered the muzzle of the Winchester to cover them. Three sets of eyes followed his every movement.

"You ain't gonna shoot us, are you, Marshal?" Milo Clagg asked, eyes glued on the business end of the Winchester.

"Not unless you give me a reason. Now you and the big fella load your brother on his horse and tie him tight. We're heading for Fort Smith." Jack caught a momentary pleased smirk slip across and quickly disappear from Milo's face.

Both Flint and Bo walked their horses forward, joining Milo at the body of their dead brother. All three were grim faced as Milo and Flint swung down. They carefully lifted the body, trying to keep from getting his blood on them. The two men worked quickly and in moments had their brother tied across his saddle. They stood looking at the dead gunman.

"Back on your horses, boys."

The two outlaws swung into the saddle, and Flint threw Jack a threatening look.

The continuing rain muted the sound of the Winchester's hammer cocking, but it still carried a chilling promise. Jack's voice, cold as the splattering raindrops, backed it up. "The three of you need to get something straight right now. You're going into town. Whether you ride upright in your saddle or tied over it like your brother is up to you. Now get moving."

2

Jack noticed a storekeeper along the boardwalk, working in front of his store. He was returning barrels to the inside of his shop, preparing to close. The man had stopped to stare at the procession.

Jack ordered the outlaws to hold up. The three stopped their horses, and he addressed the storekeeper. "Evening, friend. Can you tell me where I can find the jail?"

The storekeeper remained well under the roof that extended to the edge of the boardwalk, protecting himself from the steady rain. He wore a white shirt, now stained with sweat. Garters pulled tight over his upper sleeves to keep his cuffs high. He pointed down the street. "At the first street, take a left. You can't miss it. It's by the courthouse. Is that Joey Clagg tied on that bay?"

"Thanks, mister." Jack turned to the three men ahead of him. "You heard him. Get moving."

Hooves splashed and sucked in the muddy street as the outlaws led the way. Reaching the first street, they made the turn without Jack having to say a word. No one was braving the rain. Jack could see faces staring from behind windows as they passed, but their curiosity wasn't strong enough to bring them outside.

He saw the courthouse first. Just past it a sign proclaimed the marshal's office, and next to it was a low building, evidently the jail. "Tie your horses in front of the marshal's office and get down."

Milo looked back at Jack. "What do you aim to do?"

Get rid of you, Jack thought. Ignoring Milo, he watched the office door open and three men step out. The last man moved past the first two and slogged through the mud to Joey Clagg's body. He grabbed a handful of hair and lifted, examining the face.

He stared for a couple of seconds, lowered the head, and turned to Jack. "Reckon he won't be killing any more helpless folks. You kill him?"

Jack nodded. "I did. Name's Jack Sage. I'd be obliged to get these fellas off my hands."

Jack could see the momentary surprise on the man's face. Beneath his soaked hat, the man's forehead wrinkled, and his mustache, following the corners of his mouth, rose. "I'm U.S. Deputy Marshal Leon Nesbit. Marshal Berry and Judge Bell are expecting you. The judge said in this weather he'll be sleeping in his office, and to send you by as soon as you come in."

Jack was cold and short on patience. He had been in this rain for two days. He'd had a gunfight, killed a man, and had to herd these varmints into town. The last thing he was going to do was to submit to a judge's demands with night coming on. He needed food, rest, and dry clothes. Plus, he wanted to get his animals sheltered and fed.

He pointed at Joey Clagg. "Deputy, I don't care what you do with the dead man. The live ones are now your prisoners. They need locking up. I've got their guns on my animals. Have your men get them, and let the judge know I'll see him in the morning." He turned and pointed at the rifles behind him. "These are their rifles."

Under his narrow-brimmed hat, Deputy Nesbit's eyebrows pulled together, and his lips pursed. "I'll be glad to take the prisoners and the weapons off your hands, but Judge Bell ain't a patient man. When he says he wants to see you when you arrive, that's just what he means."

"You've delivered the message, Deputy. I've received and understand the orders. Now, if you'll get those gunnysacks off my animals and have one of your men grab these rifles, I'll be taking my horses to the stable, finding a dry room, and getting a hot meal. If I haven't fallen asleep in my plate by that time, I might go see the judge, but my guess is I'll see him in the morning."

Marshal Nesbit waved one of his men to the rifles and the other to the gunnysacks. The deputy heading for the rifles reached Smokey and placed his hands on the rifles. Jack jerked the remaining piggin' string, the deputy's hands slipped on the wet metal, and the four rifles plummeted to the mud, splattering both the deputy and Nesbit. The two men jumped back and stared at the rifles buried in the thick mud. Nesbit finally spoke up, his voice loud and harsh. "Pick 'em up. A little mud ain't gonna hurt you."

The deputy gave Jack a sour look, bent, and fished all four rifles out of the mud. The other deputy, a wide grin on his face, untied the sacks, and with their loads, the two headed for the office.

The outlaws had been watching Nesbit. He jerked his head toward the office, and they hurried into the building.

Nesbit glanced up at Jack. "Don't say I didn't warn you. By the way, Winthrop's Stables is straight ahead on your left. I recommend the place. Pauly's a good guy. It's big, so you won't miss it." He wheeled and marched through the rain and mud to his office. Jack swung Smokey around and continued along the street. He was cold and felt a bit guilty about the rifles dropping into the mud. He sure hadn't planned on that happening.

The rain had strengthened, beating with unrelenting force against his hat and slicker, giving no indication of letting up. From under the wide brim of his soaked Stetson, he spotted a welcome sight. A large gray building with a corral to one side and a tall, wide front door. If he tilted his head slightly against the rain, he could just make out a sign on the door, Winthrop's Stables. The door was closed, but Jack could see light coming from the single window along the front at the far end of the livery. He rode Smokey to the big door and banged on it with a gloved hand. A face appeared at the window, then immediately disappeared. Moments later the door began to roll.

Jack, Smokey, and the other animals had moved as close to the door as they could get. The wind was from the northeast, and the structure gave them small protection, but even a little was welcome.

Light glistened over the street as the door slid open, reflecting off puddles and rivulets working their way through the muddy thoroughfare.

A middle-aged man, favoring one leg, pushed against the door, causing it to groan and slowly move. "Git yourself in this here stable, big feller. Looks like you and yore beasts are plumb soaked."

Jack rode into the welcome dry warmth of the stable, his animals pushing in close behind him. He swung to the ground, Smokey giving a long sigh. He patted the horse on the neck. "I know, boy, it's been a tough day. How about a cookie for your hard work?"

At the word cookie, the big grulla turned his head and nuzzled Jack's slicker. Unbuttoning and pulling his slicker out of the way, Jack reached into a coat pocket and extracted a large cookie. It was made of ground carrots, oatmeal, apples, and molasses to hold it together. The animals loved them. He held it out to Smokey. The big head dipped, lips pulled back, and teeth gently lifted it from his palm. At the sight and smell of the cookie, the other horses and mule pushed forward.

"Alright, alright, give me a chance to find one for you." His hand returned to the pocket and pulled out three more, giving one to each, Pepper his big chestnut, Thunder his gray, and Stonewall his mule.

"Don't mind me," the stableman called as he labored to push the big door closed against the driving rain. "I'll take care of this here door, as long as you and your animals are nice and dry. You just stand right there."

Jack hurried to give the man a hand. When he threw his shoulder into it, the door picked up speed.

"Not too fast, big fella. I don't want it to come off those rails. It's a bother to rehang, especially in this weather."

Jack let up enough for it to slow, and the door gently closed, sliding into its slotted facing. Straightening, he gave the man a wry grin. "Sorry." He nodded toward the horses and mule. "Those boys have traveled a long way and were in this for the last two days. I wanted to give them a treat, and I honestly forgot about you."

The man grinned. "Well, shoot, feller, I'll take one myself if they're that good."

Jack pulled one out and handed it to the man. "Fact is, mister, they're real good. I eat them on the trail when I'm hungry."

The man took it with his left and held out his right hand. "Name's Paul Winthrop. Folks around here call me Pauly." He took a bite, turned, and picked up Stonewall's and Thunder's lead ropes. Around a mouthful of cookie, he said, "Let's get these darlin's some feed and get 'em dried off."

"I'm Jack Sage, U.S. Marshal. Mighty fine meeting you, especially since you have such a nice dry barn."

His response was greeted by a deep chuckle. "Yeah, it's amazing how much folks appreciate a stable when the weather's bad."

Jack picked up Smokey's reins and the lead for Pepper and led them into two adjacent stalls. He concentrated on getting the gear off Smokey. He could hear Pauly stripping Stonewall.

"Tack room's over by the office. Yore stuff'll be safe in there however long you want to leave it."

Jack had begun wiping Smokey down. The horse was soaked, and though the barn had felt warm when they first arrived, it was feeling colder. *I'll get blankets on these boys before I leave,* Jack thought. "Pauly, what can you tell me about Deputy Marshal Nesbit?"

Pauly didn't stop working. He talked while he worked. "Nesbit's a fine feller. He takes some proddin' to get his mad on, but when he does, look out. He's honest and a good man with a gun."

"What about Marshal Berry?"

The stableman chuckled. "You mean Strawberry?" He noticed Jack's puzzled frown and laughed. "Don't you go callin' him that. His first name is Strawn, and he just naturally got the handle of Strawberry. Growing up, it caused a lot of fights." He shook his head, his mouth still spread with a wide grin. "He still doesn't like it, but he's another good man. He's tough as nails. There ain't no backup in him, but like Leon Nesbit, he's honest. A real churchgoing man. But don't let that fool you. He'll shoot or hang an outlaw without flinching."

Pauly worked swiftly drying Stonewall. The wet mule occasionally pushed a side or hip against the rough cloth, clearly enjoying the rubdown.

Jack continued working on Smokey. "Pauly, what's a hotel and a good hash house you can recommend? I'm a mighty hungry man."

"I can set you straight on that. The Palace Hotel is the best in town." He moved to Thunder, stopped, and looked across the top of the stable wall. "But it's also the priciest. Depending on what kind of room you get, it can set you back anywhere from three to seven dollars a day. Now if you don't mind dropping a little of the fancy, you can't beat Ma Nelson's Bed and Eats. It sits right next door to the Palace. She's a fine woman, with a heart of gold. Her place is clean, and I'd eat there every day if my wife would let me."

"Sounds good to me." *I need to get cleaned up,* Jack thought, *eat, and go talk to the judge. All of that sounds good except the last part. I'm not up to a longwinded discussion tonight.* Jack shook his head. He was tired, and even though President Grant had emphasized the importance of giving the new judge a hand, he still wanted to get back to Texas. Fortunately, President Grant, in their last meeting, had assured him when this was over he could hang up the badge. Just the thought brought a lighter feeling.

He finished Pepper and straightened. With both hands on his waist, he leaned as far to the rear as his stiff back would allow. The popping was audible. Next, he tilted his upper body from side to side.

Pauly was watching his antics. "Been in the saddle for a while?"

Jack turned to Pauly and grinned. "Too long, and I'm not getting any younger."

Pauly's wide face broke into a knowing grin. "Reckon I know what you're saying. I ain't got the get up and go I had twenty years ago, but what I've lost in steam, I make up for in smarts."

Jack nodded and looked around. "You have any blankets? These boys have put in a long wet day, and with this rain, I don't want them to get chilled."

"I sure do." He gave Jack an apologetic look. "They'll cost you a nickel each a day. It costs to get 'em washed."

"More than fair." Jack pulled out a twenty-dollar gold piece. "I'm thinking I'll be here for quite a time. This should do for a start. If you would make sure they have all the water, oats, and hay they need, I'd be much obliged. They've earned it."

Pauly took the gold coin and held it up in the light. "Gold is mighty pretty." He dropped it into a front pocket. "I'll take good care of your animals. If you don't mind my saying, it looks like they've come a long way. They're good-looking stock, but they've lost themselves a bunch of weight."

Jack carried his gear to the tack room, rifle tucked under his arm. Pauly followed behind with Stonewall's sawbuck packsaddle, harness, and both nearly empty panniers. After hanging his saddle over a rack, Jack began drying it.

Pauly dropped the panniers. "I'll empty those and dry out what needs it, no charge. Won't be much trouble. Looks like there's little left in them."

"Yep, just about empty. We've come a long ways."

Pauly chuckled. "Horses ain't the onliest ones who are showin' signs of a long trail. You're lookin' a little scrawny yourself."

"I aim to take care of that right now. What's the quickest way to Ma's?"

"Out my side door. That'll put you a few steps from the boardwalk and a roof. The Palace is about four buildings down. You'll pass a saloon, the Whiskey Barrel, before reaching the hotel. Right on the other side of the Palace, you'll find Ma's place."

"I'm obliged, Pauly. Thanks."

Jack picked up his rifle and saddlebags and headed for the side door. Before opening it, he pulled his hat tight on his head, brim low. Pushing the door open, he was pleased to not be met with a blast of rain. The tall building would provide him protection for a few steps. He took a deep breath and launched into the muddy alley. He was across it quickly and onto the boardwalk. Lamps from still open stores and always open saloons cast their pale light into the glimmering streets, giving him more than enough light to make his way to Ma's.

The dull thud of his boots on the sodden boards was overpowered by the rain pounding on the roofs of the town. Jack passed the Whiskey Barrel, drunken laughter, shouts, and the piano's incessant banging reminding him of the noise of civilization. He had been enveloped in the silence of the trail for almost two months. It would take getting used to the grip of humanity.

He was again bathed in light from the windows of the Palace Hotel, but was quickly past and standing at the door of Ma's Bed and Eats. Jack pushed it open, removed his hat, beating it on his leg to remove most of the water. Out of habit, he stooped to keep from ramming his head into the door facing and stepped inside to the welcome scent of hot coffee, spices, and faint perfume.

He was greeted by a middle-aged woman with an angular face and wide smile. She sat in a large blue wingback chair, her long gray dress covering legs extended and resting on a matching blue footstool. Her hands gripped two knitting needles, now stopped. Wrinkles crinkled at the edge of green eyes. Those eyes examined him, traveling from boots to face. "My, you are a big chunk of man." The smile disappeared. "And wet." Her feet went to the floor, and she dropped the knitting in a basket next to her chair. Rising gracefully, she moved to his side.

Jack became conscious of audible dripping. Water, accumulated on his slicker from the heavy rain, was now running to the bottom of the raincoat and dripping on the floor. "You're right, ma'am. Sorry about the water. I'm pretty well soaked."

"Well, let's take care of that. Give me your rifle and saddlebags, and you can remove that wet coat." She took the rifle, leaning it in a corner, and dropped Jack's saddlebags alongside it while calling, "Billy."

Moments later a young man of about twelve arrived through a hallway door. "Yes, ma'am?"

"Just a moment." She turned to Jack. "I assume you will be staying the night with us?"

"If possible. I could be here for quite a while, so I'd like a private room if you have one available."

She nodded, her graying brown curls gently rocking over her ears. "You're in luck, Mister...?"

"Sorry, ma'am, Sage, Jack Sage, U.S. marshal."

"Oh, Marshal Sage. I've been expecting you. Judge Bell said you were coming in and you might elect to stay with us. He gave you high marks, Marshal. I'm Mary Nelson. You can call me Ma or Mary, whichever you prefer. This establishment belongs to me."

"Nice to meet you, Mary. You can drop the marshal. Just call me Jack or Sage, whichever feels best."

She turned to the boy. "This is my grandson, Billy. He and his mother, my daughter, help me with this place. It can get quite busy."

Jack nodded at the boy. "Hello, Billy. You think you could find a place for this slicker before I flood the whole parlor?"

Billy hurried to Jack and took the slicker, his eyes on the barrels of the two Smith & Wessons extending below the edge of his coat. "Yes, sir, Marshal. I'll hang it up out back. It'll dry there, and the drips won't matter." He took the coat and turned to leave.

Mary Nelson stopped him. "Billy, when you get the coat hung, would you come back and get the marshal's rifle and saddlebags? Put them in the room we've been saving."

The boy's eyes lit up. "I sure will, Grandma." With Jack's slicker over his arm, he took off at a jog, his grandmother smiling after him.

"Follow me, Jack. We'll go into the kitchen. I imagine you could use a cup of coffee and some food." They walked through the dining room, which held a clean and shiny walnut table long enough to seat at least sixteen people, with three smaller tables against the wall, each seating up to four. "We could eat here, but we've already cleaned the dining room. It'll be much easier in the kitchen, and we have room in there."

"Ma'am, you can put me anywhere. As long as there's coffee and food, I'll be a happy man."

Mary continued, "You'll have plenty of both. Isn't my grandson wonderful? He is such a good boy. He never complains no matter what we have him do, except he has this fascination with guns. That boy's always wanting to shoot something, rifle, pistol, shotgun. You name it, he's always ready when someone offers to let him shoot. Though I must admit, his love of guns doesn't sit well with my daughter, Gracie."

"Did I hear my name mentioned?" A tall black-haired woman at the sink turned as they entered the kitchen.

3

Jack was a world traveler. After the loss of his parents to scarlet fever, he lived with his uncle in Norfolk, Virginia. Upon reaching fifteen, he shipped aboard one of his uncle's clipper ships and sailed across the oceans. By nineteen he had survived life aboard a seagoing vessel, storms, several pirate attacks, and even a shipwreck. Looking for an opportunity to contribute more, he disembarked at Algiers and joined the French Foreign Legion. After several years with the Legion, rumors of war in the United States made it to his outpost, and he returned to fight for his country.

Throughout his travels, he had met many beautiful women, and also in the last two years in Virginia. However, this woman, standing tall and regal before him, with her long, pitch-black hair tied back and her sleeves pulled up to stay clear of the dishwater, ranked among the loveliest.

Mary spoke up. "You did hear your name. In that same conversation, I told Marshal Jack Sage about my wonderful grandson."

A dark eyebrow arched while a skeptical smile played at her full red lips. "Thank you, Mother, though I think you may be just a tiny bit biased." Her large eyes, the same green as her mother's, turned to Jack and sparkled with humor. "I'm Grace Blakely, Marshal. Either you've been swimming in the Arkansas with all your clothes on, or riding in the rain all day. I wouldn't think either was pleasant."

"I think I would've preferred the former, but you're right. Not my most pleasant day." He glanced at the coffeepot. "Your mother was kind enough to mention hot coffee."

She grabbed a hand towel from the counter and began wiping her hands as she moved toward the pot. "I am sorry. Of course, you are probably freezing." She flashed a smile as she filled a cup and, placing the pot back on the stove, quickly covered the space between the wood stove and the table. "Please sit, Marshal. I'll bet you're hungry." She leaned across the table, placed the cup in front of Jack, and slid a small pitcher of fresh cream and a bowl of sugar toward him.

Jack hadn't missed the graceful hands and long fingers she had protected the cup with while placing it on the table in front of him. The hands were red from hot dishwater, but the fingers were slim and strong. "Thanks, Mrs. Blakely. You'd win that bet."

"Call me Gracie, and if venison stew will satisfy those pangs, I'll have some warmed up for you in no time. I may even be able to find a piece of apple pie to go along with it."

"Thank you, stew and pie sound great." He paused for a second. "But do you mind if I call you Grace? For me, that seems to fit you much better."

She paused for only a second. The emerald green eyes seemed to probe into Jack's soul for an instant, and then the moment was gone. "That would be nice, Jack." She spun around to a large pot.

Her mother missed the exchange. "Gracie, take good care of Jack. He's come a long way to help Judge Bell. I'm going to make sure his room is ready." She turned and disappeared down the hall.

Jack drank a few sips of black coffee to lower the amount in the cup. When the level reached a satisfactory point, he picked up the spoon and added three spoonfuls of sugar. After stirring until the sugar was dissolved, he picked up the pitcher and filled the cup with cream until it was filled almost to the edge. He carefully stirred and took a sip. *Just the way I like it,* he thought. His eyes caught the green eyes of Grace watching him.

Her head tilted slightly to the right, her eyes twinkled, and her lips pursed in a teasing smile, bringing out dimples in both cheeks. "You like a little coffee in your sugar, Marshal?"

Jack grinned back. "Most times I use more. I thought I'd save you folks a little, since I suspect you'll have a large clientele in the morning."

She threw her head back, exposing a long graceful neck, and gave a melodic laugh.

Jack took another sip and watched her.

She stirred the stew occasionally to keep it from burning while it was heating. When steam was rising, and just before it began bubbling, she filled a large plate and brought it to Jack. She placed it in front of him and lifted a cloth from a loaf of bread. She cut several slices, placed them on a saucer, and set them in front of him. Then she poured herself a cup of coffee and sat across from him. When he saw she was going to sit, he began to rise, but she waved him down. "Eat. Don't let me interrupt you. I just need a few minutes' rest before I finish tonight."

Jack had taken a bite of the bread. Swallowing, he shook his head. "The bread is delicious."

Grace gave him a tired smile. "It is, isn't it. It's my mama's recipe, and not only do I love making it, I love eating it."

"Sorry I increased your workload. I'm sure you've had a long day."

She shook her head, gave a low, husky laugh, and waved a hand across the space between them. "Don't you worry a bit about it." She watched him continue to make the stew and bread disappear. Her smile faded, replaced by a slight touch of melancholy. She said, almost to herself, "I love watching a hungry man eat."

Jack caught the sadness. "I know I'm a stranger, and if I'm being too forward, tell me, but I seem to detect a bit of woe."

The green eyes looked into his now soft gray eyes. "Sorry, I sometimes feel a bit somber when I think of my husband."

Jack looked around. "Has he already gone to bed?"

"No, he was killed in the war. Billy was only four. His memories of his father are pretty foggy, but James was such a good man. I hated that he had to go to war. It was so senseless."

Jack nodded. "Both sides believed they were right. That's what made it so bad."

"Were you involved, Marshal?"

"I was, ma'am. I truly believed I was doing right to save the Union, but I've wondered many a time if it could've been prevented if the politicians had been more anxious to work out their differences."

She nodded. "Young men fighting old men's wars."

She saw his plate and cup empty. "More?"

He gave her an embarrassed grin. "If you don't mind, both would be good. Only maybe not so much coffee this time."

She stared at him, returning his grin. "Don't worry, Jack, I'll leave you plenty of room for sugar and cream." She stood, refilled the plate, cut more bread, and placed both in front of him. Then she carefully filled the coffee to about the two-thirds point, returned and set it down in front of him, and he went to work preparing his coffee.

Grace returned to the sink to finish the dishes she had been washing, and Mary walked in. She looked first at Jack and then Grace. With a faint shrug, she sat.

"Jack, your room's ready. I figure you're whipped, otherwise we would've fixed you a tub tonight, but get some sleep, and you'll have one waiting on you in the morning."

He was having a difficult time keeping his eyes open, but he wanted to finish both his coffee and the stew. "Thanks, Mary. I really appreciate it. What do I owe you?"

"It's three dollars a day. That's breakfast and supper. We whip up a light lunch for anyone here, but most of our boarders are out working during the middle of the day. Any idea how long you're planning on being here?"

Jack shook his head. "I'd planned for as short a stay as possible, but after eating that stew and drinking Grace's coffee, I may have to rethink my decision. It might be a lot longer."

Mary slapped him on the shoulder. "Ahh, lad, you are truly full of it, but you are welcome as long as you need or want to be here."

"Great." Jack pulled a small bag from his coat pocket and counted out five gold double eagles. "Will that do for a start?"

Mary scooped the five double eagles into her small hand and slapped him on the shoulder again. "Shoot, big fella, for that kind of money, I'll serve you breakfast in bed."

Grace spun around, sudsy fists clamped on her hips, her head thrust forward. "Mama!" There was the faintest grin trying to break through at the corners of her pursed lips.

Mary winked at Jack and turned to her daughter. "Don't you mama me, girl. I mean what I say." She turned back to Jack, now serious. "I can see you're just about dead to the world, Jack. Why don't you come with me. I'll show you your room, and you can get some sleep. I'm sure you've got a busy day tomorrow."

Jack stood. "That sounds good, Mary. I am whipped." He looked over at Grace, who had turned, a hip pressed against the counter. "Mighty good food, ma'am, and great coffee." The last was said with a faint grin, though he could barely keep his eyes open.

A faint smile pulled at the corners of her mouth. "Get some sleep, Marshal. See you in the morning."

Jack followed Mary down the hallway and into a large

bedroom. The bed had been turned back, and Jack could see his rifle, dry and leaning against the rack his saddlebags were hanging on. *Good job, Billy,* he thought, while Mary nodded at the bed and was gone, pulling the door closed behind her.

Stepping over to the rifle and saddlebags, Jack started to go through the bags, but quickly changed his mind, finding himself unable to concentrate. He yanked his shirt over his head and sat on the edge of the bed to pull off his boots. He grasped one and tugged. It was tight. He gathered strength to try once again, and sleep overcame him. He collapsed across the bed, sound asleep.

AN ENERGETIC ROOSTER was letting go of his third wake-up call when Jack's eyes opened. He was under two heavy blankets and a sheet. Moving his feet, he realized his boots were gone. *How'd I get here?* he thought. He looked around his room. Lying neatly on the clothing rack were his pants and shirt, freshly ironed. His boots sat just inside the door, cleaned of all the mud and polished. Clean socks draped over their tops. Seeing his pants and shirt, he looked under the blankets at his long johns. He definitely had not undressed.

A knock sounded at his door, and he recognized Billy's voice. "Marshal Sage, breakfast will be served in thirty minutes."

"Much obliged, Billy." He tossed back the sheet and blankets and, swinging his legs to the side of the bed, sat erect. This morning he felt like a new man. His exhaustion had disappeared with his deep sleep. He was still puzzled as to who might have undressed and tucked him into bed.

He walked across the room and picked up his shirt. It didn't smell like man-sweat, it smelled good, and his trousers also looked good. He didn't know how they'd accomplished that feat, but he was glad of it. He had not relished the idea of showing up at Bell's office looking scruffy and dirty this morning. At the thought, his hand went to his jaw. He was working on a full-blown beard. He moved to the dresser, where a mirror hung behind a washbasin, pitcher, scissors, and a razor. A shaving cup containing soap and a brush also sat alongside the pitcher, which felt warm to the touch. The smell of bacon grew more intense. Jack grabbed the scissors and went to work on his beard. Once it was short enough, he lathered the soap in the cup, stropped the razor, and went to work.

Twenty minutes later, a much more presentable U.S. marshal stepped from his bedroom. He felt like a new man. Instead of slipping on his gunbelt, he had shoved one of the revolvers behind his trousers' waistband. The butt was well hidden by his vest but ready for quick use should it be needed. Both of the weapons, like his rifle, had been wiped down and oiled, then wiped down again. *It had to have been Billy,* he thought. *I owe that young fella.*

The hum of voices increased as he neared the dining room. Entering, he saw Grace, who was replacing an empty plate with another, rounded with hot biscuits. She smiled and nodded toward an empty chair. His stomach growled in response, but only he was aware. The conversation was loud enough to drown almost anything except a gunshot. He seated himself between a drummer, who was pitching his wares to another man, and a quiet young man. The younger man looked like a bank teller. "Morning," Jack volunteered as he pulled out the empty chair, sat, and slid it forward to the table.

As Jack was reaching for his first biscuit, Deputy Marshal Nesbit entered the arched entry of the dining room from the parlor. He motioned with his head for Jack to join him.

Jack noticed the deputy was without a slicker, though he was wearing a coat over his vest. "What's up, Deputy?"

"Quite a bit. First thing, Judge Bell is raisin' Cain. He wants you in his office right now. If you don't come voluntarily, I'm supposed to arrest you."

Jack couldn't stop the faint grin that slipped across his face. He was over a half foot taller than the deputy and a third again as wide. "I hope you're not by yourself."

Nesbit remained deadly serious. "I am. If you want to get your gunbelt and your other gun, I'll wait on you, but we need to go now. I don't aim for the judge and Marshal Berry to both be chewing on me."

Resigned to missing breakfast, Jack returned to his room. He swung his gunbelt around his waist, dropped both revolvers in their respective holsters, and grabbed his coat. He was again surprised when he picked up his hat. It was almost totally dry and had been brushed, bringing it back to a respectable-looking Stetson.

Gripping the brim in his left hand, he pulled the door closed and strode down the hallway, meeting Grace before entering the dining room. In her hand were two large biscuits sliced in the middle and packed with an egg and at least three slices of bacon each. She gave him a warm smile and pressed them into his big hand. Her cool fingers pressing against his thick wrist felt like a jolt of St. Elmo's fire racing up his arm. Her smile widened at his reaction.

She felt it too, Jack thought.

"Give one to Deputy Nesbit. He likes our cooking. We'll save a plate for you. Don't be too long." She spun around before he could utter a word, and disappeared back into the clamor of the dining area and then the kitchen.

Jack saw Nesbit's eyes lock greedily on the two biscuits. "If you promise not to arrest me, Deputy, I'll give you a biscuit."

Nesbit reached for the trophy. "Deal."

The biscuits were big, but half of each disappeared with the first bite.

Sunshine greeted Jack as they stepped onto the boardwalk. The street was still muddy, but the streams that had been cutting through it last night had vanished. Though it was a little nippy in the shade, the sunshine felt good on his thick shoulders.

"You said first, back there when you came in. What else is going on?"

"After you meet with Judge Bell. There'll be plenty of time. He's mighty sore you didn't come by to see him last night, but I think I convinced him you needed rest first. That cooled him down a bit, but he's still at a slow burn."

"Humph," Jack said. *I'm doing this as a favor to President Grant,* Jack thought. *I won't be taking any guff from a newly appointed judge. If he pushes me too far, I'm off to Texas.*

Reaching the courthouse, Nesbit pushed open the door. "This way. His office is on the second floor."

Inside the double front doors, the stairs loomed straight ahead, wide enough for four big men to climb shoulder to shoulder. Reaching the second floor, Nesbit turned right. At a door marked Judge Ronald T. Bell, he grasped the handle, turned it, and stepped in. Inside, another deputy marshal sat at a desk in front of a closed door.

He looked up. "Is this him?"

Nesbit nodded. "Marshal Jack Sage."

The man stood and offered Jack his hand. "I'm glad you're here. Wait just a moment, and I'll let him know."

Jack shook the man's hand, "Not necessary," and headed for the judge's chambers before the deputy could object. He opened the door and stepped inside, with the deputy and Nesbit right behind him. A man sat on the corner of the wide desk, with a document in his hand. He wasn't the pale, slight individual Jack had expected. Instead Bell looked to stand over six feet. He had the sunburned color of a man who, at one time, had spent much of his days in the sun, though the color was fading. His dark brown frock coat did little to hide the wide shoulders and thick biceps residing beneath the cloth. "You've been looking for me?"

Judge Bell looked up at Jack's entry. There was surprise on his face but no fear. If anything, there was irritation mixed with humor.

"Are you U.S. Marshal Jack Sage?"

"I am."

"Then yes, Marshal Sage, I have been looking for you. I see you are just as brash as President Grant said you were, and I have a job for you. You're late."

"By whose timetable?"

Bell stood, still grasping the papers in his right hand. "Mine, of course. President Grant sent me a telegram stating you would be here over a week ago."

"I doubt that."

Incredulous, Judge Bell stared at Jack. "You what?"

"I said I doubt that. I know the president, and he would not give you a definite date for me to arrive. He would only give you the estimate I gave him. I had to travel by train back to Denver, and from there by horseback to reach here. I suppose I could probably have arrived sooner, but I would have killed my horses in the process, and I had no desire to do that for the president, you, or anyone else. However, I'm here now, so what can I do for you?"

Jack could see Judge Bell's color darkening. The judge looked at the other men standing at the door. "Thank you, Deputy Nesbit. By the way, it would appear you have a biscuit crumb at the corner of your mouth. Would you and Frank step out, and close the door, please?"

Nesbit said nothing. He wiped his mouth, glanced at Jack, and pulled the door closed.

I'm in for it now, Jack thought, *but I'm too old to let some judge browbeat me.*

Once Jack and the judge were alone, Judge Bell moved to a large leather couch and took a seat, motioning for Jack to join him. Puzzled, Jack stepped to the opposite end of the couch and dropped onto the rich brown cushioned seat.

4

"Tell me, Sage, do you always charge into a judge's chambers?"

"Only when I'm summoned."

The two men stared at each other. Jack noted the set of the man's square chin and the flint-hard blue eyes. The judge sat straight, shoulders back. *The president said he had been in the war,* Jack thought, *and you can see the military in his erect posture. There's little give in this man.*

Bell's stiff posture relaxed, and he cleared his throat. "Yes, well, you've been needed. Don't get me wrong, I have some fine men working for me, but I need your expertise. This is a big job I've been assigned to."

Jack said nothing.

"I understand you brought in the Clagg gang?"

"Yes. I caught them about to kill three families going west. They won't be doing that again."

"Unfortunately, they might."

Jack sat up straighter. "What do you mean?"

"Early this morning, before daylight, they escaped." The judge paused. "A deputy marshal was injured."

Jack was on his feet. "I've got to get moving."

Judge Bell shook his head. "Sit down. Marshal Berry is putting together a posse. They'll be caught and brought back for trial. This territory is in a lot more trouble than the Claggs can stir up, but first I want to talk about you. I understand you've just returned from Virginia."

Jack eased back onto the couch. This was the first time in a long while there was anyone other than himself to enforce the law, but he needed to advise Berry about the Franklins and the three wagons. "First, Judge, I have information Marshal Berry needs before he leaves, and he needs to be getting on the trail fast."

The judge leaned forward. "Jack, Marshal Berry will be coming to my office before his departure. You can tell him then. Now relax, and tell me about Virginia."

Jack took a deep breath. It had been a bittersweet return to his home. The last time he had seen his uncle was just after the war. The man who had raised him after his folks died had been healthy. When he had returned this time, he was dying. The man was surrounded by family. Jack had a number of aunts and uncles, but they were all aging, and their time was nearing.

"Norfolk was different. Of course, it had been rebuilt after the war, but that's not necessarily what I mean. I guess it's hard to go home again."

"Of course, you left when you were fifteen."

Jack was surprised the judge would know about his life in such detail, but he didn't show it. He nodded. "Yes, I shipped out on one of our ships."

The judge gave Jack a conspiratorial smile. "Jack, I know about most of your life. The president sent me a confidential briefing folder. I know about Algiers and your wife. I am sorry. I know about your return and the war. I even know about South America and all that's gone on since then, and I know about the scar around your neck." He paused.

Jack could see the judge was looking for a reaction, but he would get none. He didn't like the fact the president had shared such personal details, but it was done. There was no sense worrying about it.

Observing no reaction, Bell continued, "The president has followed your career. That's why you're here now. I need your help. Now fill me in about Virginia."

Jack was about to begin when there was a firm knock at the door, and it jerked open. A stocky man, just short of six feet and wearing a marshal's badge, stood in the doorway, holding his hat. The judge rose along with Jack.

"Marshal Berry, this is Marshal Jack Sage. He tells me he has some information for you."

Berry stepped forward and extended his hand. "Glad you made it. That's a long haul all the way from Wyoming Territory, but we can sure use you here."

Berry glanced at the judge. "We're ready. I'm taking three of the deputies. We could be gone for a while." He looked back to Jack. "What information?"

"I'll make this quick. When I caught the Claggs, they were holding up three wagons. The first team was driven by the Franklin family. All of the wagons were trying to catch up with the wagon train that left a few days ago."

Berry nodded. "I'm familiar. Those three stayed behind till one of the men recovered from an illness. The wagon master waited as long as he could."

"I talked to him at Fort Gibson. They weren't holding up. The Franklin group would have to catch up with them. I think Milo Clagg and his gang are set on finishing what they started. They're after gold."

The marshal's eyes narrowed. "You think the Franklin party is carrying gold?"

Jack nodded. "I suspect so. His wagon is carrying either gold or lead. The tracks were cutting way too deep in the wet ground.

He had something heavy on board. He and the wagon master should know better. Those animals will never get that wagon across the mountains." Jack shook his head. "When will these pilgrims learn? They aren't dealing with the hills back east."

Berry's angular face was grim. "Judge, the Claggs have at least six hours on us. We've got to get moving if we have any hope of stopping them before they catch up with those pilgrims. You know what they'll do to 'em."

Judge Bell's face was as grim as Berry's. "Go, and God be with you and the Franklin group."

Berry nodded, spun, and was gone. His boots and spurs could be heard clunking and ringing in his rush down the stairs. Moments later the sound of horse hooves racing out of town filled the judge's chambers.

It was hard for Jack to remain seated. He had again joined the judge on the couch. The pull of responsibility fought to drag him down to his horses, but he knew the marshal would do just as good a job as he could. Common sense reminded him his horses needed to rest for a couple of weeks after traveling so far. If he needed a horse before they were ready, he'd rent one from Pauly.

Judge Bell cleared his throat. "Back to our conversation. First, I have to ask you these questions to ensure your heart is still in this job. The president informed me that you are quite well off financially, and in fact, your family members asked you to stay in Norfolk and manage the shipping firm."

Jack was uncomfortable. He didn't like talking about his business dealings and especially family relations. The last two years he had spent returning his uncle's company to profitability. In fact, he had sailed to South America to confirm certain contracts were intact. It had been a pleasure being on the sea again, but it was not the life for him, nor was that of a manager. "Judge, rest assured, though I do make a comfortable sum from the company, I have no desire nor need to travel back east—for any reason."

Bell gazed at Jack in silence. The big clock on the wall ticked away the time. Finally satisfied, he spoke. "Good. That's what I needed to know. How soon can you travel?"

Jack thought of the breakfast that was waiting for him back in Grace's kitchen. "As soon as I get some food under my belt."

The judge let a grin play across his face. "I understand. Sorry I pulled you away from one of Ma and Gracie's wonderful breakfasts, but I needed to talk to you." His grin disappeared. "I would like for you to leave today if you're going to be of any assistance to Marshal Berry. Of course, you'll need fresh supplies. We have an account at the Far West Emporium. See Nathan Gideon. He'll fix you up with whatever you need. Your horses are at Winthrop's Stables?"

Jack nodded.

"Good. Pauly has excellent riding stock." He looked Jack over. "He even has some that can carry your weight. I imagine you'll be wanting to leave your animals with him until they recuperate after the long trip."

Jack nodded.

"Fine, so you can depart today?"

"Sure I can. I'll have to resupply, but I can definitely be out of here today."

"Good. You had something to do with catching and hanging the Haley gang, didn't you?"

"I had something to do with catching them, but not a one was hanged."

The judge's face stiffened, and his eyes drew tight, his voice rising. "We may be finished before we start. I will not brook a liar."

Jack didn't move. Only the additional tension at the corners of his eyes gave away his anger. He could feel his scalp begin tingling. His scalp always had the strange crawling feeling when his temper was rising. In a low cold voice, Jack spoke. "Judge Bell, this is the only time I'll ever say this to you. All I've got is my reputation, and I'll allow no man, judge or not, to accuse me of lying."

The judge didn't move. "I'm calling Frank to bring up a prisoner."

Jack gave a slight nod.

Bell raised his voice. "Frank, could you come in, please?"

Almost immediately the door opened, and the deputy stepped in. "Yes, sir, Judge." The deputy first looked at Bell and then Jack.

Unless he's green as grass, Jack thought, *he can see the tension between us. Leave it alone, boy. You don't want a piece of this.*

The judge cleared his throat, and Frank, whose mouth had opened to speak but snapped closed, focused on his boss. "Would you go to the jail and bring Harvey Shine up here?"

The deputy nodded, his concern disappearing. "Sure, Judge. Give me a few minutes, and I'll have him up here." He glanced at the two men again, stepped back, and pulled the door closed.

Jack could see the strain in the judge's face. *Well,* Jack thought, *he brought it on himself. He should know better than to call a man a liar unless he knows it for sure.*

Bell continued to stare at Jack. "Are you threatening me, Jack?"

"I'm making you a promise, Judge, so you won't make the mistake of ever suggesting I'm lying again, because I don't."

"I have a witness."

"Harvey Shine?" Jack gave a sharp cynical laugh. "If we hanged everyone out there, how did that kid get past us?"

Jack could see Bell's sincerity. That made it even worse. The man was willing to take the word of a thief over his?

"He said he escaped, otherwise he would have been hanged."

Jack was silent, seething inside. He would never kill a judge, but his sense of justice was being sorely tested.

There was a knock at the door, and Frank shoved the door open and pushed Shine into the room. The manacled man staggered and jerked to a halt in front of Jack. His eyes flew wide, and his mouth hung open like a fish on a bank.

"Hello, Harvey. What's it been, two or three years? I see you didn't follow my advice."

Harvey's eyes were glued on Jack's marshal badge. "Hel-hel-hello, Marshal. I tried to follow your advice. I really did, but it was too hard with all my friends getting rich. Who could blame me?"

"What'd you do, Harvey?" From the corner of his eye, Jack could see Judge Bell searching both his and Shine's faces.

"I, uh . . . Marshal Jack, I tried to rob the bank."

"In what town?" *Surely not here,* Jack thought.

"We figured with all these marshals around, the last thing they'd expect was a bank robbery."

"How'd that work for you, Harvey?"

"Not too well, Marshal. Seems they like their bank. We never made it off the boardwalk."

"Why are you lying about us trying to hang you, Harvey?"

"I swear, Marshal, I tried. I really tried. But my friends always wanted to do something illegal. What are you gonna do?"

"Leave your friends? You think they'll volunteer to serve time for you, Harvey?"

The still young outlaw looked at the floor and shook his head.

Jack leaned forward where he could see Harvey's eyes. "What did I promise I'd do the next time we met if you were still an outlaw?"

"You said you'd kill me."

"I did, didn't I? Here's what's going to happen, Harvey. You're going to tell Judge Bell here just what happened to you the day we caught you robbing the trail boss and his crew. You think you can do that?"

Harvey Shine ducked his head and stared at the floor. "Yes, sir."

Jack waited, and Shine said nothing. "Go ahead, Harvey. Don't make me get off this couch."

Shine looked up at the hard-faced judge. "Mr. Judge Bell, sir, I might have got it a little wrong when I told the story about being caught by Marshal Jack here, a couple of years ago."

When Shine stopped talking, it was Bell who said, "Well, go ahead. Get on with it."

"Well, sir, we had caught up with this here trail boss after he sold his cows. We'd heard he had a big herd, so we knew he had a lot of money. We stopped 'em and was funning with them a bit."

This time, Jack's voice was cold and harsh. "Tell it like it happened, Shine. Remember, we were lying on the hill above you, watching every move you made."

Shine straightened. "After Haley was shot trying to escape, you told me if I would go straight, you wouldn't hang me."

Jack nodded. "So you were the only remaining outlaw, and we turned you loose."

"That's right, Marshal. I sure wish I had followed your directions."

"How many years did you get for robbing the bank, Harvey?"

"No time, Marshal. I killed a teller. It weren't really my fault. He moved too fast, and I thought he was goin' for a gun. So I had to shoot him. You see that, don't you?"

Jack turned to Judge Bell. "You convinced?"

The judge nodded. Jack turned to the deputy. "Get him out of here."

Frank grabbed Harvey by the arm, and the man tried to pull away, but Frank held tight, dragging him through the door.

"Cain't you help me again, Marshal Sage? You know, like you did last time. I'll go straight, I promise."

Frank slammed the door, and Jack turned back to the judge, waiting. He knew he was well aware of the importance of a man's reputation out here.

Finally Bell shook his head. "Jack, I'm sorry. I thought—"

"That doesn't cut it, Judge. You either trust a man, or you don't. There are men out here who have never met me but know my reputation. They'll never doubt my honesty. You let a known felon persuade you I was a liar." Jack was close to yanking the marshal's badge from his vest and tossing it on the judge's desk, but this man hadn't given it to him, the president had. He kept his seat and waited.

"I'm sorry I said what I did without solid proof. After talking with you, I firmly believe you are the man you say you are. Give me another chance. I need you out here. This country needs you out here. We need law and order in the territory. It'll be a slow process, but I believe it can be done."

Jack sat silent, staring at Bell. The clock's ticking seemed to reverberate through the room. A decision was needed. The man had made the kind of mistake that could get someone killed, but he was honest, sincere, and had been appointed by the president. *I don't think he'll be making that mistake again,* Jack thought. "Alright, Judge. I'll hang around, but you've got to understand, President Grant has released me after I'm done here, and I make the decision when I'm done."

"Good. I do have rules, Jack. Any men you capture will be brought to trial here. Also, do your very best to bring them in alive. I know there will be some who will make it impossible, but other than the most hard cases, I want every outlaw to face justice here in my court. Can you work under those rules?"

Jack didn't have to think. The judge was talking about the way he applied the law. He'd bring them in to face the court. "I can do just fine with your rules, Judge."

Throughout the time Jack had been in the office, Bell had been holding several sheets of paper. Now he handed them over to Jack. "These are specific arrest warrants for three men and four John Doe warrants in case you need to make additional arrests. They are settlers on the Kansas border who seem to think thievery beats plowing. Several witnesses, in the jail here, tell me these men are rustling cattle from the Texas herds headed for Wichita. They only take a few, then hold them until they have enough to drive east. They sell them cheap and return and repeat. A couple of cowhands have been murdered. I want it stopped and those men tried. If you can arrest any others involved in the theft, feel free to do so, buyers too, if you have proof."

"You know where these thefts are taking place?"

"Talk to the prisoners. Frank will take you to them." Judge Bell stood, along with Jack. "You'll be heading along the same route as the Franklins and Marshal Berry until you reach Kansas. If you'd like to give the marshal a hand, feel free. Though I'd like to put those rustlers out of business as soon as possible, there won't be many herds moving north this late in the year. I'd like to get them off the trails, but the Franklins take priority. Luck to you." The two men shook hands, and Jack went through the two doors and headed down the stairs. He had a lot to do and not much time to get it done if he was going to be on his way today.

Frank stood as the office door opened, but Jack waved him off and headed for the boardinghouse. He was starving. The promise of the breakfast plate was preying on his mind. He was also thinking about the Franklins. Bell and his men were on the trail. Would it be possible for them to reach the settlers in time? He prayed those folks took his advice and were armed and ready.

5

Other than his concern for the Franklins, Jack was feeling much better. His stomach was full, he was on a good horse, and he had gotten a smile and a concerned look from Grace when she found out he was leaving. She was a mighty pretty woman, but he had known a lot of pretty women. *Get your mind where it belongs, Jack,* he told himself. He was in hostile country. This territory was full of outlaws and Indians. Neither would turn their noses up at the opportunity to pick up two fine horses and a scalp.

Jack patted the big palomino's neck. "Blaze, you're a fine piece of horseflesh." He glanced back at the horse he had on a lead. It too, a red roan, was big and looked like he could run for a week. Earlier in the afternoon he had started on the red roan and switched to the palomino after a couple of hours.

Picking the roan from Pauly's selection had not been difficult. Red, the pale red animal, had walked over to him when he had entered the corral. Blaze had been completely disinterested until he smelled the cookie, but the palomino's color was not Jack's favorite. It was too bright and difficult to hide. However, Pauly had insisted on the merits of the horse, and the man did know horseflesh.

It had been hard to leave his animals, especially Stonewall and Smokey. Jack had built a strong bond with the grulla and mule, though he'd also miss Pepper and Thunder. But those four animals needed to rebuild lost muscle and put a little fat on their tired bodies. A couple of weeks of rest and food would do wonders for them.

Jack bumped Blaze into a lope. He had been on the trail for several hours, having gotten out of Fort Smith faster than he expected. He hated to push the horses this hard, but he had to make sure the Franklins were safe. He felt an ominous foreboding he couldn't throw off. *If those folks have been harmed,* Jack thought, *there's no place the Claggs can hide that I won't find them.*

The tall hickory, elm, and black walnut trees blocked much of the sunlight along the Arkansas River. Jack was anxious to leave the densely forested river bottom. His time on the high seas, deserts of North Africa, and rangeland of Texas, New Mexico, and Wyoming had molded his dislike for thick forests. He liked to be able to look across an expanse of land, not thick tree trunks blocking vision and light.

This type of country also provided numerous opportunities for an ambush, so he rode ready. The rain had moved on, and temperatures had risen, allowing him to ride without his coat and slicker, making quick access to his weapons possible. Though in this forested river bottom, a damp chill penetrated everything, but better to suffer a little cold than absorb several ounces of lead.

As much as he wanted to break out of the forest, he knew it wouldn't be today. The sun barely slipped through the trees, though except for the pines, they stood barren of foliage. Unfortunately, it would disappear within the hour. Having traveled this same trail inbound to Fort Smith, he knew, no more than a mile ahead, there was an open area off the trail. The posse had probably pulled up there to camp for the night.

He slowed the horses to a walk and swung to the ground. His legs, especially the right one stiff from the old bullet wound, could use a little stretching. He had walked less than a half mile when he began to hear the sounds of men preparing camp. The stop had been expected, but part of him had hoped they'd pushed on, not resting until later into the night. However, these were experienced lawmen, and he knew they wanted to protect the Franklins as much as he did. Traveling at night was dangerous for the animals. A hole, a wrong step and a horse could be badly injured, putting a man afoot. Sure enough, when he spotted the camp, he recognized Berry among the men. "Hello the camp," he called.

Only one of the men watched him approach, Marshal Strawn Berry. The others glanced up, but quickly went back to what they were doing. They were busy taking care of their horses or getting their bedding ready. Jack recognized one of the men preparing the fire. He was the one who had retrieved the sacks of guns from his horses yesterday.

"Come on in, Jack," Berry called. "Didn't expect you this soon. You must've been pushing it."

Jack nodded to the man as he passed the camp and led his horses to their picket line. He dropped the leads and began stripping the gear.

Berry walked over. "You headed up to Kansas after those rustlers?"

"I am, but Judge Bell also authorized me to help with the Claggs."

"Good. We'll move out just before daylight. I plan on riding hard until we reach them. Hopefully Clagg figured we would be on his trail, and decided to escape rather than bother with the settlers."

Jack dropped his saddle and gear near the fire. He straightened and, with a raised eyebrow, glanced at Berry.

The other marshal shrugged, his brow wrinkled in concern. "I know, but a man can hope. I feel for those folks. All of the honest ones are tryin' to start a new life and give their family a chance to succeed out here. It's a shame we have scum like the Claggs trying to destroy those dreams."

"Then let's keep movin', Marshal." It was the man from last night speaking.

"Jack, that young feller who's vying for my job is Buck Walker."

Jack nodded to the man in acknowledgment and turned to head back to his horses. They still needed water.

Berry ignored Buck and joined Jack as he led the animals to the river. "Water's high after the rain. You can water them right at the edge. The bank's pretty solid here."

Jack walked the horses to the edge of the Arkansas and waited while they drank. "Seems mighty high, Strawn. You think it's safe to camp here tonight?"

"Yeah, it's already crested and headin' down. We'll be fine." He laid his hand on Red's back as the horse drank. "Buck's a good man, just young and brash. He doesn't realize how it would affect our mission to have a man's horse break a leg in the dark."

Jack nodded. "You're right. I even considered going on tonight, but I need my rest. I am getting up a little after midnight and heading up the trail. I plan on walking the animals until daylight. I figure with us moving slow, especially in the moonlight, the horses will be able to pick out any problem." He looked across the horses' backs at Berry. "I know this is your command, and I'm not trying to horn in, but I do have two horses. Would you consider letting Buck join me? We can wait when we catch up with the Franklins."

Berry stood silent, his hand resting on the palomino's back, and watched the debris, logs and branches, twist and turn in the current as it coursed down the swollen Arkansas. Finally, he turned to Jack. "I think that'd be fine. I wouldn't let him go by himself for fear he'd go racing through the night and break his and his horse's neck, but yeah, I think he'll be fine with you. You'll hold up with the Franklins no matter what you find?"

It was Jack's turn to stare at the fast-flowing muddy water. *If I find them harmed,* Jack thought, *I'll want to get on the trail of Clagg and his worthless bunch right away. I wouldn't want them to have an opportunity to divide their bounty and split up.* He looked back at Berry. "You asked a good question. I'd want to get on their trail as soon as possible if they've harmed any of the members of the wagon train." He thought for a few more moments. "How about if I leave Buck to help the survivors or do whatever may be necessary, and head on out after them? Would that work for you?"

"Yeah," Berry said, "that'll work. You say around one o'clock?"

"Yep."

The horses had stopped drinking, and darkness was falling fast. Marshal Strawn Berry took Red's lead while Jack took Blaze's, and the two returned to camp. The flickering flames could be seen through the trees, and the low voices of the three men reached Jack. He didn't know Deputy Buck Walker, but his first impression was good. Buck was stocky, wide-shouldered and narrow-hipped, with the look of a man who grew up in the saddle. His youth would play against him, but Jack could control the younger man's brashness, and the young fella had a sense of humor. Jack had seen it in the rain. This could work out well.

Horses fed, tied and grazing, the two marshals joined the three men. Buck had whipped up beans and tossed jerky in the pot to soak up a little fluid and soften the rock-hard strips of meat. Each man had filled his plate and nodded as Jack and Strawn returned to the fire. Jack brought two sacks, along with his plate and spoon, with him. One was filled with Grace's large and delicious biscuits, while the other was filled with donuts she had made to go along with breakfast this morning. They were both large sacks. Jack dropped the biscuit sack in front of the deputies. "That might make those whistle berries taste a mite better."

Buck reached out and grabbed the sack, opening it and looking in. "You stayed at Ma's last night, didn't you?"

Jack nodded, already chewing his first spoonful of pinto beans.

The deputy pulled out two large, thick biscuits and passed the sack around. "Gracie's biscuits, boys, they don't get any better." He took a big bite of one and grinned at Jack while trying to mumble around the biscuit. "Much obliged, Marshal."

Jack nodded again and kept eating. When the sack got to him, he took two and passed them on to Strawn.

The men concentrated on the business at hand, eating. Beans and biscuits disappeared quickly. When everyone was finished and leaning back against their saddles, Jack opened the other sack. "Gracie said you boys probably wouldn't care for these, so I was welcome to eat all of them." He had the attention of every man sitting around the fire and the one on guard.

Buck was quick to respond, "Whatcha got there, Marshal?"

Jack reached into the bag and pulled out two donuts. "Bear sign, boys, but the way you went aboard those beans and biscuits, I'm doubting you have any room left." He tossed the sack toward the men.

Buck caught it and stuck his head in the open sack, audibly inhaling. One of the other deputies yelled, "Git yore head out of that sack, Buck, or you're liable to lose it."

Grinning, he pulled his head out and grabbed two donuts before reluctantly passing the sack to the next man. Jack thought about saving a few, but decided to let the men eat. It wasn't often they had this kind of treat on the trail.

When the donuts were finished and the men were leaning back on their saddles, Jack sloped forward so he could see around the deputy sitting next to him. "Buck, how do you feel about losing a little of your beauty sleep?"

The deputy had been relaxing against his saddle. He jerked erect. "What's on your mind, Marshal?"

"I'm thinking of pulling out of here around one o'clock this morning and getting a little head start, thought you might like to ride along."

"I'm your man, Marshal. I'll leave right now if you like." He shot a glance at Marshal Berry.

"It's alright, Buck. Jack and I talked about it earlier. I asked him to take you along so I could get you outta my hair for a while. It'll make life a lot more pleasant for all of us."

One of the other deputies grinned. "It'll sure be a lot quieter around here. I'll be able to hear myself think again."

Buck jerked around. "Gil, if you had a thought, it'd be rattling around in that empty head of yours. You'd never sleep. You need me to explain everything for you."

"Alright, boys," Marshal Berry said, "settle down and get some sleep. The trail will come mighty early for some of you."

Jack checked his revolvers, stretched his long legs, and pulled his blanket up to his neck. His eyes closed while Buck was still talking.

HIS EYELIDS JERKED OPEN PRECISELY at one o'clock. A waning quarter moon was hanging directly overhead. The fire was down, and Gil sat on the opposite edge of the fire, eyes open, rifle across his legs. He nodded. Returning the greeting, Jack rose, laid out his blanket on his ground cloth, and rolled the two together. Once they were tied, he stepped to Buck and nudged the sole of the deputy's boot. The man's eyes popped open, and he gave Jack a nod.

With the acknowledgment, Jack grabbed his saddle, rifle, and bedroll, starting for the horses. Gil intercepted him and, speaking in a low whisper, said, "Horses have been watered. I gave each one a little of your feed. They're both ready."

"Much obliged, Gil. See you in a few hours."

Gil nodded. "Hopefully those folks are alright."

Jack nodded and continued to the horses. He saddled Red while Buck was doing the same with his horse. Jack leaned toward the younger man and whispered, "We won't mount until we're a ways down the trail. Might as well give these fellas as much sleep as possible."

Surprising to Jack, Buck was silent, only nodding.

A few hours and we'll know, Jack thought. *I sure hope those folks aren't hurt.* He led Red and Blaze away from the picket line and, with Buck alongside, walked the two horses down the trail.

They walked for at least ten minutes. Stretching his legs felt good. Figuring they were far enough down the road, Jack swung into the saddle, followed by Buck. He could see Buck tense, about to kick his horse into a run. His long left arm shot out, grabbing Buck's right bicep. In a loud whisper, he said, "Walk!"

In the moonlight, Jack could see the quick frown appear, then disappear. *Yeah,* Jack thought, *I'm disappointed too, Buck. But you'll learn to bridle your impatience.* Time passed slowly as they walked their animals along the trail. They passed several deer in the thickets. A family of pigs crossed ahead of them, grunting softly among themselves. Daylight began to break. A bobcat started across the trail, saw them, and spun around, disappearing into the dark forest.

Jack didn't like the forest's silence. It was too quiet and only added to his foreboding. As daylight lit the trail, they kicked the animals up to a trot and listened. Always listening. Jack yearned to hear the clank and rattle of wagons ahead, or the laughter of children as camp was broken. Maybe they had made it to Fort Gibson and decided to rest there. If that was the case, Clagg might have ridden on, knowing with the marshals on his tail, time was running out.

They reached the fort only to learn the wagons had passed through yesterday, and no, there was no chance they could have caught up with the other wagons. The officer in charge said it would still take them three, maybe four days to reach the main wagon train.

They continued to ride, now listening in anticipation for gunfire. Anything that would give them hope there was still time to save the families. But listen as they might, the only sounds coming to their ears were the singing of birds and the occasional bark of a squirrel.

The first indication they might be nearing the wagons was the buzzards circling high above the forest. Jack felt his stomach turn, and despair set in. His thoughts were for Charlotte Franklin, her baby, and the two boys standing up front in the wagon, directly behind the adults, fearless in their desire to see everything.

The thick trees had begun to thin and give way to prairie. Jack was able to see farther, and now he caught the dull white of a wagon's canopy. He dropped his right hand to the stock of his Winchester and pulled it from its boot. Holding the forearm with his left, he slid the lever down far enough to see the back end of a .44-caliber cartridge in the chamber and returned the lever to lock in place while pulling the rifle's hammer to full cock. The small leather loops securing his Smith & Wessons in their holsters were slipped from their respective hammers. He glanced at Buck, who also had his Winchester out and ready.

Nearing the three wagons, they slowed. Pots, clothing, supplies, and bodies were scattered across the small glade. Buzzards were busy at every body. Jack fired several shots into the air, scattering the black birds up but not away. Some flew into nearby trees while others rejoined those circling above.

Buck looked at Jack and motioned toward the big black birds. "You didn't kill 'em?"

"No need. They're just doing their job. If we hadn't come along, they would have cleaned up what the coyotes and other varmints left."

Jack's head and eyes continued to move. It was always possible the killers were still close, but he knew they weren't. He knew this was the Clagg gang, killers and cowards. They were probably long gone. But he didn't operate on what probably was happening. He kept a sharp lookout, like he always had, to survive at his job.

6

Jack Sage halted Red at each body. Men, women, girls, and boys, all had been brutalized and murdered. Jack dismounted, followed by the deputy. As soon as Buck's feet hit the ground, Jack heard the younger man retching. They'd had little to eat this morning, so there wasn't much to throw up, but whatever there was found its way to the ground.

Jack said nothing. He understood. He had been in Buck's shoes, but this time his emotions had gone cold. He had only one desire, to catch and take from the Claggs what they had taken from the Franklins and the two other families. But he already knew he wouldn't be successful. The Claggs had stolen love and hope, excitement in the new lands, a posterity that would remember the pioneers' sacrifices, their virtues. *Virtues,* Jack thought. *Virtue is something none of the Claggs possess, so when I bring them in to hang, or shoot them down, they'll lose nothing but their worthless lives.*

Jack walked to each body, knelt alongside, and checked to see if there were any signs of life remaining. He found none. Reaching the patriarch of the young family, Jarrod Franklin, he looked down on the father's maimed body. He was the one suspected of having gold, and they had tried to get him to talk. Jack looked back over his shoulder at Charlotte, Jarrod's wife.

She lay next to a thick-trunked elm, her infant by her side. The baby, like his mother, was dead. Jack stood and walked to the back of the wagon. Several quilts were strewn on the ground. He picked them up, using one to cover each body. Only one was needed to cover both Charlotte and the baby.

He saw Buck doing the same thing with the other families' members. That would do until they could be buried. There would be many graves, a lot of digging.

He was traveling, so he had no shovel. "Buck, you have a shovel?"

The deputy shook his head.

"You know if Marshal Berry brought one?"

"He brought two. They're on the mule."

"Did you get all the bodies covered?"

"I did, Marshal." The deputy paused, looking down at the handmade quilt now covering Charlotte Franklin and her baby. "You ever see anything like this before?"

Jack stared at the thick brush on the edge of the clearing. "Unfortunately, yes, Buck. I have. More than once."

"Does it ever get easier?"

"No. It never does." He lifted the muzzle of his rifle skyward, for he had seen movement in a thick bramble bush at the edge of the clearing. "Is that you, Elijah? You remember me, don't you? I stopped those bad men yesterday."

Buck's head jerked toward Jack, then at the patch of brush the marshal was talking to.

Jack shoved his rifle into the boot and swung down from Red. "I'll protect you, Elijah. I remember you from yesterday. You were strong."

A small, hesitant voice spoke from deep in the brush. "Why weren't you here this morning, Marshal Sage? You protected us yesterday. Why didn't you protect us today?"

Jack heard the loss and pain in the youngster's voice. Even through the cold fury he felt toward the Claggs, he had to concentrate to keep from choking up. "I'm right sorry, Elijah. Yes, sir, I truly am, but I'm here now. Why don't you come out here, and we'll get you something to eat. You'll feel better then."

Silence filled the glade for almost a full minute. Finally Elijah spoke again, his voice quivering. "I'd like to, Marshal, but one of the bad men shot me."

"I'm coming over, son. You just relax." Jack strode to the brush. No wonder they couldn't get to the lad. The brambles were thick and appeared impossible to penetrate. From here he couldn't even see the lad. "Where are you shot, Elijah?"

"He shot me in the leg. It ain't too bad, but it hurts."

"How'd you get in there?"

"I just dove in."

Jack circled the brambles again and, down low, spotted a small hole with strips of cloth and blood on the briars. He removed his hat and lay on the ground so he could look into the thicket through the hole. He could just make out the gray color of Elijah's homespun trousers. "I think I see you, son. Can you see me?"

"Yes, sir."

"Can you reach me?"

The little voice sounded weaker. "I'll try."

Jack watched a small face change places with the homespun trousers. "I see you better now, son. Try to work toward me." Jack drew his razor-sharp Bowie knife and began removing the thorny vines.

"I can't go any farther, Marshal. I'm really tired." Elijah's words were weak, and the end of his sentence faded.

"Buck," Jack called.

"Right here."

He looked up and was surprised to see Buck standing almost

on top of him. "Good." He handed him several of the bramble vines. "I'm going to work my way in and bring that little fella out."

"Those brambles are awfully thick, Jack, and you're a mighty big man."

"Doesn't matter. You heard him. He's been shot, and he's losing blood." Jack stretched, cut, and pushed his way toward Elijah. Cutting more of the thorny vines, he passed them along his side to Buck. He was widening the tunnel. The knife-edged thorns cut and gouged as he sliced and pulled vines. He felt something rip along his left cheek. He almost let out a sardonic chuckle. As if another scar would make a difference on his scarred and punctured body.

He could see Elijah. The boy was bloody from head to toe. *Most likely from these brambles,* Jack thought. *I've got to get him out of this mess. The bleeding from his bullet wound has to be stopped.* He continued crawling forward until he was able to extend a long arm and grasp the boy's arm. He slid his other hand under his face to protect him from the bramble limbs embedded in the ground, and pulled him slowly forward.

Elijah moaned.

"It's almost over, son. Just a few more feet." Jack started backing out, thankful for his chaps, even though they were bunching and making it more difficult for him to push himself backwards. The thick leather did its job and kept most of the brambles' thorns from reaching his flesh.

He continued, slowly working himself and Elijah out of the thicket. At last, reaching the edge, he grasped the youngster in his arms, rolled over, and sat up. Buck reached out for the boy, and Jack gave a hard shake of his head. "Let's get him to the back of a wagon."

"This way," Buck said, and started toward the second wagon. Reaching it, Jack saw the gate was down. Buck jerked a quilt from inside and spread it across the wagon's lowered gate. The big marshal gently laid the bloody little boy on the quilt. Elijah's eyes fluttered open.

"How are you doing, son?"

"My leg hurts something awful, Marshal."

Jack saw a towel hanging inside the wagon. He leaned in, grasped it, and gave it a hard yank. Once he had it in hand, he started wiping the blood from the boy's leg.

Elijah let out a whimper. "That hurts, Marshal."

Jack could see why. The little tyke had been shot just below his left hip. The big bullet had cut from the back of his leg forward. It had torn through the edge of the child's thigh, exiting into the ground and blowing dirt and debris back into the wound. He gently dabbed at the ugly wound. Buck hovered at Jack's shoulder.

"How's he look, Marshal?"

"Whoever did this missed the bone, though there's a bit of muscle damage. This wound has to be cleaned out. Bring me a dipper and a bucket of water, and look around to see if you can find any antiseptic. Something to wash this wound out with."

Buck returned with the bucket of water and a dipper. He disappeared again to check the other wagons. Soon he came running back. "Will this work?"

It was a bottle of rye.

"Better than nothing, Buck." He took the bottle and looked down on Elijah, whose eyes were watching Jack's every move.

"I'm sorry, Elijah. This is really going to burn. I'll wash your leg first with water and then pour this whiskey on your wound. It's going to hurt like crazy. I want you to pretend you're an Indian, and I want you to let out the loudest war whoop you can manage. Do you think you can do that for me?"

Tears welled up in the boy's eyes, but he tried to blink them away. "Yes, sir. I think I can."

He grinned at the boy, knowing there was little humor in it.

"Make it the loudest this Oklahoma Territory has ever heard. Wake up those Texans down south."

Elijah gave him a small grin. "I know I can do that."

"Good. Let me know when you're ready."

The little boy took a deep breath. "I'm ready."

Jack slid the towel under the boy's leg and began rinsing the wound with water. Elijah let out a half-hearted yelp and quieted down. After ensuring the wound channel was clear of debris, Jack picked up the bottle.

Elijah's big brown eyes were locked on his hand. His small voice whimpered. "That's what'll hurt bad, isn't it, Marshal?"

"You're doing really good, Elijah, but I won't kid you. This is where you're going to need the biggest yell you can muster. Do you think you're ready?"

The boy's bloody little head gave a nod. "I think so."

Jack held the bottle just above the boy's leg. "You tell me when you're ready, and we'll get this over with quick-like."

Elijah took a deep breath, let it out, and said, "I'm ready."

Jack held the leg tight and immediately began pouring.

Elijah let out a long high-pitched scream, and tears streamed down the bloody little face.

"It's over, boy. We've done it. I think they heard you down in Fort Worth."

"Was that a good one, Marshal? I wanted to make it a good one."

"Son, that would've made the toughest old mountain man grab for his hair and hang on. It was the best whoop I've ever heard."

The boy gave Jack a little smile. "That's good. I'm tired, Marshal. I'd like to go to sleep now."

"You go right ahead, boy. I'm here. You're going to be just fine."

Elijah closed his eyes and was quickly breathing the deep breaths of a tired child.

Jack slipped what was left of the small trousers from his abused legs and finished cleaning around the wound. Buck had found a kit the family had put together with bandages and salves in it. Using several of the bandages, he covered and wrapped Elijah's bullet wound. He then removed the boy's shirt and examined his upper body. He had cuts all over his body from the briars. Jack cleaned the thorn gashes and used the salve, bandaging the worst ones. The gashes and cuts would heal, and if the bullet wound healed properly, Elijah would be all right, physically.

After he finished caring for the sleeping boy, Jack dressed him in clothes Buck had found in the Franklins' wagon. He had just finished dressing him when the sound of rapidly approaching hoofbeats came to him, followed instantly by Buck, rifle ready.

"Sounds like more than Marshal Berry and the boys."

Jack covered Elijah with a quilt and picked up his rifle. "Yep. Be ready. Don't shoot until I give the word."

The two men and sleeping boy waited as the horses approached. It sounded like there were at least ten or twelve riders. The only thing Jack could imagine was Indians. *Just what we need,* Jack thought. *I hope they're friendly.*

Marshal Berry, his men, and a patrol of cavalry from the fort burst into the clearing. The riders jerked their horses to a halt and gaped in shock at the sight in front of them. Berry dismounted along with the lieutenant and strode to Jack and Buck. "The Claggs?"

Jack spoke up. "They tortured and killed all of these people and raped all the women and girls." He nodded at the boy sound asleep on the wagon gate. "Elijah here is the only one who survived, and the Claggs managed to put a bullet into him. Fortunately it only grazed his leg. He had the good sense and courage to dive into a bramble bush where they couldn't get to him. It looks like whoever was after him threw a shot at him and took off back to the wagons. Probably afraid someone would find the gold and he'd miss out."

The lieutenant turned to the sergeant still with the patrol. "Dismount the troop. Take a count, and start digging graves."

"Yes, sir." The sergeant called, "Dis-mount!" The troops stepped to the ground. "You heard the lieutenant. Break out those shovels."

"Lieutenant, this is Marshal Jack Sage and Deputy Marshal Buck Walker. They came on ahead. Jack, this here is Lieutenant McMillian."

Jack looked the man over. He appeared to be his age. *Probably reduced in rank after the war,* Jack thought. *That's what I would've had to look forward to if I had stayed. The man will never get rich, but he's serving his country.* "Lieutenant McMillian, a pleasure to meet you, though I think we'd both prefer different circumstances."

The officer greeted Buck, punched his cavalry hat to the back of his head, and looked up at Jack. "Major Sage, a pleasure to see you again."

Jack's forehead wrinkled as he tried to pull long-stored memories into the present. He vaguely remembered a cavalry major. "Major McMillian?"

McMillian nodded. "Good memory, Major."

Jack shook his head. "I'm long out of the army, Major. Jack will do fine."

McMillian gave a self-deprecating grin. "Lieutenant, Jack. It hasn't been major since '65."

"A lot of good men were given the choice of getting out or a reduction in rank. I'm sure your experience pays off for your command."

The officer waved the compliment away. "The Clagg gang, I assume?"

"Yeah. They tortured and killed everyone. They were looking for gold. I don't know if they found it or not."

A small voice pitched in from the gate bed. "They didn't find anything, Marshal Jack, 'cause there ain't any. I ain't ever known of Pa having gold. At least I haven't seen it, and nobody else had any. Those men kept hurting people, trying to get Pa to say where the gold was. He tried to tell them we didn't have any gold, but they wouldn't believe him."

Jack turned, and his hand found its way to Elijah's head, thick fingers threaded through the boy's hair, gently massaging his head. "Why was your wagon so heavy, son?"

"Mama's organ. She wouldn't leave it. Pa kept telling her we wouldn't be able to make it over the mountains with it, but she swore when it came out of the wagon, she would too."

"Go back to sleep, boy. You need your rest. We'll be leaving before long."

Elijah closed his eyes and found sleep quickly. After placing bedding between the youngster and the gate's edge, Jack motioned the men away from the wagon.

Berry spoke up. "What's your plan, Jack?"

"I'll tell you my plan. It's to bring in the Clagg gang." Jack looked toward the area the sergeant had chosen for the burial of the families. It was a good place. Off the trail, but still in the glade and without much brush. He turned back to the officer. "Lieutenant McMillian, once you're through with the burials of these folks, do you think you could have a detail take the wagons and their belongings back to Fort Smith?"

"Certainly. We'd be honored to take their things back. Possibly there is enough identification to reach relatives. The equipment might be sold and the funds sent to them."

"Just what'll happen, Lieutenant," Berry said. "I'll get you a note to Judge Bell. He'll take care of everything."

The officer looked at the animals standing around. "I'm surprised the Claggs didn't take the stock with them. They could've sold them and had enough money to stay drunk for quite a while."

Jack snorted. "I'm surprised they didn't kill them. I'm thinking they figured there were marshals on their tails, and all their time was needed trying to find the gold."

"Yeah," Berry chimed in, "they were considered a rotten bunch long before they did this. The only thing that has kept 'em out of jail is their family around Fort Smith. They have a couple of brothers who are prominent in the community." He shook his head. "Though I don't know how. Those two are almost as bad as Milo or Flint."

Jack's cold, gray eyes focused on Berry. "Those brothers won't be able to do a thing for the Claggs this time. We've got a witness to everything they did. Every single one of that bunch is going to end up at the end of a rope."

"But," Berry said in a low voice so that Elijah couldn't hear him, "we've got to protect the boy. None of the Clagg bunch, including the two brothers in town, are above killing him."

Jack thought about Berry's statement. "They've certainly demonstrated that here. Any idea about where he could stay?"

Before Berry could answer, the lieutenant spoke up. "Excuse me, gentlemen, I need to assist my sergeant." He stepped out toward the burial detail.

Berry kept his voice lowered. "Mary and Grace at Ma's usually take in waifs and orphans. I'm sure they'll be more than willing to take this young colt and allow him to stay as long as needed. Of course, the court reimburses them for their costs."

Jack's voice was hard. "What about protection? Does the court protect them from the likes of Milo or Flint Clagg?"

Berry had turned to watch the digging of the graves. Jack did the same. The deputy marshals had pitched in, spelling the cavalrymen, and it wouldn't be long. There were other men wrapping the bodies in quilts and blankets. All the men's faces reflected the horror of what these innocent folks had gone through. Several of the younger or greener troops had matched Buck's actions and lost their breakfasts.

Berry shook his head. "It's not easy on anyone. To answer

your question, yes, there'll be protection. We'll post a man at their place of business. Of course, we'll have to rotate them. If we left one man there, he'd get as fat on their food as some of the drummers."

Jack couldn't help but chuckle at the thought. The drummer he had sat next to for breakfast had had way too many of Grace and Mary's meals.

Buck joined them as Jack saw Lieutenant McMillian turn, searching for them. He headed for the back of the second wagon to get Elijah. The boy needed to see his parents go in the ground and know they were given a Christian burial.

7

Jack Sage gently lifted Elijah Franklin from the wagon and carried him to where his family and friends were being buried. A brown shock of hair fell over the boy's forehead as Jack held him so he could see his father, mother, brother, and infant brother lowered into the bosom of the Oklahoma earth.

Tears filled the boy's eyes as Lieutenant McMillian opened a small Bible and conducted the service. Several of the younger cavalrymen's eyes also filled when the women and children were lowered to their final resting place. Like all such services where no minister presided, it was short. The bugler stepped forward and slowly lifted his bugle to his lips.

The clear, mournful notes of "Taps" lifted into the trees. The birds stopped their singing, and the forest grew silent, acknowledging the loss of the hopes and dreams of these families. Moments after the last plaintive note disappeared into the forest, the birds trilled their notes again. The forest's sounds returned, and the cavalrymen began filling the graves.

Elijah looked up at Jack and, with the back of a cut and

scratched hand, wiped his eyes. "Marshal Sage, what's gonna happen to me?"

The innocent gaze of the boy reminded Jack of another youth in Wyoming, but he had been surrounded by people who loved him, including his mother. This boy had lost all of his immediate family.

"Where was your home, Elijah?"

The boy gave his head a shake. "I don't want to go back there. Pa said we were leaving it behind, and to forget it. No one there could ever hurt us again."

"Alright," Jack said. " I can understand that, but where was it?"

Hesitantly Elijah lowered his head and mumbled, "Knoxville, Tennessee, but I didn't like it. People were mean to Ma and Pa and us."

"You have any family there?"

The boy said again, this time firmer, "I don't want to go back there, Marshal Jack."

"I just need to know if you have any relatives there, Elijah."

"Yes, but they aren't nice."

"Could you tell me their names and how you're related, if you know?"

The soldiers had finished filling the graves. They took care of the animals that were still in harness and their own.

Elijah made up his mind and blurted out, "They're Franklins. I have two uncles and their families, but they were mean to my pa and us."

Jack watched the boy. He could see the emotions the child was battling. It was obvious there were hard feelings there. In the past few hours, Elijah had been through more than anyone should ever have to face. Jack decided to drop the subject. "Don't you worry. Right now, we want to get you back to Fort Smith, where a doctor can do more for you than I have."

"You did good, Marshal Jack. I know you did. I'm feelin' better already."

Jack could see the lines of pain at the corners of the young fella's mouth and eyes. His normally smooth forehead was wrinkled. He needed to get back to Fort Smith quickly, see the doctor, and get plenty of rest.

"Are you coming back with me, Marshal Jack?"

Jack shook his head. "Not right now. I'm going with Marshal Berry and the deputies. We'll be after those bad men who did this to you. We want to make them pay for what they've done, and make sure they don't do this to anyone else."

The boy's grip on Jack's sleeve tightened. "I'm feeling better. I can go with you and help."

Jack shook his head. "No, son, you can't. You need to see a doctor, get plenty of rest and good food."

Elijah's tiny knuckles turned white he was gripping so hard. "Don't leave me, Marshal Jack. Bad things happen when you're not around."

Jack leaned his back against a wagon wheel, lifted a leg, and hooked a boot heel in a spoke, then carefully sat Elijah on that thigh so the boy could look into his face. "Listen, son. You're going to have the United States Army taking you to Fort Smith, and once you're there, you'll be protected by more U.S. Marshals. The Claggs are cowards. They run from the law. If they didn't, they would have stayed around when we came up, wouldn't they?"

Elijah thought about Jack's question and, with his head still down, gave Jack a small nod.

Lieutenant McMillian had walked up during the conversation. "Elijah, I'm Lieutenant Westfield McMillian. I have a whole troop of United States Cavalry here. We're going to take you and your wagons back to Fort Smith. The Claggs won't come within ten miles of us. You, my young sir, will have nothing to worry about."

As McMillian talked, Elijah lifted his head and looked at him. "You're old like Marshal Jack, aren't you, sir."

Both men felt the barbs of youth and grinned.

McMillian laughed. "Yes, I am. Do you know what that means?"

Elijah shook his head.

"That means we've been fighting bad men for a long time, and we've learned their ways. We can outsmart them." His smile turned icy. "And if that doesn't work, we'll just shoot them so full of holes, they won't hold water."

Elijah grinned. "That's funny." Then he grew serious. "I think I'd like that."

The thought flashed through Jack's mind, *I know I'd like it.*

His face must have reflected the thought. McMillian had his eyes on Jack and gave an almost imperceptible nod.

The sergeant stepped up. "Lieutenant, sir, if we're going to get these wagons back to the fort before dark, we'd better get started."

"You are right, Sergeant. Have the men mount."

The sergeant snapped off a salute, "Yes, sir," spun around, and immediately ordered, "Mount up!"

With the rattle of gear as the men mounted, McMillian reached for Elijah. "Why don't you ride with me for a ways, young fella. We can get to know each other."

Elijah released Jack's arm and held his hands out to the lieutenant. When the transfer had been completed, Elijah asked Jack, "You're coming to see me, Marshal Jack?"

"As soon as I can. First I have some business to take care of."

The boy waved as they moved back to the lieutenant's horse. Jack watched Elijah grimace as the lieutenant stepped into the saddle, and relax in the cavalry officer's arms when they were seated. Jack raised his hand in salute, and the troop turned back down the trail, followed by the wagons.

Berry waited until they were out of sight. Once they had disappeared into the trees, he stepped up. "What's your plans?"

"My goal is to see the Claggs either over my front sights or with a noose around their necks. I don't really have a preference."

"What about the rustlers?"

"They'll wait. There shouldn't be any large herds to speak of until spring. If we haven't caught the Claggs by then, I'll pull off and chase rustlers."

"Sounds good to me."

Jack looked around the glade. Other than mashed grass, ruts, and the graves, it looked pretty much the way it had when he'd passed it a couple of days earlier. "The big question is, what's your plan? You know this bunch a lot better than I do. How do you want to do this? Me, I'm for getting on their trail and staying there until I catch them, but you may want to head straight for their haunts."

Marshal Strawn Berry knelt and pulled a sprig of grass, straightened, and began chewing it. "You're right on both counts. There's a place where I think Milo Clagg will head with his gang. It's an old hangout, so he might figure no one remembers. However, he may think they need to get out of the country, so he'll head west. If I take two of the boys and ride straight for Milo's old hideout, and you take Buck and follow them, we may be able to outsmart him no matter what he does. Don't let his country-bumpkin act fool you. He's a cunning cuss."

"Sounds good to me, if Buck is good with it."

Jack turned and called Buck over and explained the plan. The deputy's eyes shone with excitement. "I'm ready. Let's go catch 'em. After what I've seen, I want to see them hanging high."

Jack shrugged. "I guess that answers our questions. I need to switch saddles and get my horses fed and watered before I'm ready to ride."

Buck shook his head. "Already done, Marshal. Those soldier boys had a bit of corn with them and read your mind. They've already fed and watered all our stock, and the sergeant had them switch your gear to Blaze. Those fellers are on their toes."

Jack nodded. "They are that." He glanced at Berry. "Marshal, good luck to you. If you get back before me, don't let the judge send that boy back to his family in Knoxville. There were hard feelings there, and the lad doesn't want to go back. When I return, we can figure out what to do with him. If he's staying with Grace and Mary, he'll be in good hands."

Berry shook his head. "I'll tell the judge, but it don't usually matter what kids want. By law, they go to the nearest kin."

Jack had started for Blaze. He stopped and swung around to face Berry. "I know what the law says. I've been doing this for a few years. I'm not asking for a lesson, I'm asking you to tell the judge not to send him back. I don't want to have to go after him."

"You planning on keeping the kid?"

"No, I'm not. I'm planning on finding a good family who'll care for him, and he'll take to."

Berry shook his head again. "I'm not trying to argue with you, Jack. I'm just telling you how the judge thinks. He's a real stickler for the law. That's why he got assigned out here. As far as he's concerned, it's mostly black and white. Not much gray atall."

Jack nodded and headed for Blaze. "Just tell him. You can also tell him if he contacts Elijah's uncles or sends the boy over there, I'll be coming back in and going after him, and I'll leave this badge with him." He looked over his shoulder to see Buck look at Berry and shrug his shoulders. "You going with me?"

"Wouldn't miss it for the world." Buck reached his horse at the same time Jack reached Blaze, and the two of them swung into their saddles. Without a word, Jack started Blaze forward, following the Clagg gang's trail.

After they covered a couple of miles, Buck rode closer. "Just my two cents, Marshal. Marshal Berry's a good man, but he don't have much backup in him. You were getting a mite brusk with him."

Jack snapped around in the saddle to respond to Buck. What greeted him was a sincere and concerned young man gazing at him. He turned back forward and took a deep breath. The younger man was right. He had gotten mighty pushy back there with Berry. *What the blue blazes is wrong with me?* Jack thought. *That family getting murdered and the boy have really gotten under my skin. There's nothing I can do for him. I can't take care of him, not with the job I do. I wouldn't know how, anyway.* He continued trailing the Claggs.

They continued on the trail for another mile. He motioned Buck up alongside and pulled Blaze to a stop. Jack pushed his hat back with his left forefinger, kicked his left foot out of the stirrup, and crossed it over in front of him. "Buck, danged if you aren't right. I got way too pushy with your boss, and it says a lot for him that he didn't push back. I'm not one to talk about my feelings, but that little fella has gotten under my skin. He's really afraid of going back to Knoxville. I don't know the reason, and right now, I don't have time to figure it out."

Buck said nothing.

"I've got to get him off my mind for both our sakes. The only thing I need to be thinking about right now is bringing in the Claggs. You agree?"

Buck grinned. "Marshal Sage—"

"Stop the marshal stuff out here. It's Jack or Sage. We get in formal situations, then it's still marshal. Does that work for you?"

"It surely does. That's the same way Strawberry handles it." He gave Jack a big grin. "But don't let him know I called him Strawberry, or he'll kick my rear end up and down the streets of Fort Smith." Buck grew serious. "Jack, I can see you're feeling something extra for that little feller, and so can Marshal Berry. That's why he didn't say much when you went a touch wild. Let's get these varmints on the end of a rope, and you can take care of the other situation. How does that sound to you?"

"Yep, that sounds mighty fine." Jack swung his leg back into the stirrup and grasped his hat with one hand on the front of the brim and the other on the back. When he had it positioned just right, he bumped Blaze. The horse started forward at a walk, Red trailing behind. "Let's go catch us some killers."

The trail followed the Arkansas north for several more miles until it came to a river ferry. Unfortunately, the ferryboat was tied on the other side. The river was too fast and wide for anyone except a fool to try to cross it. He and Buck examined the opposite bank where the boat sat. They saw no signs of life around it. Jack pulled out his pocket watch, his thumb unconsciously caressing the emerald set in the top of the watch. He snapped it open, four o'clock. "It'll be getting dark pretty soon. You know of any other crossings north of here?" He snapped it closed and carefully slipped it back into the vest pocket.

Buck shook his head. "Not for a long ways. It'll take us many a mile out of the way. Clagg and his bunch could be long gone before we get back down to pick up their trail." He leaned on his saddle horn and stared across the river. "It ain't like Homer to leave his boat. He's been running this ferry as far back as I can remember. I even helped him some when I was a boy. He don't judge folks, he just gives them a ride across the river."

Jack was uneasy. No ferryman left his boat unattended. He pulled his field glasses from his saddlebags and slowly checked the edge of the river and the treeline—nothing.

Buck continued to stare. "Maybe he went into the trees to take care of his morning constitutional. Though I've never known the old man to be shy. Usually he just hangs his rear over the edge of his ferry and lets fly."

Jack noticed a lone buzzard circling above the river. *It may mean nothing,* he thought. He raised the field glasses again and began studying the boat, inch by inch. He had seen these types of boats in operation before. It was a big flatboat, large enough to carry a prairie schooner with a team of four horses or oxen. A heavy rope attached to a tall pole on each side of the river ran through two eyelets on the boat, one at the stern, the other at the bow, and kept the ferry laterally in place. Thanks to the rope, the ferryboat wasn't pushed downstream by the current of the river. The ferry operator used a long pole or, where the water was too deep, pulled the boat across with the rope.

He saw Homer's pole haphazardly dropped so that it lay diagonally near the front of the boat. But saw no sign of Homer until he spotted a glint of white where the bow thrust against the bank. It wasn't much. There was no form to it. He strained to make out definition. What could it be? Finally his brain interpreted the fragment. It was the cuff of a sleeve, and coming out of the cuff was a hand. Jack yanked the glasses down, blinked a couple of times, and put them up again. *That's it,* he thought. *It's a cuff, and the hand is hanging on to the edge of the bow.*

"Buck, I see him, and he may not be dead." Jack tossed the glasses to the deputy. "Take a look. He's lying between the bow of the boat and the bank. A fragment of his sleeve is visible, with just a portion of his hand showing. I know most rivermen keep extra boats. Do you know if he keeps one on this side?"

"He keeps one on both sides, but most folks don't know about them." Buck spun his horse around, handed the glasses back to Jack, and rode to the treeline behind the cabin. Moments later he called, "Here."

With his glasses, Jack continued watching the hand until Buck called. Hearing Buck, he dropped the field glasses into the saddlebag, released Red's lead, and took off to join the deputy. When he pulled up, Buck was clearing brush from the boat.

"He keeps his boats hidden to protect them from thieves. Homer never was much of a trusting man."

Jack unlimbered his rope and looped it over a brace extending above the bow. He took a hitch around the saddle horn and started Blaze toward the water. The big palomino walked along as if he were pulling nothing, the boat sliding easily over the grass. Reaching the shoreline, Jack flipped the rope from the saddle horn and threw slack in the loop. Buck had been walking alongside. He unfastened the loop on his end and grabbed the rope attached to a bow ring. Jack swung down, stepped to the back of the boat, and began pushing.

The bow slid into the water, and the current yanked it downstream, but Buck held tight to the bow rope. In the boat lay three paddles.

Jack tied Buck's horse, Blaze, and Red, pulled his and Buck's rifles, and hurried to the boat. Buck was already in. He had given two wraps of the bow rope around the ferryboat's anchor post and clinched the end of the rope, waiting. When Jack made it to the back of the boat and was seated with paddle in hand, Buck released his rope and grabbed for a paddle. The rope sang as it whipped around the post, and the boat jerked with its newfound freedom.

But the boat moved with the current only for an instant. Jack's paddle thrust deep into the water, stopped the boat's surge, and slowly began moving forward. When Buck added the pull of his paddle to the effort, the boat increased its slow movement across the unrelenting river's current. Muscles bulged on both men. Being in the back, Jack had to paddle and steer. Each stroke, besides driving the boat forward, had to keep the bow from swinging between Buck's efforts. They had made this decision with little planning, thinking only of Homer. Now, each stroke against the current hammered the realization home. They were expending a huge amount of energy battling the current. The boat was moving forward slowly. It was going to take them longer than they had thought and a massive effort to get to Homer. *Hang on, fella,* Jack thought. *We're coming.*

8

The bow of the boat bumped the ferry. Holding the bow rope, Buck leaped to the steady platform, then pulled the bow of the smaller boat tight and secured it. Jack tossed the deputy his rifle and jumped from the boat. Standing on the ferryboat, they could see Homer clearly. He was grasping the rim at the edge of the bow. He raised his head to look at them. It looked like he was trying to bring them into focus.

"Is that you, Buck Walker?"

Buck leaped off the ferryboat and knelt by the old man. "Yes, sir, Uncle Homer, in the flesh. What happened, did you finally slip and fall off your boat?"

"Dang you, boy. You always had a smart mouth. No, I ain't fallen off my boat." A faint smile lifted the corners of his mouth. "I'm shore glad you're here, son. I truly thought I was a goner."

"Shoot, a mean old man like you ain't ever gonna die."

Jack kneeled next to Homer and examined him for wounds. The man had a lot of blood on the back of his head, but no bullet holes were evident.

"Uncle Homer, this here is Marshal Jack Sage."

The old man gave Jack an appraising look. "You ain't missed many meals, have you, boy?"

Jack chuckled. "More here recently than I'd like. You're not shot?"

"No, sir. Them Clagg boys said they wouldn't waste a bullet on a worthless old man like me, so they conked me on my head." He grinned again. "Course, they didn't know my head bone is the hardest thing in this part of the country."

Buck moved around to get the old man under his arms. "Let's us carry you up the slope a bit, Uncle Homer. It'll be more comfortable."

The old river pirate started flailing his arms around. "Git yore hands off'n me, boy. I ain't need'n no carryin'. Just give me a hand up."

Buck rolled his eyes to Jack and extended a hand to the old man. Homer grasped it and pulled himself to his feet. He was a bit unsteady, but made it to the log lying along the side of the trail. He sat down and gave Buck a defiant look.

The deputy rolled his eyes again. "So how many Claggs did you carry?"

"Three. They was three Claggs, Milo, Flint, and Bo. That's the ugliest bunch of humankind God ever put on this earth. It's no wonder they ain't got wives. There ain't a woman in this country who'd let one of them boys near her."

Jack squatted down by Homer. "Did they say where they were going?"

Homer shook his head. "Not so I'd notice. All they said was they planned on gettin' away from the territory. Said they've been around here too long." He turned to Jack. "Marshal, what'd they do this time? They seemed to be in an almighty hurry."

"Mr. Lester, they have good reason to be hurrying. They murdered three families, settlers headed west. They got it in their minds one of the families was carrying gold, so those Claggs, and whoever else is with them, are going back to Fort Smith—"

"And gettin' their necks stretched!" Homer shouted. "Yes, sir, I've heard about the new judge in Fort Smith. He ain't no one to trifle with. Heard he hanged five or six killers in one day. Well, I'll tell you for sure, those boys have been bad since they was born. I said old man Clagg oughta put the whole bunch in tow sacks with big rocks and toss 'em in the deepest hole of the Arkansas. He wouldn't do it, so now the government's gonna have to take care of 'em. Well, I'll say good riddance to bad seed." He finally saw his skiff attached to the ferryboat.

"You boys found my boat. You tryin' to tell me you paddled across that?" Homer swung his arm to take in the Arkansas River.

Buck smiled. "It wasn't easy."

"No, I suspect not. I'm surprised you two could get across. That's one powerful river, high like it is. So I suppose you want me to take you back across to get your horses."

Jack nodded. "We'd be obliged."

"Well, let me see. You two pull us back across, put my boat back, load your animals on, and pull across again. I reckon I can do that for two bits apiece."

Jack headed for the ferry. "Then let's get started. Buck?"

The old man rose from the log. "Give me a hand, boy. Get me on my boat, and I'll be fine."

Jack and Buck did exactly what the man had described while he talked, complained, and belittled the remaining light away. By the time they were back to where they had found him, both Jack and Buck were ready to move on no matter how dark the night became. Homer Lester wouldn't stop talking.

After offloading, Buck asked the old man, "You feel like you've recovered? You sure you can get back across alright?"

Homer placed his hands on his hips, moved his head at a quirky angle, and stared at Buck. "Boy, how long you knowed me?" Without waiting for him to answer, he continued, "I ain't never failed to make it across, and I won't tonight, trust me. Now you two git along and catch them Claggs. Bring 'em back through here 'cause I want to spit in their faces before you hang 'em."

He turned his back to Buck, stepped aboard his ferryboat, and picked up the long pole. Untying it, he moved to the end and sank the pole in the water. He put a strain on it, and the boat began slowly moving into the current as he walked along the side. When he stopped to head for the front again, he turned and gave Buck a single wave, then turned his back to them and continued to push.

The sun had set long ago, and the moon hadn't as yet risen, leaving the night lit only by the myriad of stars. Jack sat on Red, contemplating their chances of traveling in the heavy darkness.

Buck spoke up. "There's a nice little holler not far from here. Be a good place to put up for the night."

"What's the chance of you finding it, as dark as it is?"

"Good. When I was a boy, I was all over this country. It's a wonder my scalp's not hanging in some brave's lodge. We'll have to take it easy until the moon comes up, but we can do it."

"Alright, Mr. Nighthawk, I'm game for anything that gets us closer to the Claggs. Move out."

Jack could barely see the outline of the deputy as they rode slowly forward. He could tell the horses didn't like it either. Thankfully, they could see better than humans at night, but with so little light, their vision was also hampered. He could feel the big red horse's muscles jerk at every unexpected sound. He kept talking, soft and low, hoping to keep Red and Blaze calm.

After an hour of walking their horses in the darkness, Jack began to make out a few shadows developing. The moon was creeping above the eastern horizon. In its current state, it didn't produce a lot of light, but much more than there had been. He could feel Red calm, and his steps were more confident.

Buck turned in the saddle and spoke softly. "Not much farther. There's a dry creek up ahead. When we get to it, we turn right. The spot's only a couple hundred yards up the creek."

A few minutes later, Jack heard running water. Buck pulled up at the sound of the water. "I forgot about the rain. That's the creek you hear running, but it won't change anything. In fact, it's even better. We'll have water for the horses."

Yeah, Jack thought, *if the banks aren't so steep we can't get the horses down to it.* "Why don't we water them at the crossing? Then we won't have to be concerned about a steep bank where we pitch camp."

In the moonlight, Jack could see the deputy thinking. "Good idea, boss. The trail slopes gently down to the creek, so it'll work fine." Buck bumped his horse, and the animal moved down to the little creek. Jack drew up alongside Buck, and Blaze stepped up beside Jack. The three horses drank. When finished, Buck turned his horse to the right. "Follow me. We're almost there."

They rode through a border of brush, waist high to a man, running at a right angle to the creek. Once past it, the ground cleared, with the brush scattered. A flock of turkeys roosting across the creek in a tall oak clucked and fussed at them. One or two flew to different trees, their wide wings crashing and banging into limbs and making a huge ruckus, but once the riders were past, they settled down, safe in the tall oaks and cottonwoods.

After a short ride, Jack could feel the ground slope down. The incline soon leveled, forming a shallow depression. Buck pulled up. "Here we are. This is the nicest little spot you'll ever find. Nobody can see us from the trail. We can even build a small fire, and it'll be totally hidden."

Jack swung down from Red. "No fire."

The two men stripped their gear from the tired horses and wiped them down with the dry grass. Finished, they gave the animals enough slack on their lead ropes to graze, and Jack dug cookies from his bags. He gave each horse one and broke the last one in half, handing a portion to Buck.

"Horse food?"

"Try it before you complain."

In the pale moonlight, Jack rolled out his bedroll, unfastened his gunbelt, and sat, his back against his saddle. He laid his gunbelt next to his rifle, making sure both revolvers were free in their holsters. Buck crunched on his cookie. Jack relaxed and bit into his. *Pretty good,* he thought, *but I'd much rather be sitting at Grace's table in Fort Smith, wrapping myself around a pile of hot biscuits and gravy.*

The day had been long and hard, like almost every day since he'd pulled out of Laramie. It had been a long, tiring ride from Wyoming to Arkansas, and seeing those families brutally murdered hadn't helped. *I'm just glad Elijah survived. Hopefully he'll be fine when we bring the Claggs in. I don't know how long it'll take to catch that bunch, but however long it is, they'll be brought to justice.*

Jack glanced at Buck. The younger man had finished the cookie and stretched out under his blanket. *He'll do,* Jack thought, *but he needs another horse. We're going to have to push to catch the Claggs. We'll end up running Buck's horse into the ground.* Jack made one last check of his rifle and slid one of his Smith & Wessons out of its holster. With it gripped loosely in his right hand, he closed his eyes.

JACK HALTED Red and extended his hand to stop Buck. After two weeks of trailing, the deputy had learned the drill and was already pulling his mount to a stop next to him.

Before topping a ridgeline, Jack would dismount, slip to the top, and glass the next canyon or valley. The procedure had kept them from running headlong into a band of Kiowas. It had appeared the Indians were hunting, but they outnumbered the two lawmen five to one. At the prospect of fresh scalps and horses, who knows what the braves might have decided.

Jack had shown Buck how he glassed the countryside, taking

it section by section. Hunting men was much like hunting elk or deer, except men, especially the Claggs, could and would shoot back. Buck took to searching with the field glasses like a duck to water. Quite often, Jack would hand the deputy the glasses and watch as he would slip to the hillside and scan for the Claggs, but so far, nothing. They had temporarily lost the trail several times, but after searching, had found it. The killers' course was southwest, and they had managed to stay ahead, though the story the tracks told was the lawmen were closing in.

Marshal Jack Sage, field glasses in hand, swung to the ground and tossed the reins to Buck. He strode to the crest of the ridge thirty yards ahead. Placing his Stetson on the tall grass, he continued to the top, low crawling the last few yards until he crested and the ridge began to drop away. Stopping, he carefully spread the grass. He couldn't believe their good fortune.

Milo was seated, leaning back against the thick trunk of a large oak and lifting a cup of coffee to his lips. The killer was no more than fifty yards from Jack. This was more like a wide draw instead of a valley.

Jack watched the outlaw take a sip, lower his cup, and speak to the other three men. The coarse voice of the leader carried to Jack, though he couldn't understand what he was saying. In response, the other outlaws broke into laughter. Jack added his grim smile to their laughter and thought, *Keep laughing, boys. A hangman's noose is waiting for you.* He examined the draw, what little he could see that wasn't blocked by the tall grass. It was shallow, narrow, and surprisingly straight. Perfect for what he had in mind. He wanted to take them back to face trial in Judge Bell's court, but whether they faced a bullet now or the hangman's noose later would be up to them. It was time to end the chase. The day had warmed, and the upslope breeze brought the smell of burning wood and hot coffee.

Jack ignored the coffee's enticing aroma. He lay watching for a few more minutes and then began slowly backing off the ridgeline. Once far enough down, he duckwalked to his hat, made sure he was well below the ridge, straightened, and strode to Buck and the horses.

Moving close to Buck, he spoke in a low tone. "They're close. Just over the ridge in the draw. All four of them, including the new fella whose tracks we picked up a ways back."

Buck's eyes widened, followed by a huge grin. "We've got 'em."

Jack shook his head. "Let's don't count our chickens yet. They could take off in any direction. There's no brush or trees other than the big oak where they've stopped. No chance of slipping up on them."

"How far over the ridge?"

"Less than fifty yards."

"What's your plan?"

Jack secured his field glasses before tying the extra horses. Once finished, he shucked his Winchester from the boot and racked the hammer back. "Can't think of anything better than just riding over the hill and getting the drop on them. We'll walk the horses nice and easy like. After we top out, if they try to take off, we'll drop them." He swung into the saddle and patted Red on the neck.

Buck looked apprehensively at Jack. "The judge ain't gonna like it if we don't bring 'em all in alive. He's not a big believer of these fellers coming in over their saddles."

"I agree, but we've been trailing them for two weeks, and this is the only chance we've had. We're taking advantage of it. If you'd prefer to hang back, feel free."

Buck's face reddened. "I ain't sayin' I don't want to take these Claggs. I'm just sayin' the judge won't like it."

"Good. You ready?"

Buck, face still red, pulled his Winchester from its scabbard and thumbed the hammer back. "Ready."

The two men started walking their horses toward the ridgeline. When they topped the ridge, the Claggs were still gathered around Milo at the big oak. His tale gripped their attention, his loud voice carrying up the hill.

Jack kept Red at a steady walk. Within thirty yards, he saw the Claggs' horses' heads come up and a bay's belly swell.

When the bay whinnied, Jack kicked Red, and the big horse leaped forward. Buck followed suit. The camp broke into pandemonium, with Milo leaping to his feet, and his brothers spinning around and going for their guns. But they were too late. The two lawmen were on top of them. Red's thick chest slammed into Flint, knocking the big outlaw sprawling.

Jack, yanking Red to a halt, covered the group, his .44-caliber Winchester's muzzle threatening death. "Hold up, boys!"

A couple of them had their handguns partially out of their holsters, but the muzzles of the two rifles not ten feet away and the commanding voice froze the gunmen. The outlaws stood transfixed, their fear, surprise, and indecision palpable.

He felt the cold rage burning deep inside. These were the men who had so brutally murdered innocent settlers, the women and children along with the men. They had shot little Elijah. The boy would never be able to forget the attack, the pain of the bullet, and the ripping briars. Jack felt his chest swell as he drew in a deep breath. He had always believed in and defended the law, but now he yearned to pull the trigger of his Winchester and treat these animals as they had treated Elijah's family.

Flint struggled to his feet, his face livid with rage. His arm was bowed over his revolver, hand inches away.

Jack could feel the hate in the killer's stare and flashed a cold smile. "If you've a mind to pull that hogleg, Flint, go right ahead. I can't think of anyone I'd rather send to Hell." He could feel the steel of the cold trigger against his finger. All it needed was the slightest pressure, but slowly the outlaw's arms relaxed, and he straightened. "Not now, Sage, but there'll come a time."

Jack felt a momentary stab of disappointment and relaxed the pressure.

Milo stood with the other three, bunched at the tree. "How long you been trailin' us, Marshal?"

"Long enough to know I'd get more pleasure taking you back over your saddle than in it."

Milo Clagg's forehead wrinkled, and his head canted to one side before shaking. "Marshal, we ain't done nothing to make you testy like this. We're just easy goin' fellers tryin' to get to a place we can be free."

Jack leaned forward in the saddle, cold gray eyes drilling the killer. "You're a lying piece of slop. You and your worthless brothers murdered those settlers."

Milo Clagg looked up at Jack, eyes wide, his face the picture of innocence. "Now, Marshal, that ain't true. We ain't harmed a soul other than that deputy back in Fort Smith, and we was afeared he was gonna kill us. We had to protect ourselves. Reckon we did ride by those folks on our way out of here, but they was fine when we passed 'em. I swear they was."

9

The murdered settlers leaped to Jack's mind. His thick knuckles gripping the reins and the Winchester turned white. The urge to climb down from Red and beat Milo into an unrecognizable pile of flesh swept over him, but instead, his lips spread, showing a cold, humorless smile. "We have a witness, Milo. You and your brothers are going to Fort Smith to stand trial. Then the hangman will slip a noose around your murderous necks and drop you three feet. The last thing you are ever going to hear is the snap of your own necks."

Milo's eyes grew wider. He gaped at Jack, and his complexion turned white under the sun-darkened skin. A thick tongue shot out and attempted to moisten his lips.

In the silence, the lanky fourth man spoke up. "No witness can identify me, Marshal. I just joined this bunch. Figured it would be safer than riding through Indian Territory by myself. Now it looks like I made me a bad mistake."

Jack kept his eyes on the Claggs. "You're right about that. You joined up with killers of women and children. What's your name?"

"Zebadiah Long. Folks call me Zeb. I ain't lying, Marshal. I don't even know these fellers, and after spending a few hours with 'em, I'd made up my mind to take my chances and move on. I swear."

"You recognize this fella, Buck?"

"Nope. I ain't never laid eyes on him."

"Where you from, Zeb?"

"Texas. Brought a herd up several months back. After the owners sold 'em and headed back, I elected to stay in Dodge for a while. When my money was mostly gone, I figured it was time to head on back afore I got caught up here in the cold."

"What ranch?"

"The Flying J. I been ridin' for them a couple of years. They're good people. Pay's good and so's the food. I've got a job waitin' for me when I get back."

Flint had an evil smirk on his face. "He joined us right after we left Fort Smith. He's been with us the whole time."

Zeb's head jerked around. "You're lying!"

Jack's voice rose. "Hold up, Zeb." He waggled the Winchester's muzzle at Flint. "You, shut up. We'll get this worked out, but for now, I need all of you to drop your guns."

Jack kept a close watch on Flint. The man was almost as volatile as Joey had been. It wouldn't take much to set him off, though part of him hoped the big Clagg would turn loose. Jack was having a tough time restraining himself, but so far he had been successful.

The killers and Zeb dropped their weapons. Bo stood next to the cowhand. Upon hearing the name of the ranch, Jack had kept his surprise from showing. The Flying J was the ranch he and his friends, Montana Huff and Bronco Fenn, had started in Texas four years earlier. Up to now, he had heard nothing from or about them. It was good to hear the ranch was at least still in operation. He had plenty of questions for Zeb, but not yet. He knew by the outlaws' tracks, the cowhand had joined up only a few miles back. What he didn't know was if it had been a planned rendezvous. "Buck, get their guns, but leave me a clear shot. I don't want you taking a bullet meant for one of these vermin."

Buck nodded and swung down. He first collected the weapons from Flint and Milo. He ran his hands inside each boot top, finding at least a knife in each and a derringer in Flint's. With his collected bounty, he moved back to Jack, ensuring he remained clear of the marshal's line of fire, and dropped the weapons to the ground.

Flint Clagg winced when Buck dropped the gunbelts to the rocks. The butt of his revolver had struck a jagged granite edge, leaving a deep gouge in the wood. "Easy, dang it. Buck Walker, you and yore kind always was a bunch of idgits."

Ignoring the killer's outburst, Buck moved around Red, resting his hand on the horse's muscular rump. He headed for Bo's gunbelt lying at the outlaw's feet. Concentrating on the loaded belt, he began to bend to pick it up and frisk Bo. For a split second, his body blocked Jack's view of Bo. In that instant, the outlaw's right hand dropped and disappeared behind the deputy. With Buck between him and the outlaw, there was nothing Jack could do but yell, "Look out, Buck!"

Seeing Jack's attention diverted to Buck, Flint took a hasty step toward the pile of guns, but Jack, catching the movement, centered the muzzle of his Winchester on the big outlaw's chest. He stopped so quickly loose rocks were tossed up by his boots. Forced to watch Flint, it was all over before Jack could look back. Bo was stretched out unconscious on the ground, and Zeb was handing a derringer to Buck.

With the rifle, he waved Flint back alongside Milo. "Move back and sit down." The two outlaws lowered themselves to the ground, and Jack glanced to Buck. "What happened?"

The deputy shot a sheepish look at Jack. "I made a dumb mistake, stepping between you and Bo. It looks like Bo had a derringer stashed behind his waistband, and when he saw you were blocked, he went for it." Buck motioned his head toward

Zeb. "He hit Bo behind the ear, dropped him like a pole-axed steer, and grabbed the derringer. I woulda been a dead man without him."

Zeb shrugged. "Pa was a sheriff down South Texas way. Couldn't rightly see another lawman shot when I could do something about it."

Jack nodded. "You ever wear a badge?"

Zeb shoved his hat to the back of his head. "Couple of times. Truth was, it was a hard time back then, and I needed to eat. It ain't my favorite line of work."

"Where?"

"I did a little rangering. The Comanches got a mite rambunctious around Eagle Pass, so I signed up for a few months. After that, I did some town marshaling, deputy that is, in Oatmeal."

"Who'd you work for?"

"With the rangers, it was Captain Nelson, and in Oatmeal it was Marshal Wilhelm Klein."

Jack knew neither man, but it didn't mean the man was lying. Oatmeal was settled by German colonists, so the marshal's name was authentic. Either he was a quick-thinking liar, or he was telling the truth.

Bo began moving.

Jack nodded at the outlaw. "Buck, tie him up first and then Milo and Flint."

Milo cleared his throat. He began speaking in what he must have thought a persuasive manner but came across to Jack as whining and irritating. "Now wait a minute, Marshal, that ain't necessary. How about if we give you our word we won't do nothing?"

Buck let out a sharp laugh, and Jack gave Milo a cold stare. "I wouldn't trust you as far as I could throw you. Keep your mouth shut." He watched Buck finish with Bo and move to Flint.

Bo sat up and was giving Zeb a mean look.

"Why'd you leave those jobs?"

"Like I said, Marshal, packin' a badge ain't my favorite thing to do. I will tell you, I like workin' cattle, though riding drag ain't much fun."

Jack nodded. "I agree."

Buck spoke up. "That makes three of us," which brought a chuckle from all three men.

"Anyway, we chased the Comanches back to the reservation, and I wasn't needed any longer. As far as Oatmeal, I just got plain bored. That place never had anything happening. I swear I don't know why the marshal hired a deputy. Maybe an occasional drunk or two on Saturday night, but Marshal Klein had it well under control. He didn't need a deputy except maybe to sweep out the jail and make late night rounds. I got plumb bored, so I gave the marshal back his badge. He told me anytime I was looking for work to look him up."

Jack liked the cowhand. He had discarded the idea that Zeb might be part of the gang. He and Buck had seen where the horse had joined the outlaws. The man had nothing to do with the murder of the settlers. "Zeb, you're free to saddle up and be on your way. However, I do have a proposition for you. We've got about a week's ride back to Fort Smith. It'd make it a lot easier on us if you'd let me deputize you, and you give us a hand with this bunch. Once they're back in jail, you can take off for Texas." He glanced at Buck. "What's the starting pay for a deputy marshal?"

"Forty a month plus expenses."

Jack turned back to Zeb. "There you go. I'll make sure you get a month's pay for a week's work, and you can head on for Texas."

Zeb's lips spread in a wide grin, showing a missing tooth. "Marshal, I ain't never been a deputy U.S. Marshal, but better yet, I ain't never been paid a month's pay for a week's work. I'd be a blamed fool to turn that down. Sure, I'll trail along with you."

"Good, raise your right hand." Once the deputy's hand was raised, Jack continued, "You swear to uphold the law to the best of your ability?"

"Yep."

"You are now a United States Deputy Marshal." Jack pulled a leather pouch from his saddlebag. It contained several deputy marshal badges his liaison with the president, Carter Schofield, had given him upon his swearing in. He pulled one out, closed the pouch and dropped it back into the bag, and tossed the badge to Zeb. "Alright, let's get to work. I don't want to hang around too long out here in the open. We're way too exposed. Let's get the prisoners in their saddles and start back."

Buck had finished tying Milo's hands behind him. He grabbed the outlaw by the arm and pulled him toward his horse.

"I need my hands free, Buck. I ain't able to get on this horse without 'em."

"I bet you can, Milo." He pushed the man against his horse and held the outlaw's left arm. "Put your foot in the stirrup." He shoved the Clagg gang leader upward, and the man swung his leg over the saddle, settling in with a wobble.

Milo looked at Jack, who had Flint by the arm. "We cain't ride like this, Marshal. We need our hands. There's a goodly chance we might fall off."

Jack shoved Flint against his horse. "Get in the saddle."

Flint leaned against the animal, lifted his boot to the stirrup, and pushed himself up. He almost toppled over the saddle, but managed to get his leg across without falling. When he had stabilized himself, he glared at Jack.

Ignoring Flint's glare and Milo's complaining, Jack went to the fire and poured the pot of coffee over it, making sure the flames and hot coals were completely out. He swung the pot a couple of times to dry and cool it and tossed it to Zeb, who hung it on Bo's saddlebags. The rifles had been pulled from the outlaws' scabbards and hung across Jack's saddlebags for the short ride back to where the other horses were tied.

Each of the lawmen had the reins of an outlaw's horse.

Jack motioned to Buck. "Why don't you lead out. Get us back to the horses, and once there, we'll make a few changes."

Buck nodded, leading Milo, with Zeb and Bo following and Jack and Flint bringing up the rear. Within minutes, they were out of the draw and dropping down the opposite side of the ridge.

Jack breathed a sigh of relief to see Blaze and Buck's other horse still tied and calmly grazing on the dry bluestem. It would take them a much shorter time to return to Fort Smith, since they weren't trying to trail the outlaws. He figured a week, maybe a couple of days more or less. *It's a good move,* Jack thought, *to hire Zeb. Three men will make it easier to keep watch on these outlaws. We'll all be more rested, alert, and able to get them back to jail faster.*

Reaching the horses, Jack dismounted, followed by Buck and Zeb. He stepped to Flint's fat saddlebags and began going through them. Buck and Zeb followed suit.

"Look for weapons and especially things like jewelry and money they may have taken from the settlers."

The killers were frowning, and Milo spoke up. "Marshal, you cain't do this. We got our rights."

Jack continued his search without looking at Clagg. "Milo, if you don't shut up, I'm going to gag you. If that doesn't work, I just might leave you out here for the coyotes and buzzards."

"But, Marshal, it ain't right for you to treat us like this."

Jack glanced at Buck. "Gag him."

"Gladly." Buck stepped forward, reached up, and grabbed the outlaw's coat, yanking him sideways. With his other hand he jerked the dirty bandanna from around the man's neck. Milo, hands tied, fought to remain in the saddle. Buck tied a knot in the middle of the bandanna, shoved it in the man's mouth, and tied the ends behind his head. Finished, he shoved the grunting man erect and stepped back to the saddlebags. Milo's forehead was running with sweat from the effort he had expended to stay balanced.

Jack was silent as he lifted a dainty lace-edged linen handkerchief from Flint's saddlebags. The ends had been tied together, forming a pouch. He removed his gloves and shoved them behind his gunbelt. It felt wrong to handle these personal items with his dirty gloves.

Flint sat in his saddle, twisted around, and stared down at Jack and the contents. Seeing the handkerchief, his face stiffened. He watched Jack as if he could not tear his eyes away.

Jack laid the handkerchief on the saddlebag's strap and gently untied the lace ends. There were two gold bands, the size indicating one was a man's and the matching ring a woman's. The word love was written on the inside of each. Jack could picture the young woman when they had first met, holding her baby, her face a mix of fear and relief. He felt his throat thicken with emotion, embarrassed to be intruding on these most personal items between a husband and wife. There were several more rings, with different stones, one a brilliant green emerald whose cut caught the light, bent it, and reflected a green ray against the handkerchief.

However, a simple silver locket caught his attention. It was held by a soft brown ribbon. Jack remembered seeing it around Charlotte Franklin's slim neck when she was clutching her baby close. He noticed his hands were steady, though it felt like his entire body was quivering with the desire to lead the Claggs to the nearest tree, throw a rope around their necks, and leave them for buzzard bait. He took a deep breath and picked up the silver locket in his big calloused hands. It took him two tries to release the delicate latch. Inside, Jarrod Franklin and his wife, Charlotte, who was holding the baby, smiled up at him. The opposite side held a picture of their two boys.

Zeb was the first to speak. "There's quite a bit of money in here, Marshal."

Bo, his voice nasal and whiney, said, "That there money's mine. Don't you go stealin' it."

Jack retied the handkerchief and placed it gently inside the saddlebags. He fastened the strap holding the flap closed, stepped around to the front of the horses, and stared silently at the killers. Each of the three had watched him move to their front, and now all eyes were focused on the big, threatening lawman.

"I'm going to say this one time. Right now, I'm battling the urge to lead all three of you to the nearest oak and save Arkansas a few dollars. You want to make it back to Fort Smith, say nothing and try nothing." Jack motioned for Buck and Zeb to join him, and in a low voice continued, "Buck, you lead out. You know this country. Take the straightest shot you can back to town. I want to get rid of this bunch as soon as we can. We'll make camp before dark."

Buck nodded, and Jack turned to Zeb. "You follow Buck. You'll be leading the Claggs, single file. I'll bring up the rear with the extra horses."

Zeb also acknowledged with an almost imperceptible nod.

Jack continued, speaking low, "I want to make this trip back as quiet as possible, no sense attracting any unwanted visitors. However, if, for whatever reason, one or more of our prisoners breaks loose, don't hesitate to shoot. Don't let them get away or overpower you. Questions?"

Both men shook their heads.

"Let's hit the trail."

The afternoon passed quickly. Late in the day, they crossed a small creek, and Buck turned south, remaining inside the treeline made up of elm, cottonwood, and willows. Reaching a suitable clearing, he pulled up. Jack tossed the lead ropes of the two horses he was leading across a low limb and rode forward to Buck, who was stepping out of the saddle.

"Jack, this'll do for tonight." Buck pointed to a shallow depression with the blackened remains of several fires. "We can build a fire there. The smoke will drift up through the trees. By the time it reaches the sky, it'll be so faint even a Comanche won't spot it."

"Good. The horses need a rest." Jack looked around, examining the timber. "Looks like we've got some perfect trees for what I have in mind for our prisoners." He waved Zeb over. The cowhand had been waiting by his saddle, rifle in hand, keeping an eye on the Claggs. He strolled over. "What's up, boss?"

"Stopping here. Buck's going to keep a lookout. First we'll get our guests taken care of. Then we'll feed, water, stake the horses, and whip up some grub." He glanced at Buck, who acknowledged with a nod.

Jack grabbed Milo and dragged him out of the saddle while Zeb was doing the same with Bo. Milo stumbled, regained his balance, and turned with his back to Jack, lifting his tied hands toward him.

"You're kidding, right?" Jack yanked the man's gag from his mouth and waited while he tried to get his dry mouth working.

"You've got to untie us, Marshal. This is just plain mean. I'll be telling the judge what's—"

Clagg's words became muffled and unintelligible behind the bandanna Jack jammed back into his mouth. He shoved Clagg toward the depression and, once there, pushed him to the ground. Zeb followed with Bo, and Jack stepped to Flint's side. He reached for the outlaw's arm. Flint yanked it away, swung his leg over the saddle horn, kicked his left foot from the stirrup, and dropped to the ground. Without waiting for Jack's grasp and shove, he strode to the depression and dropped beside his brother Bo.

Bo had been watching, and as soon as Flint was seated, he looked up at Jack. "We need food."

"Shut up, or I'll gag you like your brother."

Bo glared back at Jack but said nothing.

Jack shot Buck a quick glance. "Keep a close watch on this bunch. We're taking the horses to the creek."

In acknowledgment, Buck touched his hat with a forefinger, and Jack, along with Zeb, began stripping gear from the horses.

10

While the prisoners ate, Jack examined several of the elm and cottonwood trees. Satisfied, he pulled six piggin' strings from the saddles. First, he went to Flint. The hostile outlaw watched Jack approach.

"Stand up, Clagg."

Flint glared at Jack for a moment longer, then shoved himself first to his knees and stood.

Jack pointed to a tree. "Over there."

Flint was almost as tall as Jack and a bit heavier. His eyes stayed locked on the lawman as he pushed himself up. "When I get loose, Sage, you're a dead man."

Jack grasped his arm and gave him a shove toward the tree he had designated. "More moving, less talking."

The toe of Flint's boot caught on an elm root. He stumbled, did a quick two-step, and regained his balance.

Quick on his feet, Jack thought and moved on with his prisoner. Reaching the cottonwood tree Jack had picked for the outlaw, he pointed at the trunk. "Sit."

"You gonna leave me like this? I can't lean against the trunk with my hands fastened behind me."

"Don't worry, you won't be leaning against anything. Sit facing the trunk, and wrap your legs around it."

"Are you crazy? That's no way to tie a man."

"Sit down, Clagg, or I'll knock you down. While you're hugging the tree tonight, think of the dead women and children you left behind you."

Flint Clagg glared at Jack. Even in the weak firelight and through slitted lids, the intense hate burned into Jack. Clagg slowly lowered himself to the ground and, with legs spread, scooted against the trunk. Jack moved to the opposite side of the tree, whipped one end of the piggin' string around the man's ankle and pulled it tight. He grabbed the other ankle and yanked. Clagg's heavy legs were pulled tight against the elm's trunk.

When Jack had the man's legs tied securely, he stepped behind him, knelt, and untied his prisoner's hands. He let him flex the hands and fingers for a minute. "Enough. Hug the tree."

"I swear, Sage, when I get loose, I'm gonna slice you like a piece of sausage."

Jack grabbed the man's wrist. Clagg jerked and almost yanked the hand away, but he held tight. For a few seconds, the two tussled for dominance, but Clagg, his legs tied around the tree, was at a huge disadvantage. Jack slammed the man's forearm against the trunk.

"Alright, Sage. That's enough, but was I loose, it'd be a different story."

Jack tied the wrist and looped the string around the other, pulling it tight and drawing Clagg's hands together on the opposite side of the trunk. The outlaw's cheek reared back from the trunk, and his eyes followed Jack as he returned to the fire. "Bo, stand up." He guided the brother to another tree and repeated the process. Next it was Milo's turn.

"Come on, Marshal. You wouldn't do that to a dog."

"You're right, Clagg, but the three of you earned this." He walked him to an elm. "Sit."

"Marshal, I'm too old. My joints won't take it. My back's already hurtin'. You cain't do this."

Jack's face was grim as he shoved Clagg to the ground. "We'll see about that."

Working quickly, he had Clagg tied, and in no time, the outlaw was hugging the elm.

Clagg moaned and wiggled his shoulders as if to find a comfortable position. "Marshal, have a heart, man. This is worse than what the Injuns would do."

Jack turned back for the fire, but Milo Clagg wouldn't be ignored. He called in a plaintive voice, "Buck, don't leave us tied like this. You've knowed us for a long time."

Buck, finishing his beans, watched Jack approach. He waited until Jack had poured himself a cup of coffee and taken his first sip. "You gonna leave 'em like that?"

"Of course I am. You want to get some sleep tonight? That's not near as bad as Milo's making out, and it removes most of the opportunities for them to get loose. If by some miracle they get their hands loose, they can't reach their feet without making enough noise to wake us. They'll be a little stiff in the morning, but we won't have our throats cut in the night. Watch and learn."

"Milo's sure moanin' a lot."

Jack watched the gang leader while he took another sip of the hot coffee. After swallowing, he turned to Buck. "You've known him for a long time. Have you ever known him not to complain a lot?"

The deputy gazed into the flickering flames. "Now that you mention it, the truth has a tough time finding its way out of his mouth."

Zeb spoke up. "How do you want to do the watch tonight, Marshal?"

"We'll make it two-hour shifts. Why don't you two get some sleep, and Zeb, I'll wake you in a couple of hours, then you can do the same for Buck. I'd like to be ready to move at first light."

The two deputies nodded and immediately stretched out. Jack picked up his rifle and moved to a log in the shadows. It was well back from the dying fire and located where he could keep an eye on the prisoners. He seated himself on the log and leaned back against the adjacent elm trunk. Milo hadn't shut up. Jack spoke only loud enough for his voice to carry to the prisoners. "Milo, another word, and I'll have that bandanna in your mouth for the night."

At the mention of the gag, Milo abruptly quieted down, and the only sound from the prisoners was the deep snoring of Flint and Bo. Their hats were crunched between the trees and their heads, providing a cushion against the trunk. Jack chuckled to himself and thought, *I guess they're used to the sound of their brother's voice. That's probably the last thing they've heard every night.*

The fire slowly died until only glowing embers were visible. The continuous trill of a whippoorwill carried through the timber, and Jack could hear the shuffling of an armadillo nearby. In the quiet of the night, he could pick out the soft steps of deer in the leaves, and their musky smell drifted to him. Moments later the rattle of stones in the creek was followed by the lapping of water. The small herd was satisfying their thirst.

His mind drifted to little Elijah. *I wonder how he's doing, almost healed, I hope. I'm afraid the poor lad's life has been shattered by these animals. His whole family is gone.* Jack's heart went out to the boy, for he had faced a similar situation when he was about Elijah's age.

His parents hadn't been taken by violence, but by disease, and it had been hard, even with the loving care of his uncle's family. *Elijah will get past this. He'll never fill the loss, but the pain will subside. Though he may not realize it now, our catching the Claggs will help him heal.*

A gray fox slipped into the faint light cast by the bright coals of the fire. Jack watched as the little animal's nose worked busily, separating the smells of the camp and the humans. Bo jerked against his tree, and the fox disappeared as if a phantom in the night.

Jack's mind drifted to Grace. *She's a beautiful woman. There might be an attraction there, but I've known so many good women and had the chance for a different life so often. I don't know if I could even make this one work, and how would her son, Billy, take to me?*

For a moment, he gazed at the stars twinkling through the branches of the thick trees, and then lowered his eyes to examine the sleeping Claggs. *As much as I detest dealing with butchers like them, someone has to do it, and though I hate to admit it, I'm good at it. The Good Lord has given me the size and temperament to handle their kind, and also the ability to face death with a calm and calculating mind. Though I'd rather be in another line of work, I'm useful here.*

He pulled out his pocket watch, his thumb rubbing over the inlaid emerald in the cover. He took a deep breath, momentarily seeing the dark beauty of his dead wife, Yasmina. Jack tilted the watch to get the light from the fire's embers, pushed the latch, and gazed at the face. It was time to wake Zeb. His thumb gently closed the cover, and he placed the prized watch back in his vest pocket while returning Yasmina to her special place in his heart. He stood and gently tapped Zeb's boot sole with his toe. This had been a long day. It would feel good to stretch out and close his eyes.

FORT SMITH LOOKED NO DIFFERENT. The wide main street bustled with activity. Immediately, when they were sighted, citizens flooded to them. Jack was glad Buck was in the lead, and everyone knew him, because most of the crowd ran to him, asking questions. Jack couldn't see the prisoners' faces. Zeb rode ahead with them while Jack brought up the rear with the spare horses, but he could see their backs. Bo hadn't changed, he rode along following his brothers, but Milo's back was slumped, his shoulders pulled in as if to protect himself from the verbal assault he was receiving from the citizens. Flint rode tall, ignoring the sharp verbal jabs, his shoulders back and head high, as if he were above all the commotion.

Jack watched the outlaw and brutal murderer. *When kindness was handed out,* he thought, *Flint must've been out killing something or someone, but I'll have to admit, the man hasn't let out a single whimper. I'd bet he'll face the noose with a firm jaw.*

Word traveled fast. Marshal Strawn Berry and Judge Ronald Bell waited for them on the boardwalk in front of the jail. Both men had satisfied grins on their faces. The judge, animated, was talking and slapping Marshal Berry on the back, while the marshal, less enthusiastically, nodded in agreement. Several deputies waited as the entourage pulled up at the jail and, as soon as they stopped, pulled the prisoners from their saddles.

Jack sat on Blaze, the palomino's golden coat glistening in the morning sun, as the judge hurried back to him, stopping only for a moment to say something to Buck before proceeding toward Jack.

He jogged to Jack's right side and pounded him on the leg. "You did it, boy, you did it. When a week had passed and there was no sign of you, I told Marshal Berry you'd follow those miscreants to the doors of hell and inside if you had to. Yes, sir, I told him that. Good job. You'll be the talk of the country all the way back to Washington. The president will hear of this. I'm telling you that for sure, he will hear of this."

Jack nodded to the judge and started to swing down. He was watching Flint jerk loose from one of the jail guards and turn to stare at him. He held the man's stare until the guard, joined by another, grabbed his arm and jerked him back toward the jail, shoving him forward. All three of the prisoners had difficulty walking, since they had spent the past few days with their legs over a horse and the nights with them wrapped around tree trunks.

"I'm telling you, boy, your name will be known across this United States."

"Howdy, Judge. I don't need that, but I do need to get these prisoners inside and take care of my deputies. I hired another one, temporarily, while we were on the trail."

The judge took his hand and pumped it like he was working a dry pump handle. "That's fine, Jack, that's fine. Whatever you need. The court will take care of it."

Jack got his hand back and managed to continue, "Judge, I promised him a month's pay for a week's work."

The judge waved off the comment.

People had surrounded Jack, patting him on the back and asking questions. Before he had dismounted, he had seen Grace, Billy, Mary, and Elijah standing on the boardwalk in front of Ma's. The two women were smiling, and both boys were waving. He had grinned at them and waved before being pulled down by the judge and the crowd. Thanks to his height, he could still see them. The boys' enthusiastic waves had increased with his acknowledgment.

A photographer stood in the middle of the dusty street, taking pictures. The judge waved an arm in an attempt to open a lane to the camera. "Move out of the way, folks. Let this good man get a picture of the returning conqueror."

The press of people opened to allow the photographer to get his shot.

"That's it, folks, move, move. Thank you."

The thank you came as he pushed several people away to make a clear shot for the camera. The man nodded to Judge Bell.

"Thank you, folks. This will only take a moment." The judge, with his arm around Jack's shoulders, backed the two of them against Blaze to use the beautiful horse as a backdrop.

Jack could see Buck and Zeb standing on the boardwalk, grinning at his discomfort. He leaned his head close to the judge so he could be heard in the din of excited people. "Judge, is this necessary?"

The judge, a stern frown on his face for the camera, kept his head facing the photographer and spoke through barely moving lips. "Of course it is, Jack. This is big news. It's always wonderful for the people to see justice overcome evil. That's what you've done, boy. You've overcome evil. These men will go to trial, and these fine folks will get to see them hang, as they deserve. Now hold still for the camera."

The photographer's head disappeared under the cloth hanging behind the camera. He held up a hand, counting down with fingers, and at last, stepped out smiling and nodded to the judge. Bell immediately turned to the nearest men and started shaking their hands. "That's right, folks. We'll have a trial very soon and see justice done. You won't have to worry about this kind of vermin bothering your family. This is a great day in Fort Smith."

He turned back to Jack. "Come on, boy, let's go to my office."

Jack shook his head. "I'll be there in a minute, Judge. I've got to say hello to some folks first."

A frown crossed Bell's face, but when he saw who Jack was indicating, he nodded and motioned to the photographer. "Yes, yes, let's get a picture of you and the boy. That'll go quite well with the others."

Jack had had enough. He spun around to the judge. "No. There will be no pictures of the boy. He doesn't need publicity. He needs peace in his life." He pointed at the photographer. "Keep him away from us."

He turned back around and strode toward Elijah, leaving a stern-faced, disappointed judge in his wake. The folks in his path backpedaled quickly to clear a way for him, and he was soon out of the press of bodies. Nearing the boardwalk, he saw Elijah was standing without assistance, and he also saw the bright smile Grace was rewarding him with.

Jack stopped at the edge and scooped up the boy, holding him high. "Look at you. I swear you've grown a foot. How're you feeling, boy?"

Elijah grinned down from his lofty height. "Mighty fine, Jack. My leg's healing real good. In fact, the doctor let me stop using the crutches. I can walk on my own."

Jack set him down. "Show me."

Elijah stepped out, limping slightly, but Jack was surprised he was doing so well. "That looks real good, Elijah. I'd say you'll be good as new in no time."

The boy nodded. "Billy's been helping me. A lot."

Jack turned and scooped up the other boy, doing the same with him.

Billy whooped. "I can see clear to Texas from up here."

Jack lowered him to eye height, his face serious. "I sure appreciate you helping Elijah, Billy. That's mighty big of you."

The boy's brilliant blue eyes gazed back at him. "It weren't nothin', Marshal. He's my friend."

Jack nodded. "That's good, but it's still big of you." He lowered him to the ground. "Now let me talk to your ma and grandma."

He turned to Grace, the radiant smile still on her face. Her emerald green eyes sparkled with unshed tears. "Jack Sage, I'm so glad you made it back safely. When Lieutenant McMillian and his men returned with Elijah, I was afraid you and Buck would be lost to those killers."

Jack grinned at Mary when he responded, "You haven't known me long enough to know that a few bad eggs weren't going to harm this thick old skin."

Mary laughed and opened her arms. "Give this old woman a hug, Jack. It's glad I am to see you back. Now come on in, and we'll see if we can find a few crumbs and a cup of coffee to work on the growl I hear from your belly."

It was Jack's turn to laugh. He had a hand resting on each of the boys' shoulders. "I'd really like that, Mary, but you see the judge over there in that press of people? I think he's a little miffed with me for not going with him to his office right away. I best go see what he has on his mind before he sends his deputy after me again."

She laughed. "Aye, lad. You best go on, but we'll have a tummy-tickling meal ready for you when you return." She called to the youngsters, "Come on, boys. Let's go see if we can find a cookie." Without another word, the boys, one on each side, charged through the door, leaving Jack and Grace alone.

The two smiled silently at each other. Finally Jack spoke. "It's good to see you again."

Her smile changed to an impish grin. "I should hope so, after I sent you away with all of those tasty doughnuts."

Though she stood on the boardwalk and Jack on the street, she was still several inches below him. It allowed him to look down on her beautiful black hair, and gave the sun a perfect angle to glint on her sparkling green eyes. Jack shook his head. "I thought of you often while on the trail, and not because of those delicious doughnuts."

Her grin changed to a wistful smile. "So did I, Jack. I prayed for you constantly."

Jack felt the jolt of realization that she might be feeling the same as him. *Can I be so lucky?* he thought. *I've turned away from so many since Yasmina. Could Grace be the one?*

Grace reached out and touched Jack's arm. "We can talk more later. You need to meet with the judge." Her grin returned. "He's not a patient man."

"I'll see you in a while." His hand touched hers where it rested on his opposite arm. He let it lie for just a moment before turning for the judge's office.

11

Entering the judge's antechamber, Jack saw Deputy Nesbit busy at his desk. The deputy glanced up and stood. "Welcome, Marshal. Congratulations on a successful hunt. We were beginning to wonder whether the Claggs added you and Buck to their list."

"Nope, they actually made a pretty stupid mistake. They stopped in the open to have coffee under a big oak. That was one of the easiest captures I've ever made. Thanks to Buck, we stayed on their trail, and I don't think they ever suspected we were following. That bunch should never have decided to ride the owlhoot trail."

Nesbit shook his head. "I've known the Claggs since I was a boy. Most of 'em are dumb as a rock. The exceptions are their two brothers, Ben and Barrett Clagg. They started a freighting business and are smart as whips. They've been mighty successful, but they spend it all keeping their brothers out of jail. Don't think their money will help them this time."

The judge stepped out of his office. "Ah. I heard voices. Come in, Jack."

Jack followed the judge into his office, closing the door behind him.

"Have a seat," the judge said, pointing to the couch.

Jack dropped onto the sofa and waited. The judge stepped behind his desk and dropped into his dark brown leather chair. "You've done a great job, Jack, twice. I want you to know I appreciate your efforts."

Jack said nothing.

"Normally, I would discipline a deputy marshal for taking it upon himself to hire another deputy unless he was in dire straits."

For some reason, this judge had a great knack for irritating Jack, but he remained silent. Nothing was gained by starting an argument.

The judge continued, "But, as we both know, you do not work for me, you work for the president, and you are a marshal. Therefore I have already authorized the Arkansas National Bank to pay Mr. Zeb Long."

Good thing, Jack thought. *I was planning on paying Zeb if the judge didn't come through, but money's running low.* Jack leaned forward on the sofa. "Judge, I'm not big on your photographer. I don't need or want publicity."

The judge also leaned forward, placed an elbow on his desk, and pointed his index finger at Jack, emphasizing his words. "As far as photographers, you might as well get used to their presence. This is how we let people throughout the country know the law is working out here in the west. There are many places in this western country where outlaws have taken over. Our publicity spreads hope to those who do not yet have the law available to them, and comforts those citizens back east who believe the west is made up of nothing but killers and rapists."

Jack's back stiffened, but his good sense kept him quiet, and he continued to listen to Judge Bell. What the man was saying actually made sense. As much as he detested publicity, he could see the judge's reasoning. He raised a finger.

"You have something to say?"

"Yes, Judge, I do. I think I understand your explanation for the need for publicity. In the future, you will get no argument from me. However, I'd like to keep Elijah Franklin out of the news. The boy has gone through a terrible ordeal. The scene of his family's death was horrible. I'll tell you the truth. It was all I could do to keep from hanging all three of the Claggs when we caught them. Elijah doesn't need any additional reminders of what happened out there."

The judge nodded. "I completely understand. I believe we can keep him well clear of any publicity."

Relief flooded Jack. He wanted to protect Elijah from as much as possible. "Thanks, Judge."

The judge continued, "I need you to hang around town for a few days. I was hoping to have the Claggs' trial tomorrow, but Nesbitt reminded me we have a full docket tomorrow and the next day. That'll take us through Saturday, and we don't hold court on Sunday, so the next available time for their trials will be Monday."

"What about the rustlers I'm supposed to be after?"

"Don't worry about them. I've already sent two other men after them. You can relax for a few days. Don't worry, something always comes up."

A few days to get all of my gear cleaned, he thought. *And some time to spend with the boys and Grace. I'm liking this more and more.* "How long do you think I'll be here?"

The judge, a knowing look in his eyes, gazed out his big window. "I noticed some interest between you and Grace. I'm thinking it might be long enough to strengthen that bond."

Jack frowned. He didn't like others delving into his private affairs.

Bell chuckled. "Relax, Jack. I'm not prying. I like to see good things happen to good people."

Jack relented with a lopsided grin. "Thanks, Judge, I think."

"I will tell you, several good men pursued her after her husband's death in the war. None have been successful. She's a very independent woman when it comes to men. I understand her husband was a fine man."

Jack squirmed on the sofa. He didn't like talking about personal things. "We'll see."

The judge gave him a knowing smile. "Yes, we will, but if you are successful, there will be a bunch of sad men in this town. They love her cooking."

Jack had to change the subject. "What about Elijah? What's going to happen to him?"

The judge moved some papers around on his desk until he came to the sheet he was searching for. He stopped, nodded, and pulled a pair of glasses from a vest pocket. "Yes, the boy. I have a letter from an uncle who claims he is the guardian in the event Elijah's parents are lost."

Jack sat forward. "That's a lie. I talked to Elijah. The boy says his father fought for the North, and the rest of the family stayed with the South. There was no love lost between the brothers. That's why Mr. Franklin brought his family west. He was trying to get his wife and kids away from their hateful family in Knoxville."

"This letter paints a completely different picture, and the uncle says he's coming out to get the boy."

"Judge, did Marshal Berry deliver my message about Elijah?"

The judge fixed Jack with an icy glare. "Yes, he did, but the law is the law, and the boy has lost his family. For his protection, it is my job to ensure his next of kin is contacted, so I followed the law. The law cannot be dictated to, not by me and certainly not by you. Furthermore, this man's claim on Elijah is perfectly legal. If there are no closer family members, he is the legal guardian until

Elijah reaches the age of majority, and there's nothing I, you, or Elijah can do about it."

Jack jumped to his feet. "Judge, it seems like dealing with you is all in one direction. You get what you want, but you never bend for anyone else. I'm getting tired of coming up here. You seldom have anything but bad news. Tell me this uncle's name, and when's he supposed to be here?"

Judge Bell's eyes narrowed, and his brow wrinkled. "What are you planning, Jack?"

"I'm planning nothing. I'm trying to figure out what to do. Just tell me his name and when he's supposed to show."

The judge considered for a few moments longer and held the sheet of paper in the light from the window. "It looks like his name is Abel Franklin, and he should be arriving any day."

Jack gave a sharp nod. "You need me for anything else?"

The judge shook his head. "Just be available to testify on Monday against the Claggs, and leave Franklin alone."

Jack turned and marched out the door, slamming it behind him. The glass panel, with the judge's name etched across it, rattled in the door, momentarily threatening to shatter, but remained intact.

Jack was seething. *Elijah's not going to be forced to go anywhere he doesn't want to,* he thought. He must immediately find out when the next stage from the east was scheduled to arrive. The rapid and heavy clump of his boots accompanied by jingling spurs could be heard throughout the building as he raced down the stairs. Reaching the main door, he threw it open and knocked Zeb Long against the railing that framed the court building's entrance, jarring the man's hat to the ground.

"Whoa, Marshal. You on the prod?"

Stepping forward, Jack retrieved Zeb's hat and handed it to him. "You all right?"

The tall rider slapped his hat on his head and tossed Jack a lopsided grin. "Yeah, I'll live. Though I feel like I've been run over by a thousand pounds of angry steer."

Jack shook his head. "Sorry, Zeb. I guess you could say I was in a bit of a hurry."

"Marshal, I was looking for you. The judge told me to go to the bank to get paid, which I did. But while I was there, this high mucky-muck banker, who I'm sure ain't never missed a meal, comes out of his office and tells me he'd appreciate it if I'd tell you he'd like to speak to you. Yes, sir, that's his exact words, 'Speak to you.'"

Jack was taken aback. He knew no banker in Fort Smith. "Are you sure he was talking about me?"

"Well, sir, he says U.S. Marshal Jack Sage, from Wyoming. Reckon you fit the bill about as close as anyone I know."

"You get your money alright, Zeb?"

"I sure did. It's nice to have a little jingle in my pocket again. It'll be more than enough to get me to Texas and back to the ranch." He gave Jack a sly grin. "In fact, it might be enough to make a stop at a saloon or two along the way."

Jack shook the man's hand. "You did a fine job, Zeb. If you're looking for a place to hang your hat, you can't beat Ma's Bed & Eats. The beds are clean, and the food's top-shelf. Tell them I sent you. By the way, which bank?"

"Thanks, Marshal, I might stop by, and it's that one right there." Zeb pointed across the street to the Arkansas National Bank.

Jack gave Zeb a quick wave, checked the street, and crossed between wagons. He pushed through the front door and walked up to a teller, who sat at a counter behind a barred opening. A space beneath the framed bars allowed for passing documents or money back and forth. "Someone sent for me. I'm Jack Sage."

The man behind the counter was young and wore a green visor and glasses. He responded immediately. "Yes, sir, Marshal

Sage. I'll let Mr. Gleason know you are here. Wait just a moment." He hurried off to a back office.

The young man returned quickly. "Please step to the end of the counter, sir, and I'll let you through."

Jack walked to where the pony wall began. There was a latched swinging door in the wall that locked from the opposite side. It was low enough, at his height, he could step over it, but he waited. The man unlocked the door and swung it open, almost bowing as Jack walked past.

Wonder what that's all about, Jack thought.

A well-dressed, portly man stepped from the back office the teller had momentarily disappeared into, a wide smile on his pasty face. "Marshal Jack Sage?" he asked, stepping toward Jack with his thick hand extended.

"Guilty as charged." Jack took the hand only to find it was limp and clammy. He dropped it quickly. "What can I do for you, Mister...?"

"Gleason, Marshal, Marley Gleason. Come in."

Jack followed Gleason into his office. The banker pushed the door closed and motioned for Jack to take a seat. There was a soft-looking couch and two straight-backed wooden chairs. Jack chose a chair, while the banker stepped around the corner of his desk and dropped his bulk into a thickly padded leather chair. It groaned in protest but held.

"Mr. Gleason, can you tell me what this is all about?"

"Yes, Marshal Sage, I am happy to be able to fill you in on my request to have you meet me here in the bank. I have money for you."

Just in time, Jack thought.

"We have received two wire authorizations. One from Montana Huff of the Flying J ranch in Texas, and the other from a Mr. Henry Marsden in Silver City, New Mexico. Both are substantial amounts."

Jack leaned forward and locked Marley Gleason in one of his interrogator stares. "Don't keep me in suspense, Mr. Gleason."

The banker, suddenly uncomfortable in his own office, cleared his throat. "No, of course not. One is from the Flying J, a ranch in Texas, and is for forty-five thousand dollars, and the other is from a Mr. Marsden, representing a gold mine in Silver City, New Mexico, and it is for one hundred and twenty-five thousand dollars." Gleason took a handkerchief from his suit coat pocket and wiped sweat from his forehead before continuing somewhat hesitantly after clearing his throat again, "Marshal Sage, I do hope you don't plan on withdrawing the total amount today. We don't keep that kind of money on hand. If you need it, we'll have to send for it."

Jack had been taken aback at the amounts of money. He had been hoping for something either from Montana or Hank, but this amount boggled his mind. "Relax, Mr. Gleason. I can't picture any situation where I'd need that kind of money in cash. If I need it sent somewhere else, you can do that for me, right?"

The man nodded hesitantly. "Yes, we can, Marshal Sage. We are a national bank and can wire funds throughout the country. In fact, from the record of the wiring orders, it appears both parties have been trying to locate you for quite a while. There were messages attached to each transfer notice."

Gleason held the two transfers while slipping on a pair of spectacles. "From the ranch, the message reads, 'Doing good. This is your part of the last four drives. Come back anytime,' and from New Mexico it simply said, 'Don't be a penny-pincher. Deep vein. More to come.'" Removing the spectacles, he slipped them into his vest pocket, laid the messages on another pile of papers, and, looking pleased with himself, smiled at Jack. "It seems things are going well at both ends."

He laid both of his hands on the desk in front of him. "I am most pleased to be your banker while you are here, and let me assure you, Fort Smith is a growing city with numerous investment opportunities."

Jack stood, relieved on hearing Montana and Bronco were doing well, at least at the time the wire had been sent, and stunned to hear his gold discovery hadn't run out and looked like it might continue. "Thank you. I'll keep your information in mind. For now, I'd be grateful if I could withdraw a couple of hundred dollars today."

Relieved, Gleason gave Jack a big smile, showing three gold teeth. "Marshal, we would be most pleased to accommodate you." He scribbled a note and, reaching across his desk, handed it to Jack. "Give this to the teller."

Jack stood. Gleason followed and extended his hand again. Steeling himself, Jack took the hand, shook, and quickly released it. He turned and opened the door. Another well-dressed man, in a black frock coat and black bowler hat, stood with his hand stretched to open Gleason's door.

At Jack's sudden appearance, the man withdrew his hand and straightened. Surprised, not at the man's sudden appearance, but at his size, Jack looked directly into the stranger's hooded gray eyes. He was Jack's height. The frock coat he was wearing fit wide shoulders perfectly and accentuated his slim waist. Jack felt sure he had seen him before, but couldn't place him.

Gleason stepped to Jack's side and extended his hand to the newcomer. "Good morning, Mr. Clagg, it's good to see you. Please come in. Marshal Sage was just leaving."

Jack watched the man's face. At the banker's mention of his name, the only expression change evident was the corners of Clagg's eyes tightened.

Once Gleason had released his hand, Clagg extended it to Jack. "How do you do. I am Barrett Clagg. I believe you brought my brothers in this morning."

Jack took the man's hand. It was hard and calloused, still a little damp from the previous encounter with the banker. There was a glint in his eyes. He tightened down on the grip, but Jack met it, squeezing only enough to stop Clagg. The faint smile disappeared, and he released the grip. "I did. I don't know how close you are to your brothers, Mr. Clagg, but were I you, I'd be spending as much time with them as I could."

Clagg stepped closer. "Why's that, Marshal?"

Jack surveyed the man's face. "Because they'll soon be stretching a rope."

"You're assuming they'll be found guilty. It's my understanding they weren't involved in the unfortunate murder of those settlers."

Jack gave not an inch. "They were involved. They are all guilty as sin, and they will hang."

Gleason stepped in close to the two men. His bulk actually pushed against Jack, who could smell the man's unpleasant odor.

"Gentlemen, I'm sorry to interrupt, but I do have a busy day. Thank you, Marshal, for coming in." He turned to Clagg. "Barrett, why don't you come in. What can I do for you?"

Clagg broke the eye contact between the two men and turned to Gleason. "I'll only take a minute, Marley." Gleason led Clagg into his office and, nodding at Jack, closed the door.

Jack moved to the pony wall. He passed the slip to the teller and, forgoing the gate, stepped over the wall. At the teller's window, he asked, "What's your name?"

The young man looked up from the paper, surprise on his face, as if it was a wonder anyone would care about him. He grinned at Jack, showing a mouthful of white teeth. "My name's Casey Carter, Marshal Sage. Thanks for asking." He looked back down at the slip. "How would you like your money?"

"Make it a hundred in coins and a hundred in bills. You break it up the way you'd want it."

Casey's grin widened. He opened a drawer and quickly extracted gold and silver coins and paper money, carefully counting it out.

"You from this part of the country, Casey?"

The boy shook his head. "No, sir, I'm from Norfolk, Virginia. My folks wanted me to go to college, but I wanted to go west. This is as far as my money would take me."

Jack swept the coins into a wide hand and dropped them into his left vest pocket. "Figure most fellas from Norfolk would go to sea."

Casey gave a self-conscious grin. "I get seasick."

Jack returned the boy's grin with an understanding smile. "Nothing to be ashamed about. Lots of folks can't handle the motion, but there aren't many who figure money as quick as you do. You must have a good mind for numbers. Is that how you got the job?" He folded the paper money and shoved it into his right vest pocket.

Casey shoved his green visor up and leaned against the back of the tall chair so he could look Jack in the eyes. "That's part of it, Marshal. My predecessor quit. Mr. Gleason was in a panic for someone to take the job. I'd never worked in a bank before, but I figured what the heck, I need money to go west, and this keeps me out of the cold and wet."

Jack, building rapport with the young man, continued, "You getting close enough to pull up stakes and keep going?"

Casey shook his head. "Not yet, but it's growing. I should have enough by the time spring comes around."

"If you don't mind my asking, how much more do you need?"

"No, sir, I don't mind. I figure when I've put aside another two hundred, I'll be set."

Jack started to ask where the boy would head, but the door of Gleason's office opened, and Barrett Clagg stepped out with Marley Gleason in tow. Clagg's eyes immediately found Jack and watched him for only a moment before he turned to answer a question from Gleason.

"Good luck to you, Casey. You can tell me more next time I come in. Maybe I can buy you lunch sometime."

Casey was all business now with Gleason near. "Yes, sir. That would be fine. Thank you for stopping by, and have a good day."

Jack nodded and stepped to the door. He had begun turning the knob when Clagg called.

"Marshal, would you hold up? I have a question."

Jack opened the door. "I'll meet you outside." He stepped through. The chilly north wind hit his cheeks, and he pulled the door closed.

12

Waiting for Clagg on the boardwalk, Jack buttoned his coat. The wind was picking up. He watched heavy clouds sail overhead.

The bank door opened, and Barrett Clagg stepped through, pulling the door closed behind him. His voice cut through the air, cold and penetrating as the north wind. "Walk with me." He stepped from the boardwalk into the street. After several steps he was aware Jack hadn't joined him. He spun to face the big marshal. "I said walk with me."

Jack leaned against the front of the bank, one boot heel resting against the wall. "Anything you have to say, Clagg, can be said right here."

"Don't try me, Sage. My time is valuable."

"And mine isn't?"

Clagg stood in the street, considering the marshal. After a few seconds he looked up and down the boardwalk and moved back to Jack. "It's getting cold out here."

Jack said nothing.

Clagg moved closer. "Why don't we at least go to Ma's and get a cup of coffee?"

Jack had to get to the stage and find out when the eastbound was due. "I don't have time. If you want to talk, do it now."

The brother of killers stiffened. "People don't talk to me like that, Sage, at least not more than once."

Jack picked up the veiled threat and didn't like it, plus his patience was running thin. He had to find out about Elijah's uncle, and Clagg was right. It was getting cold. He dropped his foot from the wall and stepped forward. "Don't waste your breath threatening me. Just tell me what you want, and we can be on our separate ways. This is your last chance."

Two cowhands, coats pulled close, approached on the boardwalk. Seeing the two big men, they stopped and stepped into the street to give them a wide berth.

Jack was fed up. He needed to get to the stage station.

Clagg watched the cowhands hurry along the boardwalk, turning in to the nearest saloon. Once they were gone, he turned, focusing his piercing eyes on the lawman. "What can you do to help my brothers?"

The question surprised Jack. "What do you mean?"

Clagg leaned closer. "Look, Sage. Don't play dumb with me. I know lawmen don't make a lot of money. If you help my brothers, I can help you."

The blatant attempted bribe surprised Jack. He expected violence first, but it made sense, with Clagg's money, bribery would be the first move. If the bribe was unsuccessful, then came violence. "Listen closely, Clagg. There are two things you don't know about me. I don't take bribes. Furthermore, I can send you to prison for just making the suggestion."

Clagg glared at Jack. "What's the second?"

"The second thing, even more important than the bribe, is that I saw what your brothers did to those three families. I would pay the government out of my own pocket to allow me to hang them myself. Is that clear enough for you?"

Clagg's face had reddened from the cold north wind, but at

Jack's last statement, the big man became livid. "You bleed just like any other man, Sage."

Jack shook his head. "And there's a threat. I'm going to do you a favor, Clagg, and not arrest you for attempting to bribe and threaten a federal officer. This is my gift to you, but this is the first and only time. Stay away from me. Don't approach me. Don't try to talk to me. You just mention the weather and I'll throw you in jail. Now I've got things to do. Get out of my way." Jack motioned Clagg away.

Clagg stared, as if unable to believe anyone would talk to him in such a manner, then turned and marched off along the boardwalk.

Jack headed in the opposite direction to the Butterfield stage office. He pulled his hat tighter. The wind was picking up, and he felt an occasional drop of rain.

Reaching Butterfield's office, he pushed the door open, allowing a blast of wind to fill the interior, and was met with a wall of heat. The rock fireplace roared, pumping out heat like a train engine. A counter, stacked with packages, ran along one wall, with an agent standing behind it.

When the wind blasted into the room, the stack of papers he was working on flew from his desk like a startled flock of birds. The agent grabbed at them and yelled, "Close that danged door. You're lettin' a norther in here."

Jack pushed the door closed, the wind fighting him. Before turning back, he removed his coat, exposing his marshal's badge. When he turned, the agent looked up and recognized him.

"Sorry, Marshal, didn't realize it was you." He picked up and stacked the papers that had blown to the floor. Once satisfied with the papers' positioning, he spoke again. "Good job, you catching those Clagg brothers. There's still a couple more floating around who need to be in jail, if you ask me. What can I do for you?"

Jack stepped up to the counter. "When's the next stage scheduled in from the east?"

"That'll be about ten o'clock in the morning." The Butterfield agent looked out the front window. "Dang it, I was hoping we wouldn't be gettin' any more of that kind of weather."

Jack heard the sudden roar on the roof before he turned to see the street disappear in heavy rain.

The agent shook his head. "Just about the time everything has dried out from that last frog strangler, here it comes again. I'm glad I don't have to go out in it. Everything that's scheduled has already come through."

Jack stared at the rain. He'd be soaked before he made it three steps into that downpour.

"Was that all I could help you with, Marshal?"

"Yep. I'll be here in the morning for the arrival." Reaching the door, he put on his coat, buttoned it, turned up the collar, and pulled his Stetson down tight over his head. "Watch your papers."

The man spread his arms over the several stacks. "Good luck, Marshal."

Jack grabbed the door handle firmly, so it wouldn't be blown from his hand, and turned the knob. He felt the jolt of pressure instantly, opened it only wide enough to slip through, and stepped onto the boardwalk, yanking the door closed behind him.

Though the boardwalk was covered, it provided sparse protection, for the wind was blowing the heavy drops sideways, hammering, searching along the buildings, looking for opportunities to slip through cracks. Jack yanked his hat tighter and turned down the boardwalk toward Pauly's stable. His stomach was growling, reminding him of Ma and Grace's welcoming promise of food, but first he needed to check on the horses. Unfortunately, he'd have to cross the street. Pauly's and Ma's places were both on the other side of the wide and now muddy street.

Jack made his way along the boardwalk, the rain pelting him as he hurried across the uncovered alleyways between each building. He passed the jail and next the marshal's office, continuing until he was directly across from Pauly's. The big door was closed, so Jack aimed at the smaller entrance door. There was no problem with wagon traffic on the street. Most travelers had been driven to cover. Holding on to his hat, Jack stepped into the mud. Thankfully, it wasn't as deep as the evening he'd arrived in Fort Smith. If the rain continued, as soaked as the ground already was, soon a man would sink to mid-thigh or deeper in the muck.

Reaching the door, he pushed through and slammed it closed. It was a relief to be out of the driving rain, which now dripped from his hat and coat. The legs of his britches, below the edge of his coat, were also dripping around his muddy boots. Jack walked straight to Stonewall, his mule. "How are you doing, fella?" He patted the mule on the back as he spoke, walking along its side. He was genuinely pleased to be back with his animals and was spending time with each one when Pauly strolled out of his office.

"How'd Blaze and Red work out?"

Jack, scratching Smokey between the eyes, turned his head to see Pauly approaching. "Real good. I liked them both. Sorry I didn't get them back to you, I was a little tied up."

"Not a problem, Buck brought 'em in. He put your tack with the rest of your gear in the tack room."

Jack gave Smokey a final scratch and moved around to Pepper, who nosed at him when he walked up. "Sorry, fella, I'm plumb out of cookies. I'll have to make some more."

Pauly reached into a pocket and pulled out one, handing it to Jack. "I tried your recipe. Mighty fine treats for everyone. Haven't found an animal or human who doesn't like 'em."

"Thanks." Jack took the cookie and gave it to Pepper. The big red horse munched contentedly. "You have enough for the whole crew?"

"Sure I do."

Jack pulled out three double eagles and traded them for the cookies. "That should keep us paid up for a little longer. Anything I should know?" He dropped the extra cookies in his pocket and moved to Thunder, who had been watching over the wall of his stall. After scratching the big gray behind his ears, he handed the cookie to him. The big horse took it and began to crunch.

Pauly, his hand resting on Thunder's shoulder, watched for a few minutes before he spoke. "I saw you talking to Clagg in front of the bank. He didn't look too happy."

"I guess I wouldn't either if I had just been told my brothers were guilty of killing three families."

Pauly spit and wiped his mouth. "Listen close, Jack. That Barrett Clagg don't mind killing innocent folks any more than his brothers. If there had been money in it, he'd a been right along. You keep an eye out for him. He ain't against killing a lawman or a boy to keep his brothers safe."

Jack rubbed Thunder as the horse chewed. "Good information. What about his brother?"

"Same. Ben's average height but skinny. Being the smallest of the bunch probably made him feel like he had to make up for it. He's mean. I'm not sayin' the others aren't, he's just meaner. If any one of them was going to take a shot at you from an alley, I'd nominate Ben. He's the sneaky sort. He'll be smiling at you when he slips a blade between your ribs."

Jack nodded, moseyed to the stock room, and retrieved his rifle and saddlebags. "My horses look a lot better than they did a month ago. I'm obliged."

"Yes, sir, they'd lost a bunch of weight when you first showed up. But they've been getting plenty of corn and oats along with their hay. That'll fatten 'em up real quick. Especially when they're getting a lot of rest. I'm guessin' they're ready to head out any time you are, though I imagine they'd prefer you wait until the rain stops."

Jack strode toward the door. "I'd prefer to wait until the rain stops, but I imagine it's gonna be when the judge sends an order."

Reaching the door, Jack turned. "Thanks again, Pauly. If you need me, I'll be at Ma's." He reached for the door.

"One more thing," Pauly called over the roar of the rain on the roof. "Barret and Ben are a pair. They're pretty much joined at the hip. It's mighty seldom you see 'em without the other. I noticed you were talking to Barrett by hisself."

Jack had stopped and turned back when Pauly called. His hand still rested on the latch. "What's your point, Pauly?"

The stableman kicked a horse apple. "I'll tell you, Marshal. I'd keep my eyes peeled. The onliest time you see them apart is when Ben is up to some dirty deed. Like I said, keep a close lookout."

Jack's mind immediately went to Elijah. *Without the boy's testimony, the only evidence we have is the belongings of the families. That's damning, but it may not be enough to get them to the gallows.*

Jack, now filled with concern for Elijah, jerked the latch on the door, yanking it open, and dashed into the driving rain. Bent low, he raced to Ma's, leaped onto the boardwalk, and slammed through the door. He was met with an assortment of tasty smells and the laughter of two boys. Relief flooded him. *Both are here and safe,* he thought. *If the Claggs wouldn't hesitate to kill Elijah, they'd also have no qualms killing Billy.*

At the sound of the door slamming, the boys raced into the room, and Grace followed, a smile on her face, which disappeared immediately when she spotted him, water dripping from every inch of his body. He watched as she tried to hide a growing grin. She placed a strong and supple hand over her mouth, but a giggle slipped through, followed by another.

Ma called from the kitchen, "Who is it, Gracie?"

"Come see."

The boys looked at Jack, then Grace, and back to Jack, confused by their mother's laughter.

Jack stood silent, relieved and dripping, in the doorway, not sure whether he should join in the laughter or be angry.

Moments later, Ma stepped into the parlor. Her mouth split in a wide grin. "Jack, do you ever come here dry?" She broke into laughter. Grace couldn't resist and joined her.

Jack frowned at the older woman. "Ma'am, I'm going to have to place you under arrest for making fun of a federal officer."

The two women roared, Ma slapping her knee, and the two were soon joined by Billy. Elijah was more respectful of the man who had saved his life. He only grinned.

Mother and daughter dropped onto one of the sofas in the parlor to catch their breath. "Oh my," Grace gasped, "I don't think I've laughed that hard since . . ." Her grin turned to a wistful smile.

She's thinking about her husband, Jack thought. *At least I cheered her up for a moment.*

Mary and Grace stood. Mary turned to her grandson. "Billy, go move the tub to the marshal's room and put a couple of the large towels and a washcloth in there. Elijah, you can help."

The two boys ran from the room. Jack watched them go. "Elijah is healing fast. You two must be taking real good care of him."

Grace smiled, her full lips parting to show even white teeth. "He isn't hard to care for. Elijah is a fine lad. Anyone would be proud to call him their son. He was in real pain when the lieutenant first brought him in, but he complained little. And when the doctor had to clean the wound, anyone could see it hurt him so badly, but he was strong."

Jack felt a tug at his heart just watching the woman speak of the little boy.

Mary spoke up. "Jack, you'll catch yourself a death of cold if you don't get out of those wet clothes. You get back to your room.

We keep water boiling most of the day, so we'll start bringing hot water back there. Before you know it, the tub will be ready. After all that travel, it's time you got rid of that dirt. Throw your clothes into the hallway, and one of the boys will pick them up. They'll be clean and ready for you tomorrow."

"Mary, I've been on the trail for almost two months. I'm filthy. I can't tell you how much I appreciate a hot bath."

"Good. We were going to get the tub in your room this evening after supper, but there's no time like the present. Throw your towels out with your wet clothes. Now come into the kitchen, and we'll get those boots off while we fill the tub."

Jack knew it was no use arguing with the older woman. He rose as Billy, along with Elijah, showed up to tell Grace the tub and towels were in Jack's room.

"Thanks, boys," Jack said. "You mind taking this wet rifle and these saddlebags back there?"

Billy grinned. "Sure thing, Marshal Sage." He took the rifle, keeping the barrel up, and with Elijah helping him, carried the saddlebags down the hall.

Reaching the kitchen, Jack pulled out a kitchen chair from the table and sat in it. He started to cross his leg to get his boot off, but Grace stepped in front of him. "Hold your boot up."

Jack shook his head. "Grace, you don't have to help me with these boots. I can get them off." He began working the boot from his foot. Wet and clinging to his foot, it hardly moved.

She shook her head. "You are one hardheaded man. Give me that boot." Grace grabbed the toe of the boot with one hand and straightened his leg. Resting her other hand just above the heel, she began to pull, using a rocking motion. Slowly his heel worked past the tight leather around the ankle of the boot, allowing it to slip free.

"Thanks, Grace. You made it a lot easier."

"Good. Give me the other boot." He held his foot up. She grabbed it and, with petticoats flying, swung her leg over his so she was facing away from him. Placing both hands on the boot, she said, "Push."

Surprised, Jack did nothing.

Grace, black hair glistening in the light of the kitchen, gave him a teasing smile over her shoulder. "Jack, don't tell me you've never done this before. Put your foot on my bottom and push."

Jack looked at Mary, who had returned to the kitchen and was preparing supper. "Just do it, Jack. It doesn't mean you're married. She's just taking your boot off."

Jack place his big foot on her bottom, feeling the soft resistance as he gently pressed forward. He didn't want to push too hard. He might hurt her.

Her voice exasperated, Grace said, "For goodness' sake, Jack, you push like a girl. I don't have all day."

He could feel her gripping his boot under the heel with both hands, and his long leg shoved. Not softly this time, but with almost all of the force his leg could muster.

"Ooh," a surprised Grace called as she shot across the kitchen, her feet working fast trying to catch up with her body. Successful, she managed to stop before slamming into the chair-lined wall.

She spun around, pleased with herself, holding the boot in front of her. "We did it!"

Billy raced into the kitchen. He looked at the boot, his mother, Jack, and then his grandmother. "Did what?"

The adults laughed, to the confusion of the boy, and Grace handed his boot to him. He took it, head shaking. "We got my boot off, Billy."

The boy looked at Jack for a moment and then shrugged. "Your saddlebags are in your room."

Jack grinned and stood, picking up his other boot. "Thanks, Billy. Grace, that was quite an experience."

Her green eyes sparkling, she gave him an impish grin. "I'm glad you liked it. We did get your boots off, didn't we?"

Mary watched the two of them, and a wistful smile pulled at the corner of her mouth as she picked up a hot pad to handle the pot of hot water.

Jack turned to go to his room and stopped. Billy had run to the back. Only Mary and Grace were in the kitchen with him. His grin vanished. "Keep the boys close. Don't let them leave the house even if the rain stops. We need to talk tonight after they're in bed. It's important." He headed for his room.

13

Jack felt like a new man. There had been enough hot water to fill the washbasin. A straight razor, shaving cup and brush, and scissors lay there. He went to work. After much chopping and scraping, he looked much more presentable than he had an hour ago.

The rain had stopped, but the sound of the howling wind could be heard behind the heavy blue and gold moreen curtains covering the windows. He could also hear the busy sounds of Mary and Grace preparing supper. They would be busy for hours. First the preparation, then supper, followed by their guests retiring after dinner to the parlor for coffee and cigars. Finally the cleaning of dishes and preparing for the morning rush. *You have to admire them,* Jack thought, *doing the same thing, day after day for life. Cooking, cleaning, cleaning, cooking, repeated over and over. Then toss in taking care of Billy.* He gave a short laugh. *It makes chasing down gunfighters sound like a walk in the park.*

He had taken his gun-cleaning kit from his saddlebags and laid it on a chair. Opening the door, he called, "Elijah?"

His heart jumped when there was no answer. As he opened his mouth to call again, Elijah and Billy stepped out of a room farther down the hallway. Elijah saw Jack standing in the doorway. "Did you want me, Marshal Sage?"

Jack smiled at the boy. "Just checking to see what you young fellas were up to. We need to get this tub emptied. How many buckets do you have?"

Billy spoke up. "We got a bunch, Marshal, but would four work?"

"Sounds like a perfect number to me."

The boys dashed away and were back quickly, each carrying two buckets.

"Good job. Why don't I take two, and you boys can take one each."

They nodded their heads in agreement. Jack filled two of the buckets about half full, and the two remaining he filled far enough below the rim so he wouldn't spill water in the house. He picked up his two and said, "Lead on, boys."

Billy and Elijah picked up theirs, Elijah laboring fairly hard but managing. They led the way, and Jack followed. Jack figured the two boys could carry one end of the tub and he the other. They opened the back door and dumped the buckets.

"We can leave the buckets back here," Billy announced. They stacked the buckets alongside four exact replicas and turned back to Jack's room.

Once there, it was as Jack had pictured. He took one end and the boys the other, and they made their way to the back door. Reaching the door, the boys set their end of the tub on the floor, and Jack grasped their handle, lifted the tub, and moved to the door. He managed to get the tub and his bulk through and tossed the water across the soaked backyard. Stepping back inside, he placed the tub next to the buckets and straightened, turning to the boys. "I'm obliged for your help." He took out a pair of quarters and flipped one to each of the boys.

Both caught their quarter. Billy looked up. "Thanks, Marshal."

Elijah still stared at the quarter. "This is for me?"

Jack grinned at the boy. "It sure is. You two have been a big help. You earned it, but I do have a question for you both. If the both of you can be spared, I still need some help cleaning my guns. That's really important work and needs to be done well, so it's worth four bits apiece. Any takers?"

Both, with excited voices, chimed in together, "Yes, sir."

He looked at Billy. "Good, why don't you go ask your ma if it's alright with her."

Billy shouted, "She won't mind, Marshal," and raced to the kitchen.

Jack watched the boy run down the hall, and turned back to Elijah. "That sound alright to you?"

Elijah nodded enthusiastically. "You bet. I can be a big help. I used to help Pa." At the mention of his father, the boy's enthusiasm faded. He stopped and looked up at Jack. "I sure miss him, Marshal. Ma, too."

Jack's heart went out to the little fella. He put his hand on the boy's shoulder. "You're facing a tough situation, son. There are a lot of grownups who couldn't handle it, but you can do it. I've seen how strong you are."

The boy's wide brown eyes showed more pain and sadness than any child should have to bear. "Does it ever stop hurting?"

Jack knelt in the hallway so he didn't tower over the boy. While looking deep into the sad brown eyes, he shook his head. "I won't lie to you. It won't ever stop hurting, but it won't hurt as bad as it does now. There'll come a time when you don't think about your family every moment of every day. When the thought hits you, it'll hurt, but then it will pass. You'll have more things in your life, more happy things, like playing with Billy or riding a good horse."

Billy came running back down the hallway. "Ma said we could help as long as we were careful and followed your orders."

Jack gave Elijah a final pat and stood. "Good, let's get these guns cleaned." He stepped into his room, followed by the two boys. He pulled both Smith & Wesson .44-caliber revolvers from their holsters. Taking the first, he eased the hammer partially back, opened the top latch, and grasping the barrel, rotated it down, careful to do it slowly. The extractor gradually lifted, pushing the six rounds out of the chambers. He removed them and laid the cartridges on the counter. With one of the dry cloths he kept wrapped in the kit, he began wiping the moisture from the weapon, hitting every tiny crevice. Throughout the task, he kept the muzzle of the weapon away from the boys.

"You boys see what I'm doing?"

Each had pulled a chair from the empty room across the hall and were watching with rapt attention. "Yes, sir," they both chimed in together.

"You see how I'm doing it?"

This time Elijah spoke up. "Yes, sir. You're making sure the muzzle of that revolver never points at us or you."

"That's right. The most important thing you do when you are handling a weapon is, first, make sure it is empty, and then keep the muzzle away from anyone around you." He picked up a steel end brush and made several passes through the barrel. Then, using a pad with a string tied around it and a piece of lead clinched around the other end of the string, he dropped the lead down the barrel. Once through, he pulled the thick pad through twice. Both boys watched closely.

Jack had said nothing while he performed the first two exercises. With the third one, he asked the boys, "Do you know what I was doing?"

Elijah spoke up. "Yes, sir. That brush knocks out any lead and powder that's been left in the barrel, and the cloth thing you pulled through dries out the barrel."

Jack nodded. "You're exactly right." Jack picked up the last instrument, a rod similar to the first, but with a soft cloth brush instead of the bristles on the first. "This has a really light coating of oil on it that will help keep rust and corrosion out of the barrel." He shoved the brush through a couple of times and laid it back among his cleaning gear. "Billy, why don't you take the one I'm working on, clean the cylinders like I did the barrel, and then wipe the whole weapon until you have it completely dry. Once it's dry, take the second cloth, it also has some oil worked into it, and wipe the weapon down again. When you're finished, lay it on the chair."

He handed Billy the revolver and picked up the rifle.

Elijah pointed at the remaining revolver Jack had tucked behind his waistband. "Aren't you going to clean that one, Marshal?"

"I sure am. But I never leave myself without a loaded weapon available." He grinned at the two lads. "In case a rattlesnake sticks its head up." Jack unloaded his Winchester and confirmed it was empty before handing the rifle and another dry cloth to Elijah, who quickly began drying the rifle. Jack used the time to find out about the boys' daily activities. "What kind of chores do you two do to help your ma and grandma?"

Billy spoke up. "We do plenty, Marshal. We're up at five and, first thing, milk the cow and feed her and the horses. Then we let the chickens out and collect the eggs. After breakfast, we help Ma and Grandma wash dishes. As soon as we're done, we head off to school. When we get home, we muck out the stalls and milk the cow again at five o'clock. Grandma says cows like regularity, so it's milking at five in the morning and five in the evening. After we're finished with milking, we feed the cow and horses and lock up the chickens. Then we do our schoolwork."

While listening to Billy, Jack thought, *Ben Clagg would have no trouble grabbing these boys. I have to talk to Grace and Mary tonight.* "How do you like school?"

Both boys stopped wiping to look at each other. Elijah shook his head. "Not much. We'd rather go fishing."

With difficulty, Jack kept a smile from his face and recited the typical adult line. "School's important, boys. When you grow up, you'll need to know how to write and do your numbers." The conversation went on, covering several important items, like what was the best time of day to catch fish and where to find the longest earthworms, and why girls were so hard to understand. Jack had no idea how to answer the question about girls, so he changed the subject back to cleaning the weapons.

They worked for almost an hour, until the revolvers and rifle were dry, clean, and shiny. After drying the moisture from his holsters, he allowed the gunbelt and empty holsters to lay across the back of one of the chairs so the leather could completely dry.

Finished, he pulled two fifty-cent pieces from his vest pocket and flipped one to each of the boys. Both caught their coins. Elijah, like he had with the quarter, stared at his in awe. Billy looked at his and grinned. "That'll buy a lot of hard candy, Marshal."

Jack laughed. "Yes, it will. Just don't eat it all at once. I don't want your ma after me for making you sick."

"No, sir," Billy replied. "Candy don't make me sick. It makes me feel good."

Elijah was still examining his coin, turning it over and over and rubbing the silver surface with his thumb.

"What do you plan on doing with your money, Elijah?"

The boy turned serious brown eyes on Jack. "I'm saving my money until I have enough to buy a gun like yours."

Jack was curious but also had an uneasy feeling. It wasn't unusual for frontier lads to want a gun, but usually a rifle, not a revolver. "What do you need a revolver for, son?"

The boy looked up at him again, and Jack swore those soft brown eyes had turned hard as flint. "Marshal, I'm going to get a gun, and then I'm going to kill the men who killed my family."

Concern cut deep into Jack. "You don't have to worry about them, Elijah. They're in jail. They're going to be tried. I feel certain the court will find them all guilty, and those men will be hanged. I think you can safely spend some of your money on candy."

Elijah shook his head. "No, sir, they won't be hanged."

"What makes you think they won't get the justice they deserve?"

Elijah looked at Billy. "The boys in school. They said the Claggs have been brought in before, and the court has turned them loose, so I'll do what I have to."

Movement at the door caught his attention. Grace stood in the doorway, her lips pulled tight and forehead wrinkled with concern. She held Jack's gaze for just a moment, jerked her head toward the dining room, and mouthed, "Supper." She turned and was gone.

Jack changed the subject. "You boys hungry?"

"Yes, sir," Billy yelled, jumping to his feet. "Thanks, Marshal. Come on, Elijah, let's eat." The boy dashed from the room.

Elijah stood. "Thank you, Marshal Sage."

Jack nodded. "You're welcome. Why don't you head on in, and I'll be right behind you."

With only a slight limp, Elijah trotted from the room.

A moment later Grace knocked at the open door.

Jack was busy loading and securing the clean weapons. "Come on in. I've got one more revolver to clean."

Entering the room, she brought with her an aroma of fresh bread combined with a scent of roses. A strand of thick black hair had fallen over her forehead and across her left eye. Showing a bit of irritation at the strand, she pushed it back, and it fell again.

Jack smiled. "You smell good."

"Oh my goodness, Jack. I've been slaving in that hot kitchen. I don't know how I could smell like anything but a farmhand on a hot summer day."

This time he grinned at the lovely woman. "A farmhand isn't exactly the vision I see before me."

She began to push the strand back and dropped it in frustration. "Did you hear what Elijah said?"

He had already begun unloading and cleaning the second Smith. He looked up and shrugged. "Sure I did, Grace. It was harsh, but I can understand where the boy is coming from. He had his family and friends butchered in front of him. He wants justice, and his friends have told him the Claggs have been released before. To his way of thinking, his way is the only way the Claggs can be punished. He'll see the difference when they're hanged."

Grace hugged herself, as if trying to squeeze away the picture of the little boy seeking vengeance. "I suppose you're right, but it's so terrible."

She searched his face with sad green eyes. Then her full lips split in a warm smile. "It felt good to laugh today. I think Mama needed that almost as much as I did. Thank you for getting soaked again."

Jack gave her a one-sided grin. "Yes, ma'am. Anything to be helpful."

She continued to gaze at him while he worked. Finally she stepped closer and ran the back of her fingers over his smooth cheek.

It surprised him, but he caught himself before he jerked, and looked into those emerald green eyes.

"Your skin is soft when it's freshly shaved. Jack, I'm sure you know it. You're a handsome man."

He laughed. "Yeah, if you could call the south end of a northbound jackass handsome."

She laughed. "Jack, don't be crude. You are handsome."

He grew serious. "I'm glad you think so, though I'll argue that opinion to my dying day."

She laughed, the sadness driven from her features. Her graceful hand bunched into a fist, and she punched him on his thick bicep. "You are so stubborn. Come on, it's suppertime."

The roaring fire had died to a mass of coals, and only a single log remained burning. The rocks of the solidly built fireplace continued to cast heat into the parlor. The other guests had retired to their rooms. Jack felt even better after his hot bath and delicious meal. He had made sure the back door was secured, and pitched in getting the boys ready for bed. He told them both a story of Algiers and the French Foreign Legion. Entranced, they wanted to hear more, but Grace insisted it was time for sleep. Reluctantly they lay back, pulled the cover up around their necks, and said goodnight.

Jack wished each boy a good night. Leaning against the doorway with Grace at his side, feeling her warmth, inhaling her scent, and having just tucked the boys in gave him a warm feeling he'd not felt for a long time. Carrying the lamp, she glanced up at him, her face glowing in the lamplight. She was like a dream, her green eyes dark and deep and her lips slightly parted in a tired but happy smile.

He would remember the vision throughout his life, especially when he smelled bread or roses. Jack felt the desire to take her in his arms, but fought it down. He wheeled, quickly moved down the hall, and checked the back door again. It was secure. When he turned back, Grace stood in place, watching him. As he approached, she turned for the parlor. Jack followed, and they joined Mary.

Mary had collapsed into a blue wingback chair and removed her shoes, tucking her feet under her. He marveled at how women, no matter how old they were, remained so limber. Grace dropped onto the loveseat facing the fire, and Jack took the matching wingback. He was worried. It was necessary to tell Grace and her mother, but he didn't relish loading them down with additional problems.

Jack had been silent for several minutes, enjoying the protection from the elements, a clean body, a full belly, and the warmth of the fire. *Did I just get back today?* he asked himself. *So much has happened, and most of it revolves around Elijah.*

The single lamp provided faint light, but Jack could clearly see the features of the two women, and the low flickering flame in the fireplace gave the room a comfortable, homey feel. Jack stretched his legs in front of him and watched Grace follow her mother's example and slip her shoes off, folding her long legs so that, with petticoats rustling, she slid her feet beneath her. After spreading her dress around her, she reached back and unfastened her hair. Giving her head a shake, the long dark locks cascaded around her face and across her shoulders. She smiled at Jack.

Mary broke the stillness. "Jack, you have something important to tell us about Elijah?"

Jack gave a slow nod. "I do, and none of it's good."

Grace had relaxed deeply into the loveseat, but with his answer she straightened, eyes glinting in the firelight.

He jumped in. "I talked to Barrett Clagg today."

Mother and daughter looked at each other. Then Grace turned back to Jack. "Elijah is the only witness, isn't he?"

Jack nodded. "He is."

Mary asked, "Where was Ben when you spoke with Barrett?"

"I never saw him."

Again the two women looked at each other, but this time, Jack could see fear in their expressions.

Grace dropped her feet to the floor, slipping them back into her shoes, and leaned toward Jack. "What did Barrett say?"

"He offered me a bribe."

Grace frowned. "That's against the law. Did you arrest him?"

"No."

Grace's frown intensified, her brow creased with wrinkles. The tone of her voice disbelieving, she asked, "Jack, he's probably the worst of the bunch besides Ben. Why didn't you throw him in jail with his other filthy brothers?"

Jack, taken a little aback at the vehemence, shook his head. "Grace, it would've done no good." She started to say something else, and he held up his hand. "It would have been my word against his. The court would toss it out."

She looked away from Jack, crossed her arms, and stared into the fire.

Mary spoke, her voice softer. "What did he say when you refused, Jack?"

Jack thought about it. There was no reason to mention the man's threat against him, but they needed to know Elijah was in danger. "He made no direct threat against Elijah, but when I talked to Pauly, he told me there was a concern with Ben missing. I'm worried for Elijah. If they kidnap him, they're home free."

Grace turned back, her voice softer. "What can we do?"

"I'm going to be around at least through Monday. That's when the Claggs' trial will be scheduled. I'll stick with the boys."

Grace relaxed more. "Oh good. You mean you'll take them to school tomorrow?"

Jack grinned. "Yep. I haven't been close to a school in a long time. Maybe I'll learn something."

Mary smiled at him. "Oh, Jack, that is so nice. Would you really do that?"

"Of course I would. I like those boys, and I don't want to see anything happen to either one of them, but that's not all of the bad news."

Grace folded her arms again, as if protecting herself from Jack's words. "What do you mean?"

"This may be harder to deal with than the Claggs. Elijah has family in Knoxville, Tennessee. That's where his folks are from."

Grace shook her head. "Oh, no, that's not bad. His family can help him get through this horrible loss."

Jack's big head shook from side to side. "I'd agree with you, in most cases, but that isn't what is happening with the Franklin family." He went on to explain. "Elijah's pa fought for the North. Being from Tennessee, all of his family were with the Confederacy. It sounds like the whole Franklin clan turned against him and his family. Elijah told me that was one of the reasons they were going west. It seems they were constantly tormented by his brothers." He paused to let his statement sink in.

Taking a deep breath, he continued, "Elijah's uncle, Abel Franklin, is on his way to take Elijah. From the timing of the telegraph Judge Bell received, the man should be arriving tomorrow morning."

Grace had slid forward to the edge of the sofa. "Jack, is there anything we can do to prevent Franklin from taking Elijah?"

"The judge won't let him take the boy until after the trial. He'll want him to testify. But we had a real blowup in his office over Elijah. He's a stickler for the law. He said Franklin is kin, therefore Elijah has to go with him."

A small voice pierced the parlor. "Go with who, Marshal?" Elijah, barefooted and looking frail in his nightshirt, stood at the entrance to the parlor, rubbing his sleepy eyes with his knuckles.

14

Jack stood, walked to Elijah, and scooped him up. They returned to the wingback, and the sleepy boy leaned against his chest. "We've got some challenges coming up, son."

"Marshal, you'll protect me. You can beat anything."

Jack felt his heart wrench. He cleared his throat. "I wish I could, but there's two things happening soon. The first is that you're going to have to testify in court about what the bad men did to your family."

Elijah stiffened and sat erect, looking at Jack. "You mean like a trial?"

"That's exactly what I mean."

"Will the bad men who killed my family be there?"

"They will, son. It's their right."

The boy sat still. "If I tell what they did, will they be punished?"

"You think you can recognize them if you see them again?"

Elijah nodded. "Yes, sir."

"Did you see what they did?"

The little boy began to shake. "Will I have to tell, Marshal? It's really bad."

"You just tell the men in the jury what they did, and they'll be punished."

"I'm scared."

Jack patted Elijah on his thin back. "All brave men feel fear, Elijah, but they push through it. You're a brave boy. I've already seen that. I know you'll do well, and I'll be there. You won't have to worry because I won't let anyone harm you."

Elijah threw his arms around Jack's neck and squeezed with all of his tiny strength. "If you're there, Marshal, I know I'll be safe."

Jack returned the hug.

The young fellow calmed and stopped shaking. He leaned back. "But I thought I heard something about someone coming."

Jack knew of no way of telling him but straight out. He grasped Elijah's shoulders. "Your uncle Abel is coming after you, but—"

Elijah began shaking his head violently. "No. No. No. I won't go with him. I'll run away. I won't go back. They hate us."

Both Mary and Grace jumped to their feet and raced to Elijah. Grace wrapped her arms around the desperate lad, lifting him from Jack's grasp. She carried him back to the loveseat. Mother and daughter sat with the boy between them while they comforted him.

After several minutes he calmed down, wiped his eyes with the back of his hands, and stared across the room at Jack. "I mean it, Marshal. I won't go back to Tennessee."

Jack racked his brain. This problem was unlike any he had encountered in his career as a lawman. He would have a talk with Franklin when he arrived. Maybe something would come to mind.

JACK PULLED the stage office door closed and slid his hand beneath his coat, dropping his watch back into its vest pocket. The station master had assured him he could expect the stage on time. Adding emphasis to the man's forecast was a second team of horses, driver, and shotgun rider waiting. He joined them. Within seconds of his stepping out of the office, the stage rattled into sight and began slowing. The horses were breathing hard when the stage pulled up and rocked to a stop.

A flurry of action began. The arriving team was unhitched, and the fresh animals led and fastened into place. Passengers disembarked, two couples and three men. Jack stepped up to the passenger who best fit Elijah's description. The man was of average height, which meant Jack towered over him.

The traveler had turned away to pick up a weather-beaten suitcase removed from the stage luggage boot and set on the boardwalk by the station manager. When he reached for the handle, Jack examined the man's hand. It was large for his size and calloused. *A hard worker,* Jack thought.

Under a round brimmed hat, the man's jaw jutted out like that of a bulldog, giving him a naturally pugnacious appearance. The bulge beneath his coat told Jack he was carrying a weapon, which wasn't unusual for the average western traveler, though unexpected for an easterner. The man turned and started at Jack's presence.

Jack nodded. "Morning, Mr. Franklin?" Jack extended his hand.

Franklin's jaw extended farther. Beneath his thick salt-and-pepper mustache, his lips pursed in a frown. Slowly he extended his hand. In a languid drawl, Franklin responded, "Who's askin'?"

"I'm U.S. Marshal Jack Sage."

Taking Jack's hand, his frown changed to a smile. "Well, Marshal Jack Sage, you just about black out the whole sky. How tall are you?"

"About four inches over six feet, Mr. Franklin. Do you have some time? We need to talk."

"I'll tell you what I need. I need a cup of coffee and a drink. If you can talk over that, then I'm your man."

Jack glanced at the man's bag. "You want coffee or a room first?"

"I'm hankerin' for something to wet my whistle, first thing. Then we can flap our jaws."

"Follow me." Jack led Franklin to the Whiskey Barrel saloon while listening to a continuous tale of the man's trip west interspersed with colorful descriptions and an occasional laugh. *Franklin has a gift for gab*, he thought. *He's not anything like Elijah described.*

Several of the Whiskey Barrel customers congratulated Jack as they made their way to a table. A couple of the more enthusiastic ones slapped him on the back, offering to buy him a drink. He declined, telling them maybe later.

When they were seated, Franklin leaned back in his chair to assess Jack. "Sounds like I'm sitting here with a dyed-in-the-wool celebrity."

Jack shook his head. "No, I led a posse who just brought in a bunch of killers. Just doing my job."

The bar girl swished over to their table. She was a buxom, blonde lass with a wide smile. "What can I get you and your friend, Marshal?"

Jack returned the smile. "Coffee for me." He nodded to Franklin.

The Tennessean matched her smile and raised her a gold tooth. "I'll tell you, honey, I'd like me a whole pot of coffee and a bottle of rye. You think you could get that for me?"

She gave him a teasing smile and tilted her head, allowing her long blonde hair to fall over one shoulder. "Why, mister, I can get you whatever you want."

Franklin winked at Jack. "Thirst before pleasure, honey. Let's start with the coffee and rye."

"Coming right up, *honey*." The girl made an exaggerated swish of her hips and awarded Franklin a sparkling smile. The man's eyes were glued to her as she made her way across the saloon, disappearing into the kitchen.

"I'm likin' Fort Smith already." He turned his head and grinned at Jack. "Now what can I do for a U-nited States Marshal?"

Jack didn't much care for the man or the way he asked his question, but held his temper. Before he could answer, the girl was back with a steaming pot of coffee and two cups. She had also brought a chipped pitcher of cream and a bowl of sugar with a single spoon. These she set on the table along with a bottle of rye and a glass, then followed with a cup in front of each of them and began to pour. Jack stopped her when his cup was little more than two-thirds full. After pouring the coffee, she gave Franklin another promising smile and headed toward a table surrounded by men who were yelling for her.

Jack completed his standard coffee preparation by filling the space remaining with four spoons of sugar and cream. A quick sip told him it was just right.

Abel Franklin watched. When Jack was finished, he picked up his cup and took a long sip of the hot coffee, chasing it by snapping back a shot of rye. He shook his head at the whiskey and blew. "Whew, that's the way I like my coffee." He reached for the bottle and poured rye into his coffee, then looked at Jack, eyebrows raised in question.

"You're out here to pick up your nephew?"

"That's right, Marshal. That poor boy is all alone out here, but he's got himself family back in Knoxville. I aim to make sure he's taken good care of and grows up knowing what Franklins believe in." The man took another sip of his spiked coffee.

"That sounds like a righteous endeavor, Mr. Franklin." Jack

leaned forward, placing his forearms on the table. "Maybe you could tell me exactly what the Franklins believe in?" His tone was a little sharper than he had intended.

Franklin took another sip of his coffee. The rye was already beginning to take effect on his empty stomach. He leaned back in his chair and gave Jack a big grin, showing off his gold tooth. "I sure can, Marshal. We believe a man has the right to own what he wants, believe what he wants, and do what he wants, without the government sticking its long nose into his business." An emphatic nod emphasized his statement.

"Of course, you mean within the limits of the law."

The man took another sip of his coffee and wasn't satisfied. He filled the shot glass with rye and tossed it back again, followed by the head shaking. When he was finished, he turned back to Jack. "Marshal, you took the words right out of my mouth. In fact, I don't think I could've said it better."

Jack watched Franklin as the alcohol took effect. *The guy must've missed breakfast this morning,* he thought. *He's getting drunker than a skunk.* "Abel, what you said sounds really good, and you seem like a fine fella, so maybe you can explain to me why Elijah doesn't want to go back with you."

It took a moment for the question to register on Franklin. He stared at Jack with watery brown eyes. In apparent disbelief, he said, "He doesn't want to come back with me?"

Jack shook his head. "No, sir, he sure doesn't."

The man stared up at the ceiling as if he would find the solution there, and he seemed to find it.

Jack studied the drunken man as his countenance changed from happy and friendly to dark and mean. His jaw muscles began working, and his mustache moved lower as his lips pulled down in a frown. The brown eyes almost disappeared behind slitted eyelids, and he moved forward in his chair, leaning on the table toward Jack. Any intimidation Jack's size might have caused him was overcome by the alcohol.

Franklin's words, though in his drawl, were tight and threatening. "You listen to me, lawman. That boy is too much like my brother and his wife. They were all too uppity, always better than any of the folks he grew up with. He come back from the war, after fighting on the wrong side, with wrongheaded ideas. When we tried to persuade him about his errors, he ups and leaves, and you can see what that got him. Now I'm takin' that boy, and I'm gonna teach him right. It don't matter if he wants to go back or not, and I'll tell him that. All he needs is a taste of the leather. Yes, sir, enough of the leather's touch and he'll straighten up. I aim to straighten him up real good."

Jack, watching Franklin as he made his little speech, thought, *I'd like to give the leather to you. If I weren't wearing this badge . . .* and he stopped. *I can't be thinking like that. It won't help Elijah, but I'd love to throw just one punch.* At the thought, he smiled at Franklin.

The Tennessean scowled deeper at Jack's smile. "I say something funny?"

Jack leaned back in his chair. "No, you didn't. I was just wondering when you planned to head back to Knoxville."

"Reckon the first stage back. The stage driver said that would be in the morning."

Jack shook his head. "Won't work. Elijah will have to be here for the trial, and the earliest it will take place is Monday."

Franklin picked up his cup, took a sip, and stared at Jack over the rim. "What if I want to leave afore then?"

"The judge definitely will not release him into your custody, and you'll need the proper documents, until the trial is over and your brother's killers are sentenced. He may not release him until after they're hanged."

Franklin's watery brown eyes focused on Jack. "When'll that be, the hanging, I mean?"

"Understand, Mr. Franklin, I can't speak for Judge Bell. My

guess is that the three of them will be strung up on Tuesday morning."

"Tuesday, then. That's when I'll be leaving with the boy."

Jack slid his chair back and stood. He pulled a quarter eagle gold piece from his vest and dropped it on the table. "That should take care of any breakfast you might want. When you're finished here, I suggest you go to his office and let the judge know you are here for the boy. He'll appreciate your promptness."

Seeing the money, Franklin waved to the bar girl, then looked up at Jack. "Thanks for the help. Tell that boy to get ready. We leave Tuesday on the eastbound stage."

Jack thought it interesting Franklin had indicated no interest in seeing Elijah. He touched his hat in acknowledgment, turned, and headed for the saloon's door. He heard the man order a beer. He smiled to himself, thinking, *Have a few beers. Get good and drunk. You'll make a great impression on the judge. He might even throw you into his jail.* The thought gave Jack a moment of humorous relief while he headed for the school. *Hopefully Zeb and Buck are keeping a close eye on Elijah and Billy.*

His mind worked over the problem of Elijah, trying to figure out how he could keep the boy from going with Abel Franklin. He noticed a man with a rifle resting in the crook of his arm several buildings past the marshal's office and thought, *Resting in his right arm. The man's left-handed,* but didn't pursue it. A man with a rifle was not an unusual sight in Fort Smith or any other western town. He took three more long steps, puzzling over how to protect Elijah. A sharp voice penetrated his concentration.

"It's been a long time searching for you, Jack, or should I say Marshal Sage."

He had been watching the man with the rifle, but now snapped his head around to the speaker. By his demeanor Jack knew the man as a gunfighter, but he didn't recognize him. The stranger stood in a relaxed but ready stance. His left shoulder rested easy against the corner post of a general store, leaving his right gun hand free. A cigarette hung loosely from his thick lips, smoke curling up past the man's left eye, and those lips wore a smile, cold and satisfied.

Jack felt more frustration than alarm. This was something he didn't have the time or inclination to deal with right now. His plate was overloaded. The last thing he needed was a gunfighter with a grudge or looking to add a notch to his gun.

Voice cool and smooth, the gunfighter spoke again. "You don't know me, do you, Jack?"

Jack was good with people's names and faces, but though this one, with his tall black Stetson, looked vaguely familiar, he couldn't place him. Jack's patience was short and his voice demanding. "No. Is there any reason I should?"

The man's smile widened, and he shook his head. "No, we haven't met. If we had, you'd be rotting in some cheap grave, but you met my pa. In fact, you killed him and my brothers."

Can this man be Emmett, the oldest son of Elijah Rush? Jack thought. His features were similar, big head, thick lips, shady eyes.

By now people had spotted the two men confronting each other, and their stance gave an easily understood warning to clear the street.

Jack's mind was working double time. *Come on, Berry. Get out here. I don't want to have a gunfight in the streets of Fort Smith.* But neither the marshal nor any of his deputies were appearing.

"I think you might be starting to figure out who I am, Marshal. Let me give you one more hint. Silver City."

It's him, Jack thought. *The one I never met.* "I wondered if you'd ever show up."

"Here I am, Marshal, and V's with me." The younger brother he had caught in El Paso, Vern, stepped out of the general store, twenty feet from the post Emmett was leaning against.

He was grinning. "Howdy, Marshal. Long time no see. You ready to die?"

Jack's mind cleared of his Elijah problems, and he felt his body relax. His breathing was steady and slow. "Hello, Vern. How was prison? I have to admit, you've grown a mite. You probably got those shoulders from breaking rocks. Of course, I don't know what kind of job you can apply that to, maybe track laying. Would you like that?"

Vern's grin disappeared. "Sage, I'm gonna fill you full of holes."

Jack shook his head. "After all these years, that's the best you can come up with?" Jack remembered the rifleman. He was the one who worried him. He felt his chances were good against these two, but the rifle was a real concern. He needed Berry, Zeb, Buck, or one of the other twenty-five or thirty deputy marshals to take care of that rifleman.

When Vern's grin turned into a snarl, he went into his gunfighter's crouch. His gun hand hovered above the butt of his Colt .45. "Enjoy your smart mouth, Sage, 'cause you've just come up against the fastest guns in the west, and this ain't El Paso."

I've got to keep them talking until someone can take that rifleman out of action, Jack thought, and showed Emmett another wide grin, belying the fear he felt. The rifleman could shoot at any time unless one of the deputies had already taken him out. *Play it out, Jack,* he thought. *It's just like any other time facing more than one gun. You'll either get shot, or you won't. All you can do is your best.* "I'm guessing the fella down the street is Ted. I'm sure he's aching to pull a trigger on me, but he'll never get the chance. You rode into a nest of marshals, and even if you get me, which you won't, Judge Bell will have you hanging from a gallows within the week, but take a good look at me. You might get a couple of hunks of lead into this body, but I'm not going down easy. You'll be dead before you can enjoy it."

For the first time, Emmett's smile faded, like he was recognizing the truth of Jack's words. His eyes cut toward where the rifleman had been when Jack saw him. The smile completely disappeared. His eyes jerked, desperately looking for his hole card. Jack felt better.

"Throw your guns down, boys. You won't get more than a year for making fools of yourselves. If you keep this up, I'll kill you. You know I can. You know what happened in Silver City, and I'm sure you've heard about Wyoming. I have no desire to kill you, but I'm tired of humoring you." Jack's voice hardened into a command. "Drop your guns!"

15

It was like all the gunfights Jack had been in with more than one shooter. There was always one guy who felt it was his responsibility to get the ball rolling, and usually it was the one who was the most afraid. In this case, it was Vern, the younger brother. Emmett looked like he was going to call it off, but before he had a chance to say anything, the antsy younger fella went for his gun.

Slow, Jack thought. *Why do these younger guys think they are so fast when they're slow as molasses?* Jack shot the older brother, the real gunfighter, first. Emmett had begun his draw after Vern, but, as Jack had expected, was fast.

Jack's Smith & Wesson came level just ahead of Emmett's Colt. Jack fired. He paused a split second before swinging the muzzle to the other man. His opponent's weapon was barely clearing the holster. Jack could see the fear in the younger man's eyes. Had he never thought he might be shot or killed? Jack fired, the bullet striking Vern in the center of his chest. He was flung back, crashed through the general store's large glass window, and piled into a rack of women's dresses. Jack didn't worry about him. Even if he survived, he wouldn't have the will to get off a second shot, but the gunfighter might. He swung his revolver back to the first target, and, sure enough, the gunfighter was struggling, but slowly bringing his Colt to bear.

Jack could see Emmett's determination. "Drop the gun, Emmett. You still might have a chance."

Unsteady as he was, he continued to slowly bring the Colt to bear. Jack waited as long as he could. Regretting the result even before he pulled the trigger, he fired. The heavy chunk of lead slammed into Emmett's chest. He stumbled back, his legs giving way, and fell, his black Stetson flying off and rolling down the boardwalk. He slammed against the building's wall and slowly slid down into a sitting position. With two holes in him and bleeding out, but with his back braced against the building's wall, he attempted to level the revolver once again. Jack strode forward, knelt next to him, and yanked the weapon from the dying man's hand. "It's over."

Emmett let his head drop back against the wall. In his position, he could look into Jack's eyes. He was able to gasp the question, "My brother?"

Jack shook his head. "Dead."

"Too fast. Ted warned me." Blood ran from the corner of his mouth. He began to cough. Flecks splattered Jack's coat. He drew another breath. "Should've listened." His eyes opened wide and unblinking, stared past Jack, and his last breath escaped in a long sad sigh.

Jack stared at the man in silence. He laid Emmett's revolver on the boardwalk and, with his left hand, softly closed the man's eyes. He looked up to see himself surrounded by deputy marshals. He saw Berry advancing. He picked up the revolver and stood. Before either Berry or Jack could say anything, the sound of a woman's shoes running down the boardwalk raced toward them.

People moved out of the way, and Grace dashed through the opening, flinging herself at him, her arms flying around his neck.

"Are you alright? Have you been shot?"

His arms encircled the beautiful woman. The fragrance he would always recognize as hers filled his nostrils while the warmth of her pressed against him, and the onlookers disappeared. A feeling he had yearned for these many years enveloped him. He was safe. The kind of safety only the love of a good woman could bring. He felt her soft cheek against his and opened his eyes to see Judge Bell standing not five feet away, looking—pleased?

Reality returned. "I'm fine." When she didn't loosen her hug, he moved his mouth close to her ear and whispered, "I'm fine, and so is everyone watching."

It was like she had been hit with hot grease. A sharp, "Oh," escaped her, and she jerked her arms away and began to smooth her dress. "I'm glad you're alright. I was in the store. I saw everything. It was so scary, and you seemed so calm." She looked up at him. "How did you stay so calm with those men threatening you?"

He shrugged. "That's what I do. Now why don't you go finish what you were doing, and I'll see you later." He nodded at the dead man. "I've got to take care of this."

"Yes, you're right. Give me your coat. I'll clean it before that blood dries."

He peeled off his coat and handed it to her. "Thank you."

She smiled up at him. "I'll see you later." Grace spun around, her face still red as a ripe peach. Seeing Judge Bell directly behind her, she nodded to him as she passed with Jack's coat. Primly, she said, "Good morning, Judge," and with chin up, marched through the crowd and back into the general store.

Jack handed Berry the Colt belonging to Emmett. "So maybe you can tell me where all your lawmen were while I was out here getting shot at by these fellas?"

Berry took the revolver a little sheepishly. "We were all in court."

Judge Bell glared at Berry. "I guess it's a good thing the bank wasn't being robbed."

Berry's ears turned pink, but all he said was, "That's a fact."

Jack looked around. "Who stopped the character with the rifle?"

Buck stepped forward. "That'd be me, Jack. I was headin' back from the school. Figured Zeb had that job under control, and I see you in the street talking to those fellers. Then at the edge of the alley, I see this rifle barrel pointed out toward you. I just drew my sixgun, walked over there, and politely asked that ole boy to put it down." He gave a short laugh. "He ain't had no idea I was anywhere around, he was concentrating so hard on you. Gave me no argument. Unfortunately, you started shooting up the town right then, and I had my hands full." He looked at the two bodies. "Course, it don't look like you needed any help from me."

Jack gave his head a shake. "You helped plenty, Buck. If you hadn't come up when you did, it'd be me the undertaker would be working on and not them." He glanced at Berry.

The marshal nodded. "Yep, I already sent a man for him."

Judge Bell scanned the gawkers. "Alright, folks. Let's get on about our business. Marshal Berry will get this mess cleaned up." He glanced at the deputies. "Those of you participating in the trials, head on back to court. We've got a lot of work to do." He turned to Jack. "I assume you have sufficient witnesses? I want this dealt with quickly, and I don't have time today, but tomorrow is Saturday. Stop by tomorrow morning. I want a full report." The judge turned and, followed by most of the deputies, headed back to the courthouse.

When Judge Bell was out of hearing, Berry gave Jack a subtle grin. "That was quite a display you put on out here."

Puzzled, Jack said, "They drew on me. My only other option was to stand there and die."

Berry shook his head. "That wasn't what I was talking about."

Jack stared at the marshal for a moment before it dawned on

him he was talking about Grace. His thick eyebrows pulled together beneath a wrinkled forehead, turning the stare into a glare. "She was concerned I might have been shot."

Berry's smile broadened, and he nodded his head. "She sure was. The way you were holding on to her, it looked like you were concerned she might've been shot, too."

Before Jack could respond, there were several chuckles from the crowd. He turned cold gray eyes on the group, and silence erupted. "Buck."

The deputy stepped forward. "Yes, sir."

"Thanks. I'd be a dead man if it wasn't for you. I owe you."

"You owe me nothing." Buck shook his head. "You mind me asking how old you are?"

"Forty, this year."

"I thought a man slowed down after his mid-twenties."

It was Jack's turn to grin. "You shoulda seen me in my twenties."

Everyone laughed. Berry had been listening and watching the undertaker, who was loading the bodies into his wagon. "Jack, why don't you and Buck join me at the office, and I'll buy you a cup of coffee. Course, I don't think you'll enjoy it near as much as what Gracie makes."

Jack had had enough. He turned to the marshal. "Sounds good to me, *Strawberry*."

The grin dropped from Berry's face. Wheeling around, he glared at Jack. "Nobody calls me that."

Jack leaned forward until the two men were inches apart, hard men not giving an inch. Then Marshal Berry blinked and took a deep breath. "Alright, I get the point. No more comments about Gracie."

Jack smiled. "Amazing how easy it is to communicate with you . . . Berry."

Several of the deputies laughed, but shut up when Marshal

Berry turned, eyeing each deputy, then led the way back to the office.

Jack asked Buck, "Did you put the guy in the big jail or the office holding cells?"

"Office. I was in a hurry."

They entered Marshal Berry's office, and the marshal stepped up to the potbellied stove. A large pot of coffee sat boiling away on top. He poured a cup and offered it to Jack, who eyed it and shook his head. "I'm going back to Ma's place when we're through. I don't want to rot a hole in my belly before I get there."

Berry handed it to Buck, who took the cup, sipped, and shook his head. Spotting Berry watching him, he took another sip. "Hot, that's hot."

Berry took his cup and moved behind his desk, motioning to the adjacent chair for Jack.

A voice Jack remembered sounded from behind the second set of bars. "What happened?"

Jack walked to the bars where he could see Theodore Rush in the back cell. Rush looked a lot older since last he'd seen him. He sported a salt-and-pepper beard and thinning hair of the same type. When he saw Jack, he began cursing. It went on until Marshal Berry called from his desk, "Shut your face, mister."

Ted commented on the marshal's ancestry until Berry stood and walked to the bars. He turned to Jack. "Who is this filthy-mouthed feller?"

"That would be Theodore Rush, brother to the gunmen the undertaker is preparing."

Jack's statement set Ted off again.

Berry took down a ring of keys and tossed them to one of the deputies. "Take this feller over to the main jail and lock him up. I'm tired of listening to him."

The deputy dragged Ted out of the cell. When he passed Jack, he jerked the deputy to a stop. "Are they both dead?"

"Yeah, Ted. They're both dead. If I remember correctly, you're the only Rush left. You might think about changing your ways before your name dies with you."

Ted Rush stared at Jack and began cursing him.

"Get him out of here!" Berry yelled. He stood until Rush was gone, then pointed Jack toward a chair. They seated themselves, and Berry removed several sheets of paper and a pencil from his desk drawer. "Alright, Jack, tell me what happened."

Jack began the story from when he had stepped out of the Whiskey Barrel. Berry gave him a sideways glance but did not interrupt. When Jack had finished with the second shot into Emmett, he leaned back. "That's about it."

"Sounds like they knew you."

"Yep, they did. When I arrived in Silver City, New Mexico, I happened to hear Judge Andrew Coleman was holding court. I'm always interested in court cases, so I went in and had a look. One of the men on trial had killed a deputy marshal. His pa and a whole slew of hands rode into town to break him loose. I helped shoot a couple of them, and they hightailed it out of there. To shorten this whole story, I ended up killing a couple of brothers of those two dead men, and their pa. I suppose they wanted a little revenge. It didn't work out the way they'd planned."

Buck was leaning against the iron-barred entry into the room with the holding cells. He spoke up. "I saw it all, Marshal. Those two fellers thought they had the drop on Jack, I mean Marshal Sage here."

Jack interrupted. "They would have if Buck hadn't come along. They had Ted set to dry gulch me. I saw him when I came out of the saloon, but thought nothing of it until those two called me out. I figured I was a goner until Emmett started looking a little antsy when he couldn't see his ace in the hole. Buck had taken Mr. Rush out."

Buck cleared his throat. "Like I said, Marshal, I saw the whole thing. You wouldn't have believed it. Those two fellers talked way too long. I think they wanted to enjoy their moment and make

Marshal Sage squirm. It looked like the younger one started it. He went for his gun, and the older fella followed along. He didn't look too happy with his brother's decision. He was fast, just not fast enough. Jack whips out that Smith & Wesson and blasts the guy before he gets off a shot. Then he switches to the other guy, who's still drawing his gun, and blasts him. Then he switches back to the older one. The older feller looked like a gunfighter, and he ain't had a bit of quit in him. He's bringing up that Colt when Jack shot him again. He killed both of them when they had the edge on him. Yes, sir, that was something to see."

Jack was feeling a little nauseated. He wasn't going to throw up, these weren't the first men he'd killed, but it always affected him like this. Taking a man's life was a heavy weight, and he had a load of those weights pulling down on him. He stood. "You need me to sign that?"

Berry looked up at Jack.

Jack could see the man understood.

Berry turned the papers around so they were facing Jack. He had filled three pages with the testimony. "The judge likes for each sheet to be initialed by you, and sign the last page."

Jack looked at the document. It was written in pencil. "Pencil's alright?"

"Yeah, it's faster and less messy."

Jack shrugged, took the pencil, initialed every page, and signed the last, then handed the pencil to Buck and watched him initial and sign. When he was finished, he nodded to Buck and Marshal Berry. "I think I'll go grab a bite to eat. Thanks again, Buck." He turned. One of the deputies opened the door for him, and he stepped through, into the fresh air.

He looked up the street. The bodies were gone, the general store had already boarded up the window, and there was someone washing the blood from the boardwalk. People were going about their business as if nothing had happened.

Jack felt the southern breeze on his face, cool and damp. It felt good against his skin. It also felt good to be alive. How many times had he faced men who had the intent to kill him? He carried the scars to prove it.

He started for the school. Billy and Elijah would be getting out for lunch, and he wanted to be there when they came out of the schoolhouse. Striding to the school, his mind went over past events in his life. During his years as a legionnaire with the Foreign Legion and as a soldier with the U.S. Cavalry during the war, he had never been wounded. He'd even made it through his excursion in Central America and Mexico without a wound. But he carried scars all over his body, acquired after he had put on the badge of a lawman. *Ironic,* Jack thought, *to go through two wars without a scratch, and start carrying a badge and . . .* He shook his head, *Not worth thinking about,* and strode on to the school.

Zeb was sitting on a chair under a big red oak. "All quiet, Jack. Though I hear that's a lot more than can be said for you."

"Yep, I was a little busy."

When Jack didn't pursue it, Zeb stood. "I've been thinking about this badge. I don't need it to protect Elijah, so how about if I give it back to you? I don't much care for this lawman business. It's never been an attraction to me."

"Sure, Zeb. You going to keep on watching out for Elijah and Billy if I need you?"

"Oh, for sure. I'm just not much for this badge responsibility stuff, you know?"

"I do indeed."

Zeb unhooked the badge from his vest and handed it to Jack.

He dropped it into his vest pocket. "If you want to take off, it's fine with me. Thanks again for keeping an eye on the boys."

"Glad to help, Marshal. I'm headin' to Pauly's, if you need me."

Jack watched Zeb stride back to town, and sat in the chair, waiting for the boys. It wasn't long before the door burst open and kids came charging out the door. It looked like exiting was based on age, the natural pecking order. The older kids first, then gradually working down to the youngest. Elijah and Billy came out in the latter half. As soon as the boys saw Jack, they dashed down the stairs and across the clearing.

Billy beat Elijah. "We heard shooting. It sounded like it was in town. Was anyone hurt?" Billy looked worried. "Mama was going to town."

Jack dropped a hand on each of the boys' shoulders and turned them toward their house. "Billy, your mama is fine. It was only a couple of bad guys, and they won't be bothering anyone again."

Elijah looked up at Jack. "Did you shoot 'em, Marshal?"

Not a question I want to answer, Jack thought, *but he needs the truth. They'll find out soon enough anyway.* "I'm afraid so, Elijah. They didn't give me an option."

Billy skipped along beside Jack. "Are they dead?"

"Two of them are. One was captured."

Elijah asked, "What will happen to him?"

"Prison."

Elijah reached up and pulled Jack's hand from his shoulder, slipping his little hand inside the big marshal's. "For a long time?"

Billy skipped ahead, interested in a lizard crossing the street.

Jack liked the feel of a youngster's hand in his. "Not too long. He didn't shoot at anyone. He'll probably only get a couple of years."

The lizard, its long tail flying, raced away from Billy, disappearing through a crack in the siding of a house.

Elijah looked up. "That's a long time."

Jack nodded. "It is, and it isn't. While it's taking place, it seems like a long time, but when it's past, it doesn't seem long at all."

Billy turned to Elijah and yelled, "Come on, Elijah. We've got to help Mama and Grandma get dinner ready."

Elijah released Jack's hand and, without another word, raced after Billy.

16

Jack watched the little boy dash after his friend. His leg was getting better every day. Maybe the doctor was right, and it would be good as new when it had completely healed. He smiled at the thought. The two boys banged onto the boardwalk and shoved the door open. He could almost hear Grace call, "Don't slam the door," before Billy swung the door hard, slamming it into the facing. *Boys will be boys,* he thought.

His mind went to Abel Franklin. The man had been in the crowd after the shooting, staring at Jack intently. Barrett Clagg had stood near him. For no reason, Jack stepped into the alley and walked along the side of the house to the back entrance. He had no plan, no motive. At the last moment, he bypassed the front door and turned to the alley between Ma's establishment and the attorney's office. The attorney's entrance was on the second floor, with a long stairway along the outside, beginning at the boardwalk. The attorney's door opened, causing Jack to look up, but the person in the doorway changed his mind and jerked back inside upon seeing him. He only caught a brief glimpse of the man, but he had a feeling it was Franklin.

It didn't take him long to find an attorney, Jack thought, beginning to mull over Elijah's uncle visiting a local attorney. Was he planning to make sure he had no trouble getting the boy? He might be figuring if he hires a local attorney, maybe one who knew the judge, it might make it easier to get him. Jack continued to muse as he walked. *And how does a man from Tennessee find an attorney that quickly?*

Jack continued to the back. Seeing nothing out of place, he climbed the short staircase to the landing and entered the house. Arriving through this entrance put him close to his room. He passed a couple of doors and, reaching his, removed the key from his pocket and unlocked the door.

Swinging the door open, he halted and surveyed the room. Someone had been inside his room recently, like within the hour. Over the years, Jack had learned to trust his instinct. It seldom failed him. What concerned him even more was whoever had been here had been in Mary and Grace's home, which put them and the boys at risk. Jack pulled his door closed and headed toward the noise coming from the kitchen and dining room.

He stepped into the kitchen to see Elijah heading toward the loud conversation with a big platter of rolls. From the dining room, he could pick out the sound of Berry and the judge talking and Mary laughing. Several other unrecognized voices could be heard in the cacophony.

"Hi, Marshal," Billy said, returning to the kitchen with an empty tray.

"Hey, young fella, looks like you made yourself useful fast."

Grace looked over her shoulder from the large indoor stove and gave Jack a sheepish smile. "Hi, Jack."

He shot a big grin at her. "Hi yourself, looks like you're busy."

Before she turned, Jack could see the extra pink of her cheeks.

She bent and removed two pies from the oven and set them on the kitchen table on metal trivets. "We are." Grace glanced at her son. "Grab Elijah, and you two sit at your table and eat. I've prepared your plates."

Billy started toward the small table against the wall, turned his head toward the dining room, and yelled, "Elijah, come eat."

Grace glanced at Jack and rolled her eyes. He shrugged as Elijah raced back into the kitchen, with Mary following. While Elijah ran to the table, Mary came straight to Jack. Reaching him, she reacted much as her daughter had in the street, by placing her arms around him and laying her head on his chest.

"Oh, Jack. I am so glad you are safe. Grace told me what happened." She gave him a squeeze and released him. Grasping both of his thick biceps, she gazed into his gray eyes. "You were watched over, Jack. I hope you know that."

A little embarrassed, Jack answered sincerely, "I know, Mary. I've been watched over a lot in my lifetime."

She squeezed his arms with her small, strong hands. "It's good that you know." She released him and took a couple of steps back where it was easier to look up at him. "You should also know you scared the life out of my daughter."

Grace jerked around. "Mother..."

"Don't 'Mother' me, Grace. He did, and you might as well admit it." She winked at Jack. "You hungry?"

Grace's frown softened as she turned her green eyes on Jack. "You're right, he did, and of course he's hungry. Go sit down, Jack, while there's still food left. Seems a shooting activates everyone's appetite."

He nodded to her and turned to Mary. "I'm so hungry I could eat the south end of a northbound jack—"

Mary popped him with the end of the dishtowel that had been hanging around her waist. "You don't need to finish that. I've heard it more than I care to tell. Do like Grace says, and I'll fill you a dish with fresh ham, gravy, and cooked cabbage straight from our garden."

Jack headed for the dining room door. "I don't need to be told more than twice. Especially when it's by the two best-looking women in Arkansas."

He stepped into the dining room, and the conversation died. The judge was sitting at the head of the table, with Berry on one side and Buck on the other. Several of the deputies, plus business owners, lined the table. The silence was immediately broken by applause, with the judge joining in. Buck, who was finishing off his pie, took the last bite and stood.

Speaking around the big bite of pie, he said, "Come on over here, Jack, and have a seat next to the judge. I'm sure he and the marshal want to talk to you, and I'm just leaving."

The applause died, people went back to their eating, and Jack stepped to Buck's side. "Thanks, Buck. How's the pie?"

The deputy rolled his eyes and swallowed the last bite. "You ain't tasted the best pecan pie in all of Arkansas 'til you slap your lips around a piece of Grace's." A grin slipped across his face. "Course, the way it's looking, you might be eatin' a lot of her cookin'."

Jack's smile disappeared, and his eyes tightened.

"Alright, alright. I swear you ain't got a bit of humor." His grin widened. "But I reckon I can put up with you." He turned to the chair where he had been sitting and pulled it farther out and, making an exaggerated bow, held the chair for Jack. "Please sit down, Marshal Sage."

Jack gave the grinning deputy a grunt. "Thanks, now get out of here before you get into trouble."

Jack sat, and Buck shoved the chair under him. "Yes, sir, Marshal, sir."

Everyone roared, and Buck, as he exited the dining room, raised his hat to laughter and greater applause than Jack had received.

Jack pulled his chair to the table as Mary appeared and removed Buck's plate and silverware. Picking them up, she leaned over, putting her mouth close to Jack's ear. "You'd better get used to a little ribbing, Jack, boy. All these fellas are jealous of what they saw today with you and Grace. Like Buck said, get a sense of humor." He felt a solid bump from her hip as she left the room with his dishes. Moments later, she returned with a cup of coffee, filled two-thirds full, and a plate loaded with ham, potatoes, gravy, and fresh-cooked cabbage. Reaching into a pocket on her apron, she pulled out a knife, fork, and teaspoon, dropping them next to Jack's plate.

"Thanks, Mary."

Saying nothing, she bumped him again with her hip, for emphasis, and went around the table picking up plates. While she was going from man to man, speaking loud enough for all to hear, she said, "You boys need anything else?"

A particularly hefty older gent on the opposite side and near the other end of the long table spoke up. "You bet. I could go for another piece of that fine pecan pie."

Mary, stacking dishes on top of each other on her arm, looked across at the man. "Coming up, Winthrop, but don't forget, extra pie is twenty-five cents a piece."

Winthrop shook his head as he pulled out two bits to drop next to his plate. "It don't matter how much it is, Mary. That's the best stuff this old man has had in a long time."

She nodded, gifting him with a smile. "Thank you, Winthrop. Grace made the pies today. She has an angel's touch."

Several of the men nodded or mumbled their agreement.

The judge, between bites, leaned toward Jack. "Do you think Elijah will be up to testifying Monday?"

Jack nodded. "I'm pretty sure he will, Judge. He's a strong lad, and I think he's looking for a little justice for his folks."

The judge nodded and slid his chair back. "Sorry to leave so soon, but court starts in a few minutes. Normally I would be eating at home, but on these court days, it gives me an excuse to enjoy Grace and Mary's cooking. Their establishment is much closer than home. See you tomorrow." He turned to Berry. "See you in court, Strawn."

"I'll be there in just a few minutes, Judge."

Jack could see that several of the deputies were hurrying with their pie, indicating they would be leaving with Berry, who was within a bite of finishing.

Berry swallowed and leaned forward. "You need any other protection for Elijah? He's the only witness we have against the Claggs. Without him, they'll walk again. If they do, this'll be the first time for Judge Bell."

Jack gave serious thought to adding deputies. They weren't needed during the day, but it couldn't hurt at night. The only way he could guarantee the boy's safety at night was to sleep in his room, and he didn't want to increase the disturbance any greater for Elijah. It was bad enough for the boy to be aware of the approach of the Claggs' trial. However, a little additional protection outside at night might be useful. "That'd be great, Strawn. With me and Zeb, the day's handled, but night's a different thing."

Berry looked relieved. "Good. I was concerned about the nighttime. Barrett and Ben, especially Ben, are slick operators. Ben's deadly with a knife. I wouldn't put it past him to try to slip in at night. In fact, I'd sleep light were I you. He's the kind who'd try to slit your throat while you were sleeping, kinda like a bonus. I can tell you, from what I hear from the jail attendants, the Claggs would love to leave you sucking for air."

Jack halted the fork on the way to his mouth, loaded with his final bite of ham and potatoes. "That's a comforting thought. I'd hate to have to kill a man in Mary's place, close to the kids. They'd probably have nightmares for years." He continued the fork and savored his last bite. No sooner had he swallowed than Mary stepped beside him. "Elijah and Billy are ready to go back to school."

Jack rose, pushing his chair back. "See you later, Strawn." He turned to the other men at the table, "Gentlemen," and headed for the kitchen. Entering, Jack witnessed Billy trying to talk his mom into he and Elijah staying and helping her. Jack remembered his days of trying to get out of school. It mostly never worked, but it didn't stop him from trying.

Speaking a bit louder than normal, Jack said, "Alright, boys, I need you to escort me to school."

Billy immediately stopped his begging and, with Elijah, raced to his side. "Can you show us how to shoot, Marshal?"

"Well, Billy, a man needs to know how to shoot. Maybe one of these days after school, you can show me a good shooting place, and we'll burn some powder."

Elijah asked in a small voice, "Can I go?"

Jack bent and scooped him up. "Of course you can. We can all go. That'd be fun, wouldn't it?"

Both boys' faces lit up. "Yes, sir," responded the pair.

He nodded and set Elijah down. "Good, I'd like that myself, but now we need to head out for school. You boys ready?"

Elijah grabbed one hand, and Billy the other. The three of them marched proudly through the dining room to the parlor and out the front door. Jack couldn't help but notice the silence as they walked through the dining room. He could almost hear the creaking of necks as heads turned to follow the trio across the room. When they were through, the talking started up again, and chairs began to scrape as lunch patrons decided it was time to get back to work.

Jack spotted Zeb waiting at the schoolhouse as he and the boys neared. Both greeted the cowhand with, "Hi, Zeb," and raced into the school. Jack watched the door as other children filed in. "You get a chance to eat?"

Zeb was also watching. "Yep, I did. Ate over at the hotel. It was pretty good."

"I'm telling you, you ought to try Ma's place. The food is hard to beat. They had pecan pie that I hear is better than in Texas. Grace is a terrific cook."

Jack saw the glint in Zeb's eyes at the mention of Grace and raised an eyebrow.

Zeb controlled the grin threatening to burst out at the corners of his mouth. "I'll have to give 'em a try fore I head back to the ranch. I'll probably stay till after the hanging, and then head on back. I'm not big on cold weather, so I wanta get outta here as soon as I can."

Jack, knowing how Zeb felt, especially after spending a winter in the Rockies, gave him a sincere nod. "I'm like you. I've never liked the cold. In fact, when you get back, tell Montana and Bronco I'm liable to be showing up before long. You can also tell them I appreciate the money."

"I'll be glad to."

Jack scanned the area surrounding the school. It was heavily wooded. In fact, the school was surrounded with trees. There were only two paths, one back to town and one to the outhouse. Not a location Jack really liked, but this far east there was little Indian trouble to be concerned about. "I'm going to head back to town and chat with Marshal Berry for a while. If you need me, give me a shout." He looked around one last time. "Keep your eyes open. I'm starting to get a little antsy."

Zeb dropped into the chair. "I'll do it. See you later, boss."

JACK SPENT the afternoon with Berry, finding out about the Claggs, especially Barrett and Ben. He had learned the town was almost evenly split on the family, some liking, some not.

They came from a farming background, arriving on the scene in the thirties, clearing land, and planting cotton. Success came early for old man Clagg. He knew cotton and for many years was fortunate with the bugs and the weather. His crops seemed to always mature and find their way to the warehouses on the river before the heavy rains hit. He was a rough but likable old man who grew rough boys always ready for a fight. Then the war came, and he lost everything.

Old man Clagg, while his boys were away fighting with the likes of Quantrill's Raiders, came down with consumption and died on his farm, leaving Joey alone and destitute. Typhoid had taken his wife several years earlier. With all the men away at war except Joey, the farm withered and died, leaving nothing but falling-down buildings and weeds. When the other sons returned, they found an emaciated and almost wild Joey living on what he could kill in the woods and grow in the garden. Most of them, already bitter from the war, worsened, but Barrett had a head on his shoulders and a little money.

He bought a wagon and started a shipping business, using his brothers as employees. It grew rapidly, the competition mysteriously disappearing. Several of Barrett's competitors met untimely deaths, while others sold out. Rumors were heard, but nothing could be proven.

After a couple of hours of talking to Berry and drinking the marshal's coffee, Jack's ears were numb, and he felt like his stomach was ruined. Suddenly, multiple yells jerked him out of the conversation. Jack leaped to his feet and lunged for the door, for he had heard, clear and distinct, the word school. He was out the door running, joined by several of the parents. He plunged down the path, his long legs pulling him ahead of the others.

17

Nearing the school, Jack heard the teacher, Miss Hawkins, screaming for help. He burst into the schoolyard and saw nothing. The screaming was coming from the path to the outhouse, which was located roughly thirty yards from the school. Halfway to the outhouse, he saw Miss Hawkins kneeling alongside a body. Relieved, he could see the person down was too big to be either Elijah or Billy or any of the other children. Immediately after the relief, he felt a wave of guilt but pushed it away. Nearing, he recognized Zeb's hat lying in the brush at the edge of the path.

Jack slid to a halt, jumped to the other side of Zeb, and knelt. He was conscious but looked to be bleeding badly from both his head and back. The blood had soaked into the dirt of the path.

Rita Hawkins instantly quieted when Jack arrived. He took the cowhand from her arms. "Get the doc, and make it quick."

Buck slid to a stop and, hearing Jack's order, spun around and raced back through the gathering crowd. Jack pulled Zeb's shirt above the wound. He had been stabbed. It had entered his back on his right side.

Zeb's eyes fluttered open, and he gripped Jack's forearm.

"They got the boys, Jack. I'm sorry." He winced and took a sharp breath, held it for a moment, and continued, "I had my gun out and was about to shoot when everything went black." Zeb put his hands on the ground and started to push up. "Come on. We got to get after 'em, or they'll get away."

Jack gently but firmly pushed him down. "You're not going anywhere except to the doctor, Zeb. You've had a bad blow on the head and a knife stuck in your side. Who was it?"

Zeb shook his head. "Couldn't tell. Never saw the guy who hit me. Other two wore pillowcases over their heads. I'm real sorry, Jack. I told you I wasn't cut out to be no lawman."

The doctor rushed up, bag in hand. When he saw Zeb, he turned to a man in the crowd. "Blanton, you know where I keep the stretcher. Run back and get it." When the man didn't move fast enough for the doctor, he rose up from Zeb and yelled, "Hurry." The doctor added to his command, "Get three men to help."

Someone piped up in the group surrounding them, "We got enough men here, Doc."

The doctor nodded and turned back to Zeb. He quickly examined the head wound and abandoned it for the puncture in Zeb's back. He checked the front for a through and through and then began pressing gently on his belly. After a few pushes, he nodded to Jack. "I don't feel any sign of blood pooling. He may be a lucky cowhand."

Zeb had leaned back in Jack's arms. He opened his eyes and stared at the doctor. "I ain't feelin' real lucky right now."

"Yes, sorry, Mister . . . ?"

"His name is Zeb Long, Doc."

"Mr. Long, what I mean is, at this time, it looks like there may be no damage to important internal organs. Barring infections, you might heal completely from this."

Zeb grimaced. "Dang, Doc. You really know how to cheer up a feller."

The stretcher arrived, with Grace right behind Blanton.

Seeing Jack, Grace cried, "What's happened, Jack? How are the boys?"

Jack patted Zeb on the shoulder. "I'll be right back."

Zeb grabbed him again. "Tell her I'm sorry, Jack."

"Don't worry about it, Zeb. You did everything you could do. A man gets hit from behind, he's pretty much out of business." He patted the man's hand and removed it from his forearm, stood, and walked to Grace.

Seeing the look on his face, she started shaking her head. "No, Jack, don't tell me someone took my boys."

He encircled her with his arms, and she pulled herself tight against him, speaking into his chest. "You've got to get them back. They're just little boys. Why would anyone do something like this?"

"I'm not sure, Grace, but I'll make you a promise. I won't stop until I find them, and when I return, whoever took them will be with me."

He felt the old pain growing. It wasn't a friend, but more like an unwelcome relative who showed up when least expected. It felt dark and bitter and cold. *I'll find those boys,* he thought, *and I'll bring them back. If they've been harmed . . .* The rage grew, and even as he held Grace, the horrible pictures of his dead wife, Yasmina, and their baby flashed in his mind. His fury grew. "I'll bring them back, Grace. I promise, but I've got to go while there is still daylight."

He knew his voice had turned hard, and she must have noticed, for she pushed away and looked up at his grim features.

"Be calm, Grace. While I'm getting my mounts ready, pack food that will last for several days. Get my rifle. It's in the bedroom. My saddlebags are also in there. Put a change of clothes in the saddlebags, and the food, and bring it with my coat and rifle to the front door. I'll be in a hurry when I come by." His hand took one tender moment to caress her face. Then he turned her toward town. "Now go."

Mary arrived in time to hear everything. Her searching eyes examined Jack's hard features and cold eyes. She seemed to discern his rage, and placed a hand on his forearm. "Go with God, Jack."

He examined her for a moment, and when he spoke, his voice was frigid and devoid of emotion. "I don't think he'll be riding with me today, Mary."

She stood on tiptoe and kissed him on the cheek. "He's always with you. Whether you realize it or not, you're his avenging angel." Turning, she wrapped her arm around her daughter's waist, and Jack raced toward Winthrop's Stables.

The big door of the stables stood wide open. Jack plunged into the interior, hardly noting the musty smell of horses, horse droppings, and straw. Pauly was standing on the raised porch of his office, staring at Jack like he was seeing a madman.

"What's happening, Jack?"

Jack dashed by him into the tack room and grabbed his saddle and the remainder of his gear. He shouted at Pauly, "Billy and Elijah have been taken from the school. Zeb's been stabbed. I'm taking Pepper and Thunder. I need you to sack me up several days of feed and fill me a canteen." He jerked to a halt alongside Pepper, took the time to wipe the chestnut's back to make sure it was clean, and tossed on the blanket, followed by the saddle. He worked quickly. By the time Pepper was ready, Pauly had returned with a sack of feed and hung it over the saddle horn along with the canteen.

"There's a couple of feedbags inside the sack. It'll make it easier." He slipped a lead around Thunder's neck and looped the end around Jack's saddle horn. "Your rifle ain't here. You took it. You want mine?"

Jack shook his head. "Don't worry about it, Pauly. I'm stopping at Ma's. Grace has some food and clothes packed for me, and she's got my rifle."

Pauly slapped Jack's saddle. "Good luck, Marshal. Bring those boys back safe."

"I plan on it." Jack was about to swing into the saddle when a voice he hadn't heard in a while called out, "Hold up, Jack." Turning, he saw Judge Bell entering the stable with none other than Carter Schofield, and thought, *This can't be good.*

Carter had entered his life a few years earlier at Fort Bayard, near Silver City, New Mexico. To his surprise, Schofield had been the bearer of an offer from the president. Jack had served under Grant during the war. After he left the army, the general had followed his adventures in Central America, Mexico, Texas, and New Mexico. Schofield had arrived at Bayard to persuade Jack to become a U.S. Marshal, working directly for the president with the option to resign at any time he deemed it appropriate.

After his mission in Wyoming was completed, Jack had decided to step away. He had left the army after the war because he preferred his independence. He enjoyed helping people, not answering to the brass.

However, Schofield had convinced him to continue his service and help Judge Bell at Fort Smith. Justice was scarce in the Indian Territory, so outlaws flocked there. It was Bell's assignment to clean it up, and the president wanted Jack to help. He had relented, and here he was, but he knew Carter Schofield spelled trouble. He removed his left foot from the stirrup. "Make it quick, Carter. I'm in a hurry."

Judge Bell addressed Schofield as they approached Jack. "I told you he'd be chasing after those boys." He directed his next statement to Jack. "Marshal Sage, I have delegated Marshal Berry and three of his men to pursue the boys and their kidnappers. They will bring them back. You are needed here in case Elijah Franklin does not return in time for the trial."

"Judge, you can postpone the trial and set a new date after we return."

Schofield spoke up, his voice dripping with persuasion. "Jack,

I talked to the president. He has received word that you have not been exactly cooperative with Judge Bell."

Jack snapped back, his eyes locked on Bell, "I wonder how he came by that information."

Schofield, smooth as fresh cream, smiled. "Jack, that isn't really important. The important thing is the president wants you to work with the judge and follow his orders." His eyebrows rose, and his head tilted slightly for emphasis. "That means staying here for now. You are the only witness against the Claggs if the boys aren't back in time."

Jack, anxious to be on his way, directed his question to the judge. "When's Berry leaving?"

The judge cleared his throat. "Well, Jack, I believe he said he needed to get his men together and get supplies. I'm sure he'll try to get out of here today, if darkness doesn't catch them."

Jack shook his head and turned Pepper toward the big door as he swung into the saddle. "He'll be too late. Tell him to bring a tracker and follow me."

Carter stepped in front of Pepper and grasped the horse's cheekpiece. "Jack, don't do this. I have the authority to remove you as a marshal."

Time was wasting. Reins clutched in his left hand, his right flew to the badge. He yanked it from his vest and threw it at Schofield's feet. "Thanks for making it easy, Carter." At the same time he slammed his heels into Pepper.

A thousand pounds of chestnut leaped forward, lifting Carter Schofield's one hundred and seventy pounds from the ground. Knowing the danger he was in, Schofield simultaneously jerked his left hand from Pepper's cheekpiece while pressing and shoving with all of his might against the big chestnut's jaw. His quick reaction tossed him clear of the chestnut and the big gray.

The two horses charged from the stable, and Jack turned them toward Ma's place. Grace was standing in front of the entrance, waiting. He pulled up, and she handed him his coat and saddlebags. He took the coat and pulled it on. While he was tying the saddlebags, she rammed the Winchester into the scabbard.

Jack looked down into the bright green eyes sparkling with unshed tears. "Rest easy, Grace. You'll see your boys again." Spinning Pepper around, he galloped the horses past Pauly's, where Schofield and the judge stood. Carter Schofield was occupied, wiping straw and manure from his trousers. The judge glared as he passed. He continued along the path to the school and then to the outhouse. Once there, he began to examine the bushes, and found the tracks of the assailants.

Reading the sign, he found where the two men had grabbed the boys. A third had joined them after stabbing Zeb, and they'd run along a small trail to their horses. *Only three horses,* he thought. *They're going to have to ride and hang on to the boys. Keep your heads, boys. This is no time to panic.* He saw where the men had walked their horses through the thicket until they were clear. Just before clearing the trees, he found the masks and shook his head. They weren't interested in covering their faces. That wasn't good at all. Once clear, they'd broken into a gallop.

Jack jogged back to Pepper and swung into the saddle, following the trail of the kidnappers. He suspected one of them was Franklin, but it didn't make sense. He was going to get the boy after the trial, with no problems. Now he was being pursued, and he was in huge trouble even if he didn't harm the boys. Jack was extremely concerned for Billy. As far as he knew, they had no need to keep him alive. If they murdered Billy, Grace might never recover. It was bad enough for her to lose her husband, but to add losing her son would be devastating.

The men were doing nothing to hide their trail. They must have figured they would be far away before anyone found Zeb or recognized the boys were gone, or they were just cocky enough to not care. *Either way,* Jack thought, *you're making a huge mistake.*

THE SUN HAD SLIPPED below the treetops and would soon be sliding below the horizon. Fortunately, a waxing gibbous moon had risen, and Jack would have light, not bright sunlight, but enough moonlight for him to stay on the trail, especially since these morons were doing nothing to hide their tracks.

Rounding a bend, Jack could see the glint of water ahead. His hope for a quick conclusion plunged. If they had a boat, he was in trouble. The trail continued, paralleling the river. Jack was following the tracks using moonlight. Fortunately there were no clouds to interfere with the weak light, and the ground was soft from the recent rains, leaving deeper tracks. Jack split his concentration between the tracks and searching ahead for the kidnappers.

Icy doubt almost overcame him when the trail ceased paralleling the river but turned toward it. In this area, the Arkansas was wide, and though the current wasn't nearly as fast as it had been when he had crossed it, the river was much wider. If they'd crossed, it would mean they had a boat waiting, and he'd have to find a means to get himself and his horses to the other side—soon.

Coming to the edge of the river, his greatest fear was realized. A large boat or barge had put in right here, and the horses' tracks disappeared. Heart heavy, Jack swung down from Pepper. He checked his saddlebags, dug in them for a bit, and pulled out his field glasses. It was dark, with the exception of the moon, and he didn't expect much.

He put the glasses to his eyes, waited while his eyes adjusted, and then slowly began sweeping the opposite side of the river. No sign of the fugitives, but he was pleased with the brightness. He could see. The moonlight was sufficient to allow him a fair look at the opposite shore, and he was actually able to make out a log floating down the river. If he could see the log and the opposite side, he might find the boat. He examined the opposite side as far downriver as he could, until the river's edge on his side entered his field of vision.

Cheered, he swung into the saddle and made his way along the bank. From his next stop, being conservative with the distance he traveled, he examined the bank and found that he could have gone farther, almost twice as far. He picked out a point he could use as a marker, and continued. This time, when he halted, he found he had gone too far and had to backtrack to make sure he hadn't missed the boat. Nothing was there, but he was feeling more confident with his plan.

Ensuring he passed nothing as he rode, Jack began traveling in spurts. He'd glass the river until he was positive there was nothing in the river and no one on the opposite bank, then he rode as fast as the night would allow, and glass again. He had spotted several boats tied up on the opposite bank, and had run across two on this side, but neither of them was large enough for him and his horses. He kept leapfrogging.

The moon had passed its zenith, and Jack had lost count of the number of leaps he had made along the riverbank. Time passed, and the moon rose, adding brightness, making the opposite bank clearer. Jack made his next leap. He pulled Pepper to a halt and brought the glasses to his face. The barge leaped into his vision, pulling up to the opposite bank. Several horses were on it along with a number of men. When the boat touched the bank, men leaped the horses ashore. Once there, several of the men began arguing, and then a gun fired, once, twice, and then a third time.

Jack, using the field glasses, had been looking directly at the men when the weapon flamed in brilliant flashes. He yanked the glasses down with the first flash, but his night vision was gone, even without the two additional flashes. Bright spots floated across his eyes, and everything else was black. He listened and waited. He could see nothing and could only make out faint voices across the river.

Moments after the shots, he heard horses riding away. They were gone.

I've got to get across this river, Jack thought. While he waited for his night vision to return, he switched saddles from Pepper to Thunder and mulled over his predicament. *I have to get across, but it's impossible to swim here. I'll have to ride downriver until I find a narrower spot to cross or someone who can take me.* He immediately shot the last idea down and began looking around. He found what he needed.

This was no time to be subtle, and he had no fear of the men across the river spotting him, not after the three shots. Finding an acceptable spot on the riverbank, he tromped down the grass, then dragged a thick limb, ripping off branches as he moved. When he had the end clean where it looked like a giant arrow shaft, he dropped it, pointing toward the opposite bank and the boat.

He yanked his tally book from his inside vest pocket and, with a pencil stub he always kept handy, quickly wrote what had happened across the river. Finding four small rocks, he placed three in a triangle on the limb, folded the note and set it inside the triangle and carefully positioned the fourth rock on top of the note. He examined his work and, to his horses, said, "Even a crazy posse should be able to find this, boys." Jack mounted Thunder.

With his vision returned, he lifted his field glasses. To his surprise, the boat was gone. He swung the glasses downriver and found it floating, uncontrolled, slowly turning in the current. *They killed the rivermen,* Jack thought and nudged Thunder. The big horse started moving forward, paralleling the riverbank.

18

The barge had drifted toward the opposite bank, then gradually worked its way toward the middle. It had neared, almost close enough for Jack to break out his rope, but then began to turn, following the current, and swing farther away. Now it was drifting nearer. Jack had his rope ready, waiting, praying it would come close enough. It had a thick post at each corner and on each side approximately in the middle. Jack planned to get a rope on one of those posts. Hopefully, Thunder could stop the drift of the barge and pull it toward the bank.

Jack was not a good roper. His background was war and the law, not herding cattle. But when he bought part of a cattle herd in Texas, to drive to Kansas, his good friend and partner Bronco Fenn had taught him the details of roping. Bronco had never hesitated to deride Jack's weak roping skills, and his friend was right. He could occasionally daub his loop over his target, but it was usually more luck than skill, and that was what he was praying for tonight. Whether luck or skill tonight, he prayed the rope would settle over one of the posts, for two young boys' lives rested on his loop.

Jack watched and waited.

The barge slowly rotated as it drifted closer and closer. Jack had judged the boat's speed accurately. It appeared his target would be within forty feet or so, exactly where he and Thunder and Pepper waited. Both horses had their heads up, watching the river, as if they too understood the urgency. The boat drew nearer, and Jack shook out his loop for the umpteenth time. Jack's lips moved. "Lord, you know I'm not a praying man, but this isn't for me, it's for those two boys. I'd be much obliged if you'd guide this loop tonight."

The boat was almost to the point Jack had picked for his release. He calculated like it was a trotting deer. He'd have to lead it just a little. It was nearing the spot. Now! He swung his loop once and released.

Moving lightly in the night breeze, a small, almost invisible elm limb, well over Jack's head, took this moment to bow to the wind, ever so slightly. But it was enough to gently kiss the rope as it passed on its way to the post.

The loop began to wobble. Not much at first, but as it traveled, the wobble increased. Jack held his breath. He hadn't seen that blasted limb. It was so small, he'd hardly felt it when he threw the rope. But there the loop was, wobbling and about to fall apart before it reached the boat's post. It was almost there when it collapsed. His heart dropped. His quick reaction to yank the now wet rope back and give it another try, though the boat would be farther, almost kicked in, but before he could, a light gust of wind pushed the far edge of the falling loop over the post. The rope caught and cinched tight to the boat.

The slack slowly but inexorably began to pull out of the rope. Jack threw a dally around the saddle horn and felt the first pull as the flow of the current and weight of the boat stretched the rope taut. Thunder began taking the load. The rope stretched tighter until it could have been strummed like a guitar string.

"Hold on, boy, hold on."

Thunder's forelegs were locked tight, front hooves digging into the soft ground. His weight was thrown back on his hips, and he was squatting like a jackrabbit, but holding, and the barge was beginning to swing toward the bank. Jack felt the saddle move. "Don't give way now." Glancing down at the saddle horn, he was relieved. It too was holding tight.

Then Thunder took a step back. Jack looked up and, with relief, saw the barge moving to the bank. He urged Thunder farther back until the boat touched the bank. They were adjacent to a large elm. He leaped off Thunder and, working quickly before the boat could begin moving again, released the dally and wrapped and tied the rope around the elm. The boat was secure.

He took a moment to pat the big horse on his quivering shoulder. "Good boy, Thunder. You did great." He led the horses to the river and let them drink. Once they were done, he guided them on board. When they were secured, he jumped off, untied the boat, and as it began to move, leaped back on board. Jack picked up one of the long poles and began to push. Even for a man his size, the boat was heavy.

Pepper and Thunder watched Jack only for a few moments, then their heads dropped. "Yeah, get some sleep, boys. You've earned it." He bent his back to the long staff and strained. The boat moved into the current and began to pick up speed, entering the swifter portion of the river. It was his turn to sweat. He could feel the strain in his back and shoulders. He threw everything he could muster against the pole, and the boat slowly headed toward the other bank.

A clearing opened ahead, and Jack threw everything he had into pushing the barge toward the clearing. They struck the bank hard, causing both horses to jerk their heads up in surprise. Jack threw the pole down, grabbed the end of the rope, and raced toward a tree he had spotted nearing the bank. He whipped the rope around the tree, tied it, and looked back. The boat held steady against the bank. Not waiting to admire his work, he rushed on board, led the two horses onto shore, and at last leaned over, placing a hand on each knee. It took him a bit to regain his breath, but when he did, he tied the horses and went back to the boat.

He hadn't allowed himself time to check the two bodies of the boatmen until now. Each had been shot in the chest, with one receiving a final shot to the forehead. Jack shook his head. He had no love for these men who had aided in the kidnapping of the boys, but a couple of ounces of lead was a harsh payment for saving someone's life, and that was exactly what they had done for their killers. If they hadn't been waiting to ferry the kidnappers away from Jack, he would have caught them, and any way you cut it, they would have died, either from lead poisoning or a tight rope.

The two bodies would be found by passersby. Putting the dead men out of his mind, he turned to Thunder and swung into the saddle. It was time to find and rescue those boys. They were depending on him.

He started up the river, but after a short distance, he pulled Thunder to a halt and patted the big gray gently on the neck. Pepper, on his lead, stopped when he was next to Thunder. "Boys, I need to think about this. I just assumed I'd meet these fellas heading along the river, but what if they banked the boat at that spot for a reason? Maybe they're meeting someone or actually have a plan."

Jack bumped Thunder, and the gray began moving forward again, Pepper following. Continuing his ride in the moonlight, he tried to work out what the men he was following might have planned, but in every scenario, no matter what their plans, he would have to cut their tracks. The only way he could do that was to ride to where he had seen them, but he would angle away from the river. Maybe he would be lucky enough to cross their tracks early. He rode through the night, eyes searching the ground for tracks, time fading from his senses until approaching dawn pulled him back to reality. He shook his head. *Concentrate,* he told himself. *You've got to be alert and ready.*

The night had passed, and sunrise, through the broken clouds, began to tinge the dark sky with splotches of pale color. Jack suddenly smelled smoke. At the same time, he heard someone curse and the crack of a hand against flesh. He stopped the horses and, knowing movement and sound were dead giveaways, remained stationary in the saddle, listening.

He heard a small voice, but couldn't make out what was being said, followed by another crack of a hard slap. They were close, and Jack thought, puzzled, *Why did they stop?* In the dim light ahead, he caught a glimpse of a fire. *Too close. If I'm not careful, in the increasing light, they'll spot me. I've got to get out of this saddle.*

Jack cautiously shifted his weight and slowly swung his leg across Thunder's back. The last thing he needed was leather to squeak while he dismounted. His right foot touched the ground, and he lifted his left from the stirrup. He breathed a silent sigh of relief. No squeak.

He started to leave the rifle, since they were in the trees, this would be close work, but if it came to shooting, he needed absolute accuracy. Though he felt confident he would be accurate with his Smith & Wessons, he couldn't take the chance of a stray bullet hitting one of the boys. The rifle would be slower, but more certain.

A different voice spoke up. "Why don't you just kill that kid, Ben? You shoulda done that a long time ago. He ain't been nothing but a drag."

Jack had to move quietly but quickly. Daylight was breaking fast. He removed his spurs and hung them on his saddle, but he had no time to exchange his hard-soled boots for the moccasins he carried in his saddlebags.

Clagg snapped at the voice, "I'll kill him when I'm good and ready. I owe this smart-mouthed kid a little more comeuppance than he's gotten so far." He stopped, and so did Jack. Then he spoke again. "Don't I, kid."

Jack recognized Billy's voice. "I wish I coulda shot you."

There was a moment of silence, followed by loud laughter and the crack of another slap.

Jack moved forward, taking advantage of the noise from the camp. He was seething inside and balled his left hand into a fist. One good, solid, bone-breaking smash to the man's face would bring him great satisfaction.

The camp came into view. He immediately recognized Franklin, his hand gripping Elijah's arm. The boy was next to his uncle and looked better than Jack had expected. Other than sleepy and tired, he appeared to have no visible marks on his face.

Slipping sideways behind the trunk of an elm, Jack saw the laughing man. He had no idea who the laugher might be other than another enemy to handle. He moved to the opposite edge of a large sycamore. After removing his hat, he eased his head just far enough past the trunk to allow a single eye to clear the bark. He had a good view of the camp, and it was his first good look at Ben.

Despite the situation, Jack almost grinned. This guy was the perfect example of rat-faced. He was a little man, no more than maybe five inches over five feet, and looked like a scrawny bag of bones. He had almost no chin. It appeared to disappear between his tiny mouth and neck. His eyes were close-set, dark and small, almost beady. Then he reared back to hit Billy's defiant little face again.

Billy's lip was bleeding, and the left side of his face, from his temple to his chin, was swollen, bruised, and bleeding.

Jack couldn't allow the boy to be hit again. He made a quick step into the open, bringing the rifle to bear on Ben Clagg. His voice boomed in the small clearing. "Hit that boy again, Clagg, and you'll be shaking hands with the devil."

Clagg's arm froze in mid-swing. Elijah jerked away from Franklin and stood as if to run to him. "Marshal Sage!"

Jack's voice was kind, but firm. His eyes stayed on Ben Clagg, Franklin, and the laugher when he spoke. "Good to see you, boy. Sit down and stay where you are until I have these fellas thrown and hogtied." He nodded to Billy. "How are you doing, young fella?"

Billy gave him a lopsided grin. "I've been better, Marshal."

Jack admired the boy's grit and grinned at him. "Reckon you have, but all that is in the past. Why don't you back off and have a seat."

Billy nodded and backed away from Clagg, whose arm was still in the air.

Ben Clagg slowly turned toward Jack and began lowering his arm. "You must be the famous Marshal Jack Sage."

Jack motioned Clagg back toward the laugher. "And you're the rat-faced killer and brother of those worthless Claggs who're going to hang."

Clagg's ears turned red, and his eyes pinched together. He pointed to Elijah. "If he don't testify, they don't hang, and there ain't but one of you."

Jack smiled, but it didn't reach his cold gray eyes. "Benny, boy, you've got two options. One will keep you alive for a while." He took a quick look at each man. "Drop your guns or start shooting, because if I don't see sixguns hitting the ground, it'll be me shooting."

Clagg sneered. "You cain't do that. You're a federal marshal."

Jack gave a short laugh. Holding his rifle like a sixgun, he pulled his coat back with his left hand, exposing the spot where his badge normally hung. "Wrong again, Clagg. I quit before I left Fort Smith. I'm making a citizen's arrest." He dropped his coat back in place. "Now make your move."

Franklin was the first to respond. He moved in a slow deliberate manner, unfastening his gunbelt and tossing it in front of him. "I didn't want anyone hurt. I just wanted Elijah."

Jack glanced at Elijah's uncle. In that instant Ben Clagg made his move, and he was like a striking snake. His arm flicked, and Jack caught the blur of a knife coming for him. He fired and felt the sting of the knife blade entering his chest. His hand was a blur slamming the lever of the Winchester down and forward, ejecting the fired and useless case while cocking the hammer. It had no sooner reached its forward limits than he was ramming the lever back up, slamming a live and deadly round into the chamber.

He registered Clagg falling and the laugher, the man who had suggested Clagg kill Billy, going for his gun. Jack knew he was probably dying from the knife in his chest, but not before he sent this worthless scum to lead the way. Pointing the rifle like a sixgun, he fired. The bullet struck the man in his left breast pocket, stretching him out. The laugher's hand opened, allowing his revolver to fall free. Jack had slammed another cartridge in the chamber and swung the rifle on Franklin.

Elijah's uncle threw his hands in the air. "Don't shoot. Don't shoot. I'm not armed."

Jack looked back to Clagg, who was on his back, his wound pouring blood. He walked to the man's side, bent, and pulled the killer's sixgun from its holster, sliding it behind his belt.

Clagg lay on the ground, staring at the knife sticking out of Jack's chest, and gasped. "Why ain't you dead?"

That's a good question, Jack thought. He had felt the blade cut with his motion of retrieving the revolver from the ground. With his left hand, he reached for the knife to carefully pull it from his chest. When he began, he noticed it was protruding much farther than he had expected. He felt the sting of the knife coming out of his chest, but it was like any cut, not a death-dealing stab wound. Once it was out of his flesh, something seemed to grip it, hampering the knife's movement. Giving the knife a harder yank, it slipped through his coat and was free in his hand. He bent down to Clagg and wiped the knife off on the dying man's coat.

Jack examined it, double-edged and as sharp as any straight razor. He laid the knife on the ground and lifted Clagg's left sleeve. There the throwing holster lay, waiting to surprise some unknowing cowhand who was waiting for Clagg to draw with his right hand. Releasing Clagg, Jack opened his own coat again. It was a heavy coat, and the blade had had to make it through the thick wool, but that alone wouldn't stop it. The vest was leather. That would help, but with the coat and vest, the blade's penetration should still have been fatal.

Jack reached into his vest and smiled. From his inside vest pocket, he removed his tally book. The thick engraved leather cover he had bought in El Paso from a Mexican vendor, combined with the fact the tally book must have a hundred pages, had all worked together to slow the knife. And after battling to penetrate those items, it finally had to go through the back of the vest, his shirt, and his long johns. He slid the tally book back into his vest pocket and pulled his collar and the neck of his long johns away from his chest, allowing him to see the wound. From the size and amount of blood, Jack estimated it had penetrated no more than half an inch. He smiled. Like he'd always known, he was a lucky man.

He dropped his collar back in place, glanced at the laugher, who had headed on to his just rewards, and back at Clagg. He grinned and held up his tally book. "Guess my luck is better than yours, Mr. Knife Man."

Clagg saw the book and realized what had happened. The dying man began cursing. He stopped long enough to say, "I should have put it in your guts."

Jack, feeling little remorse, knelt beside the dying killer. "Clagg, you're dying. I wouldn't meet my maker with those kinds of words or wishes on my lips. I've got a feeling things aren't going to go too well for you when you get there."

Clagg started cursing again.

Jack shook his head. "You've got young ears around here. They don't need to hear that kind of trash." He grabbed the man's head with a big hand and held it still while the other pulled the bandanna up from around the scrawny man's neck and shoved it far enough into his mouth to make anything he said unintelligible.

Clagg tried to bite him.

Jack jerked his hand away, fighting the temptation to slap the man silly. He was already dying, but the desire was strong. He stood, moved over to the laugher's revolver, shoved it back into the holster, and dogged it down. Then he walked over to Franklin and picked up the gunbelt. "When did you take to carrying a gun?"

Franklin frowned at him. "Figured I needed it out here."

"Do you much good?"

Sullen, Franklin said nothing.

Jack ignored him and motioned Elijah toward Billy. "Go on over there. You don't need to sit by him ever again."

Elijah jumped up and walked with Jack back to Billy. The boy had been sitting but stood as Jack approached.

"Thanks, Marshal Sage."

Jack shook his head. "I'm just sorry you boys had to endure this." He glanced toward Clagg, who had stopped fighting the gag and was approaching the end with wide eyes and short breaths. He had stopped cursing.

"Why was he so tough on you, Billy?" But he was thinking, *Why did he keep you alive so long?*

19

Elijah spoke up. "He was really bad to Billy, but Billy stood up to him the whole time."

Jack watched Elijah beaming at his older friend, and smiled inwardly. *I think Elijah may have found himself a home, if they'll have him.*

Of a sudden, Ben Clagg, through his gag, set up a muted wail.

Jack turned to see the man's eyes open wide, staring at the sky, almost like he was staring through it. His mouth was wide, and the wail had turned into a single word, no, drawn out in a long pleading tone. It lasted at least half a minute, then every muscle in Clagg's body released, and he slumped against the ground in silence.

Jack stepped to the killer's side and gazed down at him. Clagg had looked small when he was alive, but now he looked even smaller. His face was frozen with his last expression, eyes open so wide they were almost bulging and mouth distorted in his final no, the bandanna limp across it. Jack lifted the man's upper body high enough to get his coat off and threw it across the frightening face. He did the same for the laugher. He didn't want the kids to have to stare at the gruesome visions. Once they were covered, he glanced at Franklin, who looked like he had seen a ghost. From the laugher's saddle, Jack took a piggin' string and walked to Elijah's uncle. "Stand up."

The man stood. "You don't need to tie me up. I ain't gonna run."

Jack said nothing until he finished, then pointed to the ground. "Sit."

Once Franklin was secured and sitting, Jack went back to the boys and squatted down in front of them. "Now, Billy, tell me why Clagg was so mean to you."

Billy had been staring at the dead man who had emitted such an awful sound. He looked at Jack, his trancelike state broken, and gave him a lopsided grin. "Coffee."

The boy was obviously waiting for his question. "Coffee, what?"

"I poured hot coffee on his hand when I was refilling his cup, and he claimed I did it on purpose."

Jack caught the small flash of anger from the boy. "Did you?"

Billy straightened and said defensively, "Yes, sir. Mr. Clagg was saying bad things about my mom, and I happened to have a full pot of hot coffee handy. I just naturally missed the cup and poured it on his hand." This time he grinned. "You ain't never seen anybody jump around and cuss like he did. It was a sight to see. The dining room was full, and all those men, when they figured out what had happened, laughed like crazy. He shouldn't have said those things about my mama."

Picturing the event in his mind, Jack couldn't help but grin. He gripped Billy's shoulder. "His comments gave you no option. Was I your age, I hope I would've done the same thing." Jack paused at the grin on Billy's face. "But having said that, you've got to be careful about making such decisions. Hot coffee, or hot anything, can be dangerous. You best not let that happen to you again."

Billy's shoulders slumped. "I felt kinda guilty about doing it, even to him."

"So that's why he was slapping you around?"

The left side of Billy's face was turning blue. In a couple of days, he would be sporting a myriad of colors. He nodded. "Yes, sir."

"Quite a story. Now how about we head back to Fort Smith. I think you two have a couple of ladies anxiously awaiting your return. They'll be greatly relieved to see you both."

The three of them stood and began packing the gear. The boys were a big help, and Jack soon had the two dead men tied on one horse, and the horse's saddle on Thunder. It wasn't a fit, but this would be a short day and a light weight. Thunder should be fine. Jack had also switched back to Pepper. This was going to be a fast trip. He'd take everyone west, on this side of the river, until reaching Fort Smith, then get a ferry across.

He walked to Franklin. "Stand up."

The man followed his command. Once erect, Jack assessed the man, considering whether he could trust him or not. Making up his mind, he addressed him again. "I don't usually do this, but if you'll give me your word you won't try to run or try anything else, I'll untie you."

"I won't do anything, I swear."

"Good enough." Jack untied the man's hands. "It wouldn't be smart to try anything."

Franklin nodded. "I saw you outside the Whiskey Barrel. You can trust me. I won't be a problem."

"Good." Jack watched Elijah put out the fire. The boy knew what he was doing. He poured the contents of the near full coffee pot over the still burning branches and then kicked dirt over everything. Jack examined it and patted the boy on his shoulder. "Good job. Now, did you two boys decide which horse you're riding?"

"Yes, sir. Billy's bigger than me, so he'll fit Thunder better'n me." He released a sudden grin. "But I reckon ain't neither one of us is gonna fit that big horse for many a year, if ever."

Jack laughed. "I bet you boys grow so big, they'll have to breed bigger horses for you."

Elijah's grin grew larger. "Maybe so, but it ain't gonna be today. Anyway, I've got Sawyer Shaw's horse. He's the one you been calling laugher. He was 'most as mean as Ben Clagg. I've got some welts on my back where he whaled me a couple of times before Uncle Franklin stepped in. He stopped him."

Interesting, Jack thought. *Franklin protected Elijah. I guess blood is thicker than water, and the laugher's name is Sawyer Shaw, another ne'er-do-well riding outside the law.*

"Alright, boys, saddle up. We're burning daylight."

JACK CHECKED his pocket watch riding into Fort Smith, three o'clock. They'd made good time. He rubbed his thumb over the emerald and gently closed the watch, sliding it back into his vest pocket. "Why don't you boys ride on over to your place. I think you'll be a nice surprise to the folks there."

Billy turned in the saddle. "Aren't you coming?"

"Not right now. I've got to take Mr. Franklin to jail, then do some checking and, I imagine, talk to the judge. Tell your folks I'll be along in a while." Jack watched the two boys gallop ahead.

Entering town, people gathered around him and the dead men. They immediately began asking questions.

"Are the boys alright?"

"Marshal, did you kill both these fellers?"

"Is that Ben Clagg?"

With the last question, there was a gasp from the crowd.

Jack turned to the questioner. "Yes, sir, that is the late Mr. Ben Clagg. When I caught up with him, he was beating Billy Blakely and didn't much want me interfering."

Another man in the crowd shouted, "Good riddance. I reckon he don't much like where he is right now, either."

Low laughter sifted through the crowd as they followed him through town.

Jack pulled up at the marshal's office, with the crowd still growing. Buck Walker stepped out, hands on his hips and a big grin on his face. "Been a little busy, Jack?"

"Long day, Buck. Mr. Franklin here is going to need a room."

"Isn't he Elijah's uncle?"

"Yep, he is." He threw a thumb toward the corpses. "How about sending someone to get the undertaker, then have someone else take these horses to Pauly's. They'll need to pick up Thunder and the other horse at Ma's. Special treatment for both Thunder and Pepper. They've earned it. These other fine animals probably wouldn't mind Pauly's attention, either."

"Sure, Jack." Buck stepped back into the office, said a few words, and three other deputy marshals followed him outside. One took off down the street, and the other two stood ready to take the horses. Jack knew all three of them and nodded an acknowledgment, saying, "Much obliged." Swinging down from Thunder, his leg almost gave way. The old gunshot wound was acting up again. He stood for a moment, allowing time for the stiffness to subside, then watched the people still gathering, and looked at Buck.

A couple of men walked right up to the bodies and lifted the heads by their hair. One of them spoke up. "Ben Clagg for sure, but last I heard, this feller, don't recollect his name, was up in Missouri."

Buck walked to the edge of the boardwalk. "Folks!" Buck shouted. Everyone quieted and turned to face him. "I know you're interested in what happens around your town, and you've got every right to know. However, we've got a job to do."

The crowd began to disperse. Many of the people patted Jack on the back as they walked by.

Buck continued, "The newspaper will be printing everything we know, because you know that crazy editor never saw a question he didn't like."

A soft chuckle drifted through the disappearing crowd. Jack turned to Buck as he approached. "Who's the crazy editor? He might not take too kindly to your comment."

"It don't matter. I've been telling him he's crazy ever since he was a kid. He's my brother."

"It's good you have someone smart in your family."

Buck frowned. "I could take offense to that there comment. Anyway, he can't rope."

With the mention of roping, Jack changed the subject. "So where's the marshal?"

"Where you'd expect. Off chasing this bunch. Don't know how long they'll be gone. If they're not back real soon, I imagine a riverboat will see 'em and pass on the news."

"Where's the judge?"

"In court." His eyebrows rose. "Mighty put out at you."

Jack said nothing. There were a few folks still standing around, and he felt sure anything he said would eventually make it back to the judge. There was no sense roiling the water any more than he had already.

Franklin swung down, and Jack pulled his saddlebags and bedroll from Pepper. He rubbed the animal's neck several times. He hadn't been called on to put out the effort Thunder had, but Jack knew Pepper would rise to the call just as the gray horse had. The chestnut nuzzled at Jack's coat. "Sorry, boy, the larder is dry today." He gave him a pat, motioned Franklin to follow Buck, and brought up the rear. The past twenty-four hours were catching up with him.

Having secured Franklin in the holding cells of the office and completed a two-page report for the marshal and, he speculated, probably the judge, Jack stepped from the office. He glanced at the courthouse, considered it only for a moment, and voted the choice down. He headed for Ma's place. He was too tired to take on the judge. Passing the new telegraph office, a familiar voice called from the open door.

"Jack, I need to talk to you." It was Carter Schofield. Along with the judge, Carter rated pretty high on his list of people he didn't feel like talking to, at least until he rested his tired body.

Never breaking a step, Jack glanced Carter's way. "Not now, Carter. I need some sleep."

He figured it must have been his tone, for Carter was not a man who took rejection easily. The liaison from the president waved, said, "When you can," and stepped back into the office. Jack was tired, but he would never get so tired not to realize that wasn't like Carter. He shrugged and continued for Ma's.

Approaching, he was pleased to see Thunder and the other horse were no longer tied in front of Ma's. The deputies had picked them up along with the others, and now the horses were relaxing and being treated like kings. He was smiling at the thought when the front door to Ma's place flew open, and Ma herself came running out, straight for him, closely followed by Grace.

Both women's eyes were red and puffy. Ma charged him, enveloping him in a bear hug. When she stepped back, her eyes were full again and leaking down her cheeks. "Oh, Jack, boy. We are so thankful for you bringing our boys back and your miraculous delivery from the very maws of death."

A little dramatic, Jack thought, *but women can be dramatic when the need arises.* He patted her on her ample back. "I don't know about the maws of death, Mary, but like I always say, I'm a mighty lucky fella."

She wouldn't be deterred. Stepping back, Mary looked up at the tall man. "You have been the hand of God dealing vengeance on the evil and delivering our Billy and Elijah back to us. Don't downplay your deliverance, young man."

Jack smiled. "Reckon I'm just glad the boys are safe and I'm here."

Grace was standing behind Mary. "Mama?"

Mary stepped to the side. "Of course, child."

Grace moved forward and, slipping her hands under his arms, wrapped her arms around his muscular body. Her squeeze was much less hard than her mother's but much more intense. He held her for a long moment, inhaling her familiar scent, before relaxing his arms. She stepped back, and her brilliant green eyes gazed into his, as if touching his soul. "Thank you for saving our boys. You are such a . . ." She searched for the perfect word.

He completed her sentence. ". . . tired man."

Surprise replaced the intensely grateful, and maybe more, look. Her eyes examined him closely. "Oh, Jack, I am so sorry. You look like you could drop in your tracks."

"I think I've got enough steam remaining to make it to my room. Figure I'll sleep for about a week."

Mary took his saddlebags and Grace his bedroll, and each grabbed an arm. Mary gave his thick arm a squeeze. "A week it is, then."

They led him into the boardinghouse, through the parlor, and into the hallway. Here Mary fell back and allowed Grace to help Jack navigate. Reaching his door, she pushed it open and led him in. "Is there anything we can do for you, Jack?"

He gave his head a single shake. "Nope, this bed is going to provide everything I need."

He thought it funny that her cheeks turned a little pinker.

Mary spoke up. "We'll leave you to your dreams, boy. May they be good ones." She held the door for her daughter and, following her out, closed it softly.

Jack heard a key turn in the lock, and smiled. His voice rumbled softly while he lifted a leg to remove a boot. "I wasn't so tired I needed their help, but only a fool would've turned down the help of two fine women." He worked one boot off and stood to brace his foot against the other heel, slowly prying the boot from his foot. Once his foot was past the throat, he sat back on the bed, crossed his leg, and slowly pulled the tall boot from his foot. Jack Sage never heard the boot hit the floor. He fell back on the bed, legs draped over the side, and continued falling into a well-earned dreamless sleep.

THE POUNDING COMMENCED AGAIN. Jack's mind raced, trying to figure out where he was while it labored to pull him from a deep sleep. His right hand whipped up to his holster hanging on the headboard, and he yanked out a Smith & Wesson as he was sitting up. He at last realized it was someone hammering on his door, and he had just gotten to sleep. His anger growing, he stood, seeing his image in the full-length mirror on the armoire. It shocked him. He was barefooted and in his long johns. He could've sworn when he went to bed he had all of his clothes on except his boots.

The hammering on his door began again. His voice slightly lower than a carnival barker, Jack called, "Who is it?"

"Carter."

Mystified, but resigned to getting no more sleep, Jack dropped his revolver into its holster, thinking, *I don't remember hanging up my holster there either.* Jack shrugged and headed for the door. Carter stood there dressed in a white shirt, a floral cravat with a gold stick pin, and a black frock coat, wearing a ton of frustration. Jack scanned him from head to toe. "You're either going to a wedding or a funeral, and why the blue blazes are you hammering on my door? I'm trying to get some sleep."

"Oh, I don't know. I just thought you might like to attend the biggest trial in Fort Smith history. It's Monday, the Claggs are on trial, and Elijah will be going over to testify in an hour. You think you might want to escort him?"

Jack's mind processed Carter Schofield's information. "Come in, Carter, and close the door." He spun around to see fresh clothes laid out, shined boots, and his gray Stetson brushed and looking almost like new. On the dresser was a pitcher, a basin of steaming water, the shaving cup, and the straight razor, sharpened. No longer surprised at anything that happened in this house, he strode to the shaving cup and began to build the cream. "Why didn't you wake me earlier?"

While Jack applied the soap, Carter Schofield, never a man who liked his plans thwarted or delayed, placed both fists on his hips. "I'll tell you why I didn't, and it was for no lack of trying. Those two . . . ladies did everything except pull a gun on me to prevent me from waking you. They absolutely refused to allow me access to your room. I tried to slip in through the back, but they had locked the back door. Finally, this morning, they allowed me to your room, because, as Grace said"—Carter did a bad imitation of a female voice—"'they want protection for Elijah,' as if the whole marshal contingent of Fort Smith won't be enough. Furthermore, they refused Judge Bell access. He was livid. He wanted to talk to you before the trial, but they stood up to him." Though he was angry, Jack heard respect in Carter's voice.

Jack was amazed at their successful guarding of his room and thankful. Carter, a spy for Grant during the war, was adept at going anywhere he desired. To stop him was quite an accomplishment. He finished shaving, washed and dried his face, and began dressing. When he slipped on his vest, Carter tossed him something. He caught it, instantly recognizing the familiar shape and feel. "What's this?"

In his most sarcastic tone, Carter responded, "It's a badge, Jack. I thought you should be wearing it at the trial."

"I quit."

"No, you didn't. It fell off when you tried to run me over at the stables. I picked it up and am returning it to you. Do you plan on wearing it?"

He thought about it only for an instant and stabbed the piece of metal onto his vest. "I reckon so."

"Good."

Jack swung his gunbelt around his waist, buckled it, checked each weapon was fully loaded, and headed for the door. He glanced back at his frustrated companion. "You coming?"

20

Mary was in the kitchen when they entered. "Oh my, you look much better today. I must say, Saturday you looked as if you could drop right there on the boardwalk."

Jack gave her a grin. "You weren't far wrong, though it's been a long time since I slept that long. In fact, I don't think I've ever slept for almost forty hours. I would've been surprised at twenty-four hours, but forty hours, it doesn't seem possible."

Mary smiled. "You're a big man, Jack. Big men require a longer time for repair, and you're not as young as you used to be." While she spoke, she was constantly moving about the kitchen. She pointed to two seats at a counter. "You two sit. I'm sure you both could use a little breakfast and coffee."

Carter replied quickly, "Coffee would be great, ma'am, but I already ate at the hotel."

For acknowledgment, she gave him a nod.

Jack pulled up a chair and began doctoring his coffee. "Thanks, Mary. Where's Elijah?"

"Grace is getting him ready. He's nervous. He'll be happy to see you."

"How's Billy doing?"

"That poor boy. He's handling it well, but his face must be hurting like crazy. We've been using warm compresses to relieve some of the discomfort. When I think of that man slapping him that hard, I could just..."

Carter finished a sip of his coffee. "He won't be slapping anyone else, ma'am, thanks to Jack."

Mary turned a beaming face on Jack. "Thank you again, Jack. You saved our boys. We will forever be in your debt." Noticing the badge, her eyes twinkled. "Oh, I see Mr. Schofield returned the badge you dropped. Isn't that wonderful."

Jack gave her a wry grin. "I didn't realize so many people were concerned about my employment."

Suddenly, Billy and Elijah rushed into the kitchen. Seeing Jack, both boys charged over to him. Elijah gave him a big hug, while Billy, a bit older, stopped short, leaned against the counter, and grinned at Jack. Billy's face looked terrible, but he wore it like a badge.

Jack hugged Elijah and returned Billy's grin. "You boys are pretty spry this morning."

Billy spoke up. "Feeling spry, Marshal Sage." He couldn't help a slight wince from the jaw movement when he spoke. Other than the myriad of colors along the left side of his face, he looked good.

Jack picked Elijah up and set him on his knee. "How about you, son? Are you ready for this?"

The little boy didn't look afraid, but he was definitely nervous. "I think I am. I'm not real happy about sitting up there in front of all those grownups, but Judge Bell said to just try to relax and pretend all those people were in their underwear." He giggled.

Mary added her opinion. "I can't believe the judge would tell him such a thing. That's so crude."

Jack winked at the boys. "I don't know, Mary, that might be

pretty funny, and there's several who would be downright interesting."

"Jack Sage! You're not too old for someone to wash your mouth out with lye soap."

Billy spoke up. "She'll do it, too."

Her face flushed, Mary gave her grandson a loving swat, careful to stay away from his bruised face. "You best be careful or you might be included."

Carter took his last sip of coffee and set his cup down as Grace came in with Deputy Nesbit, the judge's messenger, who was also a deputy marshal.

Nesbit removed his hat. "Morning, Ma." He turned to Jack and Carter. "The judge is going to be ready for you and the boy shortly. We best be going."

Jack lowered Elijah to the floor and took one last sip of his coffee. He stood and looked down at the boy.

Elijah wore a white shirt, a red tie, and gray pants. His coat was a dapper-looking dark gray wool that Grace had made for him.

Jack took the boy by his left hand. "Let's go take care of that bunch."

He gave Grace a smile as they passed. "Don't you worry, he'll be fine."

Jack saw her feeble attempt to override her concerns. She managed a worried smile and nodded as he passed.

Stepping through the door of the boardinghouse, Deputy Nesbit took the lead. Elijah followed behind Nesbitt, holding Jack's hand on his right, with Carter Schofield on his left. They made the courthouse without incident. There were three deputies outside. After climbing the steps, they passed through the tall doors and headed for the courtroom door.

Jack stopped. "Hold up," he called to the deputy ahead. Nesbit halted, swung around to see the problem, and Jack turned to

Carter. "I forgot in the rush to get here, but where is Barrett Clagg, and how did he react to Ben's death?"

"According to Marshal Berry, he was calm as a morning sunrise. He just stood there looking at Ben's body. When he turned away, he said, 'I told him that knife would get him killed.'"

Jack, now worried, asked, "Do you believe that? Not the marshal's account, but Barrett's reaction. Would you expect something different, recriminations, anger, accusations? Is that the normal way he operates?"

Carter shrugged. "I'm at a loss. I don't know him any better than you do, probably less."

Nesbit stepped closer. "If you don't mind me putting in my two cents, it's not like him at all. I wouldn't call him high-strung, but he's definitely got a temper. He's not one to mess with."

Jack nodded. "That was my take, but I only met him once. I can't picture Ben doing anything Barrett isn't at least aware of. I think the whole thing was planned by Barrett, and from what I've heard, the two brothers were close." Jack had another thought. "What about Franklin? I feel sure he knows something. Has anyone questioned him?"

Nesbit shook his head. "The judge said to wait until after this trial and these executions are done."

"Where do you have him housed?"

"I'm pretty sure they moved him to the main jail. The judge says no one gets preferred treatment."

The statement stunned Jack. "You need to get him out of there, now. Move him to the holding jail in the marshal's office, where he can be watched. If he knows anything, Barrett Clagg will have him killed, if he hasn't already." Jack looked down at little Elijah. There was no way he could leave him. He stewed on the thought only a moment. "Carter, go with Nesbit and get over to the jail. It may be too late, but with all of the deputies pulled out for this trial, now would be the time to kill Franklin. I've got to be here."

"Way ahead of you." Carter headed for the door. "Come on, Deputy, we've got to save a life."

The deputy had to run to catch up with Carter, for he had already disappeared out the door, at a dead run for the jail.

Elijah had been looking at the pictures in several of the big display cabinets and missed most of the conversation.

Jack called him over, and the two of them stood outside the tall doors to the courtroom. Jack offered his left hand, and the little boy took it. The sweat on the little hand made it feel clammy. "Try not to worry. This will be over soon. You ready?"

Elijah nodded. Jack saw his little chest rise and slowly expel a long sigh. He reached for the door and opened it.

BARRETT CLAGG HAD BROUGHT in a well-known Little Rock attorney for his brothers' defense. The man was finished before he started. The trial was cut and dried. Milo, Flint, and Bo Clagg had been found guilty without the jury leaving the courtroom. The jurors looked at each other, nodded, told the bailiff, and announced the verdict. Elijah's simple but strong story, told in a child's honesty, had the ladies in the courtroom in tears, especially the part about the killing of his mother and baby brother.

Judge Bell sentenced the Claggs to death by hanging Tuesday morning, which was the next day. At the last bang of the gavel, Jack instantly picked up Elijah and carried him through the mass of excited people. Flint Clagg yelled, "You're a dead man, Sage." He hoped the boy hadn't heard it. They made their way through the press of people, who separated like the Red Sea for Jack and the boy, until, finally, the two of them were outside and clear of the bedlam. Before Jack could let the boy down, Elijah turned in his arms and gazed at him with those sincere brown eyes. "Are they going to hang those men, Marshal Sage?"

"Yes, Elijah, they are going to hang them for all the evil they did."

The boy thought about it for a moment and matter-of-factly stated, "I think that's a good thing."

Jack nodded. "Yeah, son, that's a very good thing. You ever see a mad dog?"

Elijah shook his head. "No, but Pa explained to me, if I saw one, to run."

"That's a good rule. They're sick and dying. If they bite a person, that person will also die. When a dog gets the sickness, he'll bite anything that gets in front of him, doesn't matter what it is."

"Would he bite his ma?"

Jack nodded. "Yes, he would. Anything and anyone. That's why he has to be killed, and that's why those three Clagg brothers have to be hanged. If they were released, they wouldn't change, they'd just go on killing other people until they were stopped. That's what the government is doing right now, stopping them."

Elijah thought about it and gave a little nod, indicating all of his questions were answered. "Can we go home? I'm hungry."

Jack set the boy down. "That's a great idea." The two of them headed for Ma's.

Halfway there, Billy came running up. "Come on, Elijah, help me with the cow."

Elijah looked to Jack.

"Get changed first. We'll all be in trouble if you get those clothes dirty."

He watched the two boys race toward their house, shaking his head. *Kids are resilient,* he thought, and watched them until they disappeared into the boardinghouse. Once they were gone, he turned for the marshal's office.

Buck was leaning against a post, whittling a splinter to make a toothpick. He looked up at Jack. "Nice testimony, Jack, but it was the boy who hanged 'em."

Jack winced inwardly at the statement. Elijah didn't need that responsibility. "That may be true, Buck. He had a powerful testimony, but let's not get that kind of thing started. I don't want him having to carry that, and I don't want any extended Clagg family member searching for him."

Buck stopped whittling. "Dang, you're right. Sorry, you won't hear that cross my lips again."

Jack slapped him on the shoulder. "Thanks. Have you seen the new government man around?"

"You mean Carter? Sure, he's inside with the marshal and some of the boys and Mr. Franklin."

Jack entered the office and looked around. Berry, behind his desk, saw him and spoke up. "Franklin's in the back, alone."

Jack nodded. "Windows?"

Carter looked at Berry, who jumped to his feet. He hadn't locked the main door to the cells and disregarded the keys, yanking the door open. Before the door opened wide enough to enter, a gunshot rang out, then a second one.

As every man in the office poured into the jail area, Jack spun and charged through the front door, yelling at Buck, "Come on."

His revolver had leaped into his hand at the shot and was ready for action when he slid to a stop at the back corner of the jail. No one. Buck joined him. Both could see the low tree limbs still moving from being brushed by a human body, probably at a run. Jack walked to the back window, where an upside-down wooden box sat. Because of his height, he didn't need the box, but the last thing he was going to do was look through that window. There were too many high-strung gunhands in there for his comfort. He called, "Is he dead?"

Berry, dejection in his voice, answered, "Yeah. He's got two holes in his chest. The shooter was serious."

Disgusted, Jack turned back for the front of the building.

Buck stood in place. "Aren't we gonna chase that bushwhacker?"

Jack continued walking. "Maybe, but that decision is up to your boss. You can bet whoever that was had his horse waiting and knows this country. The men who go after him need to be ready for a long chase, not just a quick romp in the woods."

Buck dropped his revolver back into its holster. "Yeah, I reckon you're right." He strode after Jack.

Jack halted to let a deputy through the door. Clearing the door, he turned and began jogging.

Buck watched him for a second. "He's headed for the undertaker."

Jack entered and saw Berry returning to his desk. "Did you get anything from him before he was shot?"

Berry's voice was hollow. "No, he kept saying he wasn't involved. He just wanted to get the boy."

Jack nodded. "Has anyone checked on Barrett?"

"His office is locked, and he's gone, withdrew all of his money from the bank. He had quite a bit."

"Has anyone checked the depot?"

Berry shook his head. "Not yet. I'll send Buck over there."

In all the excitement this morning, Jack had forgotten about Zeb Long. "You know how Zeb is doing?"

Berry smiled at the question. "I can at least give you one positive answer. I talked to the doc before the trial, and he said as long as there ain't any infections, he's gonna be good as new."

"Good. That boy didn't deserve what he got. I'm mighty glad to hear that news. He say when Zeb might be ready to travel?"

Berry gave Jack an inquisitive look. "Said it would probably be about five, maybe six weeks, but he'll be up and around in a week or so."

Jack contemplated the coffee pot and decided against it. "All in all, it's been a fair day. Sorry about Franklin, but a man's gotta watch the company he keeps."

Carter, Berry, and all of the deputies nodded in agreement.

Jack reached for the door.

Berry took a sip of his coffee, looked at the cup, and frowned, then rose and tossed it out the open window. "In all the excitement, I almost forgot. The judge wants you to stop by."

"Thanks." Jack pulled the door open and stepped outside to see Buck working on his toothpick. "You need to head to the depot and find out if Barrett took the train, and if he did, where the ticket was for."

Buck folded his knife and tried his toothpick. It was still too thick. He dropped the knife and the toothpick in a vest pocket and waved a hand, "See ya," and swung into the saddle.

"Adios." Jack headed for a meeting he wasn't exactly happy to attend. In fact, as he looked back over the short time he had been here, he had a hard time remembering any meeting between him and the judge that was pleasant. As far as he was concerned, the job was done. Sure, Barret Clagg was still on the loose, but he wasn't Jack's problem. Clagg belonged to Berry, along with his brothers, and with the job completed, he was beginning to feel the itch.

Crossing the street, he thought about Grace, Billy, Elijah, and Mary. He could make a home here, or anywhere he or they wanted, with the way the ranch and mine were paying. He had real feelings for Grace, but he'd had real feelings for other women, and none of the plans had worked out. Would these? Would his past reach out to touch the people he cared for? What about Elijah? He felt a real fondness for him, but no young fella should grow up with a gunfighter for a pa, and that was what he was. Yeah, he wore a badge, but was he too good with his tools? He had to think about it, think about it hard and fast.

His boot heel hit the boardwalk, bringing him back to the here and now.

A feminine voice called, "Jack."

He turned to see Grace walking rapidly toward him, and touched his Stetson. "Morning, Grace, I didn't have much chance to speak to you this morning."

Her face carried a look of concern, though even with the burden, it was beautiful, framed with her striking black hair glistening in the sun. "What was the shooting? Are you alright?"

"I'm fine. Nobody shooting at me. It was Franklin, Elijah's uncle. Somebody shot him through his cell window. He's dead."

Grace shook her head. "Poor Elijah, he's losing all of his relatives. That bears on why I wanted to talk to you. Are you going up to see the judge?"

"I am. Would you like to accompany me?"

She shook her head in quick small movements. "Goodness, no, I don't want to bother the busy man, but would you ask him a question for me?"

"Sure, I'd be glad to." Jack could see she was uneasy.

Grace paused for another moment. "Well, I've been talking to Mama, and I think we should adopt Elijah. He doesn't have to take our name." Flustered, she continued, "I don't mean I wouldn't like him to." She paused again. "What I mean is that he can have whichever name he prefers, but I love that little boy. It just breaks my heart at what he's been through, and Mama agrees. We don't have much, but we have enough, and I feel sure he'll be happy with us. You should see how he loves playing and working with Billy. They've already formed a strong bond. We—"

Jack placed his big hand on her arm. "You don't have to explain it to me, Grace. I've seen how he is with Billy, and you and Mary. I think he would be lucky to have the three of you. He'll fit right in, and I'll be glad to pass your request on to the judge."

He could see relief wash over her. The sunlight made visible a touch of gray invading the thick black hair. He thought, *It only makes her more beautiful.* Resenting having to leave, but knowing he must, Jack said, "I've got to get up there, or the judge and I won't be doing anything but having another one of our arguments."

She smiled, bringing radiance to him, and two passing gentlemen, and moved her arm back so that his hand dropped in hers.

She gave his hand a squeeze. "Oh, Jack, yes. You need to go on up. Thank you. Thank you so much. You have been so good for all of us." Her cheeks brightened slightly, and she turned toward her house. Her shoes clicked against the planks, setting off a staccato rhythm.

Jack, still surrounded with her scent, watched her departure. His eyes followed the tall beauty, who captivated him with her straight shoulders, slim waist, and swaying hips. His mind remained on her as he turned and headed up the courthouse stairs.

21

Deputy Nesbit was sitting at the desk outside the judge's office. Seeing Jack, he jumped up and began to speak when Judge Bell rushed from his office. "What was that shooting at the jail?"

Jack removed his hat. He was determined to stay on safe ground with the judge today or at least not be the one who started anything. "Mr. Franklin, Elijah Franklin's uncle, was murdered."

The judge's eyes narrowed, and his chin thrust out. "In my town? By whom?"

Jack gave a single shake of his head. "No idea. The shooter got away."

Judge Bell took a short step toward Jack. "With the number of deputies I employ, how could that happen?"

Jack took a deep breath. This was a winding trail of questions that could go on for hours. He had no desire to become involved in it. "Judge Bell, with all due respect, this is Marshal Berry's jurisdiction. He already has a posse after the shooter, and I'm sure he can give you much more succinct answers on the situation than I could."

The judge's frown deepened momentarily, then softened. "You're right, Jack. This isn't your bailiwick. How's little Elijah? That was a good job he did today. He's a brave young man, and you can tell him I said so."

Jack smiled at the thought of Elijah beaming from the compliment from the great man, Judge Bell. "Thanks, Judge, he'll like that. In fact, it's him I wanted to discuss."

The judge took Jack's arm and led him into his office, indicating the couch, while he moved to his chair behind his huge desk. "Have a seat, Jack, and tell me what you have in mind."

Jack leaned back on the couch and laid his Stetson beside him. "Judge, I understand what you were telling me the other day about adult relatives having priority over the wishes of others when it comes to children. However, I believe you understand what a fine young man Elijah is, and he has a very good head on his shoulders."

"Yes, I believe he does. His testimony was instrumental in convicting the Claggs. I am very proud of him."

Jack winced at the mention of Elijah being instrumental in convicting the Claggs. He leaned forward, placed his elbows on his knees, and brought his hands together. "Judge, I know you have seen and convicted a lot of bad men. But over the years I have been associated with them up close and personal. Please don't be offended at what I have to say, but any compliments for Elijah need to be silenced before they're uttered. They can't get out to the general public, or the wrong folks will hear them. I don't know what kind of extended family the Claggs might have." He pointed toward the jail. "If they have any, and if those folks are anything like the ones across the street, they won't hesitate to kill Elijah, and throw in Billy, Grace, and Mary for fun."

The judge leaned forward while Jack talked, nodding. "I agree. I'll put out a note to remind everyone to choose another case to talk about. That boy needs no more problems. Now what else?"

Jack was suspicious. The judge was being much too agreeable. "I'm going to say it outright. Grace wants to adopt Elijah. He gets along well with all of them, especially Billy."

Jack shut up. He knew more talking would either irritate Bell or be a distraction. Either might lead to an argument.

The judge sat silent. He leaned back in his large leather office chair, elbows on the padded arms and fingers intertwined, with his pointer fingers steepled. He stared at the ceiling for a few minutes, then asked, "What would you like to happen, Jack?"

The question surprised him. What would he like to happen? He knew Grace was and would be a good mother, but it wasn't his decision, so what he'd like didn't matter, but the judge had asked the question. "Judge, I'd like to see Grace adopt the boy."

The judge nodded, still leaned back in his chair, staring at the ceiling. "What about the Franklin family members?"

"In our last conversation, you said the family had all the rights, so Elijah had no choice but to go with them. However, after the harsh treatment they provided his family in Knoxville, and his uncle's recent actions, Elijah is vehemently opposed to going back to them, now or ever."

Judge Bell nodded again, moving past the question. "Would he like to be adopted by Grace?"

Jack shook his head. "No one has talked to him yet. They don't want to get his hopes up, but I guarantee you, he loves it there. He loves working with Billy, and he likes interacting with the guests."

The judge smiled. "I know. I've been over several times for lunch. When he brings out a plate, he always respectfully addresses the guest he's serving by name and asks a question of him. He's quite a little front man."

The judge continued questioning Jack about Elijah, how he was doing, his relationship with the family, was he sleeping well, and finally came back to the question he had asked Jack earlier. This time he leaned forward, forearms on the table, and hands together. "So tell me, Jack, what would make you happy?"

Having come back to the earlier question, Jack was highly suspicious. What was the judge up to? He said straight out, "Judge, I have the uneasy feeling you are trying to handle me, but I don't know why."

Judge Bell smiled. "In the president's correspondence, he has warned me several times to not underestimate you. He says you have a very active mind, and you are extremely perceptive. I must say, it appears he is correct."

Jack said nothing. He had no use for frivolous compliments.

"He also said you don't take compliments well."

Jack said nothing.

"There is a gunfighter..."

Jack leaned back and looked up at the ceiling. Thoughts flashed through his mind. *I don't want another job. I planned on quitting the next time I see Carter, but now the judge is asking me to head out again, and somehow this will be tied to Grace adopting Elijah. He's going to trap me, sure as shooting.* He lowered his head, and his cold gray eyes focused on Bell. "I suppose you're going to tell me you'll set up the adoption if I take the job."

"I will admit, I was tempted to use such persuasion, but that would be extortion, and I refuse to become like the men I prosecute. No, I will need to speak to Elijah. After I have spoken to him, and he confirms his desire to join the Blakely family, then I will proceed. Normally, I would send this to a local attorney to prepare the documents, but I will take care of it myself."

Jack was not necessarily surprised, when he thought about it. The judge had the reputation of being an honest man, almost to a fault, but he could have accomplished his request of Jack so easily. "I'll tell you, Judge. I'm pleased." He grinned. "And a little irritated also. It can be awful hard to say no to an honest man."

The judge's face remained serious. "Good. We need to get this plague of violence on the territory removed." The judge continued, "I would appreciate your attendance at the hanging in the morning. You brought them in, and the people of

Arkansas need to see you there. Wear black, look tall and tough, wear your badge on the outside, and look like a lawman."

Jack gave a nod. "I'll be there. When will you give me the information on this gunfighter?"

"Carter has it. The man's not in my jurisdiction. The hanging's tomorrow. You should probably leave as soon after that as possible, but you'll need to confirm that with Carter. You don't have a family, so that should make it easier. Can you do it?"

"I can, Judge. Like you said, I don't have a family."

Judge Bell stood and extended his hand.

Jack followed the judge's example, stood, shook the man's hand, and turned to leave.

"Good luck, Jack. See you when you return."

Jack's mind was already working. *So much to do, and so little time. First, I've got to talk to Carter.* He stepped to Nesbit's side, where the deputy was feverishly working on paperwork. "You haven't, by any chance, seen Carter, have you?"

Nesbit nodded toward a closed door at the end of the room. "He's in there. He's alone, so no need to knock."

"Thanks." He walked across the hall and pushed the door open. His liaison was sitting behind a desk, legs stretched, feet resting on the desk. His hat was over his face. At Jack's entry, he casually lifted a corner of the hat. "Talked you into it, and no yelling. He's slicker than I thought. How'd he do it?"

The only other chair in the room was at the end where Carter's feet were. Jack closed the door, with a big hand, swept Carter's feet from the desk, and sat. "You'll never know. I guess I'm leaving after the hanging. He said you have all the information."

Frowning at Jack for knocking his feet from the desk, Carter pushed his hat up and leaned over his saddlebags. He thumbed through one side until he found what he was looking for, and pulled out a thin file, tossing it across the desk to Jack. "That's it."

Jack opened the file to the picture of a smiling man dressed all in black, wearing a pair of flashy nickel-plated, pearl-handled .45-caliber Colt Peacemakers.

"Looks pleasant enough, doesn't he?" Carter asked.

Jack said nothing, reading the file.

Carter continued, "It's not in the file, but he's volatile. He's your friend one moment, and you're dead the next. Be cautious, Jack. This guy is fast. From all I've heard, he may be faster than you. My point is, don't give him a break."

"He looks big."

Carter nodded. "Yes, sir. He's taller than you and just as wide."

Taller than me, Jack thought. *That's hard to do. It means his reach is longer than mine.* He felt a touch of adrenaline flow in anticipation. *It'll be interesting.* He stopped reading. "You need this file back?"

"Nope. You can keep it. I've got another one right here." He patted his saddlebags.

"When do you need me to leave?"

"Probably would be best if you left right after the hanging. No telling how many more innocent folks this character might kill before you catch him. By the way, he doesn't need you to bring him back here. Take him to whatever jurisdiction he's in, and give them this." Carter gave Jack an arrest warrant signed by the president.

"Looks like he really wants this guy."

"He surely does, and he can be tried in the nearest federal court. Catching and punishing this killer is important to him." Carter fastened his saddlebags. "I imagine the judge wants you to attend the hangings?"

"Yeah. Like the military, show of force." Jack stood.

"Wait. The main reason we're meeting is I have a message from the president for you."

"Well?"

"It's not written down, Jack, it's memorized. I have to think about it. Hang on."

Jack waited. He knew Carter was good at delivering messages verbatim. A handy trait for a spy.

Carter nodded and cleared his throat. "Alright, this is the president speaking, Jack. It's exactly what he said." He began. "Hello, Jack. I know you're ready to retire and use some of that income from your ranch and your gold mine, but as a friend, I'd like to ask you to stay for one more assignment."

Carter paused and filled a glass on the desk from the pitcher. He drank deeply, again gave Jack a nod, and continued, "This is similar to the case in Wyoming, but different. This man has killed several people, all in fair fights until his last victim. The young man he murdered was not a gunhand, but was destined for great things. His father a member of my cabinet, and he, along with the young man's mother, is devastated. I would like for you to bring this man to justice. We cannot have such killers riding our wonderful western country. Thank you, Jack. You are doing a wonderful job, and may God bless you." Carter nodded. "That's it."

"Thanks, Carter. Sometimes I wonder what turns men into the killers they become. I've caught quite a few, and I still don't have the answer."

Carter stood. "I think the war has a lot to do with it. Some it changes, and others it brings out the worst in. Most hate all the blood and gore, but a small few grow to like the killing."

Jack knew Carter was right, but felt uneasy. Sometimes he wondered if there was a part of him that liked the fighting, but he put it aside. He was on the right side and stopped animals like the Claggs. He'd also stop this man. He glanced out the window. The sun had slipped past its zenith, and he had much to do. "See you tomorrow, Carter."

Carter Schofield shook his head. "Nope. I'm pulling out tonight on the late stage. My job is done here. You've got all the information there is on this gunfighter, so if I don't see you before I leave, good luck and take care of yourself, but, right now, I have another conference with the judge." He thrust out his hand. "Thanks, Jack. I want you to know the president thinks very highly of you and appreciates all you do."

Jack took the hand in a firm grip. "Thanks, Carter. Take care of yourself, and I'm done when this job is over."

Carter gave him a wry grin and nodded.

JACK HAD BEEN busy throughout the remainder of the day. Grace and Elijah, in fact, the whole family weighed heavy on his mind. On the one hand, he hated to leave, but the other hand was the one that scared him. He felt a sense of anticipation, adventure, new unexplored country, and a new challenge. The thought passed through his mind. *Will I never be able to give this up until I am an old man? Will I face the prospect of sleeping in a cold bed, alone, with no laughing children around me? Is adventure and challenge my opium?* Later, another more happy thought arrived. *Or maybe this is a service I am providing for my country and its citizens, and this will be the last. Will Grace wait? Should I even ask her?*

The questions had gone on throughout the day while he prepared. That preparation had gone well. He had made time to visit the bank. While there, he withdrew a thousand dollars in cash and made additional arrangements, which amounted to opening another account and funding it. He had also offered Casey Carter, the young teller who was earning money to continue his journey west, a stake, but Casey had turned him down. He thanked Jack, but said he wouldn't feel right, and he'd make it on his own. Jack had understood and wished him luck.

Now he was sitting in the parlor of Ma's Bed and Eats, his body relaxed after a hot bath and a fine meal. Grace had cleaned and placed a new bandage over the knife wound. It was healing well. His clothes for the hanging were laid out, and he waited for the family. *Funny,* he thought, *that's the way I think of them.* Then it hit him. *That is the way I think of them.* A melancholy smile drifted across his face.

Billy burst into the parlor, looking a little bedraggled, smelling of soap, and his shirt out of his pants on one side. "All the dishes are done, Marshal. How about a story?"

Jack patted the couch beside him, and Billy spun and jumped back to land on the brocade seat.

He heard other little feet racing down the hallway, and Elijah burst into the room, his eyes searching. Billy said, "Beat you."

Elijah's happy expression began to fail. It was reenergized when Billy said, "Marshal Sage is going to tell us a story."

The younger boy's face lit, and he jumped onto Jack's knee. The sudden weight was like dropping a sixty-pound sack of flour across his knee. Jack let out a whoosh of air and collapsed against the back of the couch, arms thrown to his sides, head thrown back. There was a sudden look of concern on the boys' faces until Jack opened one eye and grinned. Both boys punched him.

"You boys forget how big you're getting, and I'm just a feeble old man."

Billy was the first to reply. "You're not *that* old, Marshal Sage. Anyway, if you have a hard time getting around, we'll help you."

Grace walked in with an additional lamp. Jack set Elijah down and stood. She was breathtaking. She wore a dress Jack had never seen. The dresses he had seen her wear were collared, plain dresses meant for everyday work. This one was nothing like those.

It was a brilliant emerald green, satin or silk gown. Which material, he didn't know, but it matched her sparkling eyes and definitely did not have a collar. The bodice was cut conservatively, but still exposed the swelling of soft white skin. Her long black hair flowed across her shoulders, creating a striking contrast. She wore a happy smile, apparently appreciative of Jack's gaze.

Billy was the first to speak, almost in a whisper. "Mama, you're beautiful."

She turned the warmth of her smile on her son. "Thank you, William. That is really sweet."

"Good boy," Jack said, and patted Billy's shoulder. His eyes never left Grace. "I agree."

"Anybody want a cookie?" Mary asked, marching into the room with a plate of her delicious oatmeal cookies.

Billy and Elijah jumped up, both speaking together. "I do, please."

"You each can have one, but when you're done, it's off to bed."

Both said, "Yes, ma'am," and took their cookie, sitting down on the couch, side by side, with Jack.

He collected grins when he tousled the hair of each boy while Grace spoke. "You wanted to speak to all of us, Jack?"

He could see the apprehension in her face.

Mary had placed the cookie plate on the coffee table in front of the couch. Mother and daughter had taken a chair on the other side of the table, facing Jack.

He leaned forward, his large form seeming somehow out of place in this domestic space. "I did. I thought we might ask Elijah an important question, and perhaps you would prefer to do it, Grace."

22

Grace's face tensed, her thick dark eyebrows pulled together almost imperceptibly, and her eyes focused on Elijah. She leaned toward the little boy, who was chewing a bite of his cookie, and her full lips spread in a caring smile. "Elijah, we all are so sorry about your family. I'm sure it feels at times like you don't belong anywhere, but I want to assure you we care about you."

Elijah had stopped chewing, and his dark eyes were focused on Grace. She continued, "If you would like, and only if this is something you want to do, I'd like to adopt you."

Elijah was the focus of all the parlor's occupants. The boy sat still, his mind obviously working. "Does that mean you'd be my mama?"

"It does, but you wouldn't have to call me that. I wouldn't want to take anything away from your own mother. Together, we could come up with something you could call me."

"Would Billy be my brother?"

Grace nodded. "He sure would. He'd be your big brother."

Elijah turned to Billy. "I ain't never had a big brother. Would you mind?"

"Shoot no. I think it'll be fun. Don't you?"

Elijah gave him a lopsided grin. "Yeah, I do."

He looked at Mary. "Does that mean you'd be my grandma?"

She gave him a wide smile. "I would, Elijah, and I would love it."

He looked up at Jack. "Do you think Mama and Papa would mind, Marshal Sage?"

Jack looked down at the brave little boy who had lost so much. "No, son, I think they'd be real happy you found such a wonderful family."

Elijah gazed into Jack's face for a long moment, as if trying to discern any hidden meaning. Then his head whipped around to Grace. "I'd like that. Then I wouldn't have to call you Miss Grace all the time. I could just call you mama. I don't think my own mama would mind atall."

"Oh, that would be so wonderful, Elijah." She opened her arms. "Could I have a hug?"

He leaped from the couch and jumped into Grace's outstretched arms. She squeezed him tight, her eyes filling with tears.

Jack watched the tenderness with which the beautiful woman embraced the lonely boy. *You're a lucky lad,* he thought, remembering his own mother, who had died so young.

Mary, her eyes glistening, said, "I don't want to miss any of that sugar. Come on over here and give me some."

Elijah slipped out of Grace's arms and ran to Mary. When Mary released him, he ran back to his seat on the couch next to Jack and plopped down. "I ain't never had a grandma."

Mary responded, "Oh, that's too bad."

"Yeah. My grandma Franklin hated us, so I never saw her."

Mary was about to respond, but Jack jumped in. "Let's don't get ahead of ourselves. Elijah still has to be interviewed by the judge to make sure this is what he wants to do."

"Oh, I do, Marshal Sage. I surely do."

Jack patted his shoulder. "I know you do, son, but the judge needs to know for sure before he draws up the legal documents. It's just a formality." He patted him again. "I'm happy for all of you, but I have more to say."

Everyone became quiet and turned again to Jack.

"I'm leaving in the morning." He was looking at Grace when he announced his departure.

Her eyes grew wide. "Must you? So soon? Your knife wound hasn't healed yet."

Jack shook his head and gave her a soft grin. "Grace, you know that isn't much more than a scratch, but yes, I've received another assignment, and I'm to leave tomorrow. It's not like chasing the Claggs. I'm just going after one man."

Grace sat with her back straight and shoulders rigid, her hands clutched together in her lap. "But it is dangerous."

Jack put the question off with a grin. "When you go after anyone, there's an element of danger."

Her voice no longer soft, she snapped, "Which you like."

Mary stood. "Come on, boys. You've finished your cookies. It is time for bed. You can tell Jack goodbye in the morning."

Elijah stood and placed his arms around Jack's neck. "Good night, Marshal Sage."

Jack gave him a tighter than normal hug. "Good night, boy. You sleep good, and I'll see you in the morning."

Billy jumped up. Jack could tell Billy didn't like the idea of him leaving, but was determined not to show it.

He nodded to Jack. "Good night, Marshal."

"Good night, Billy. See you tomorrow."

The two boys were herded off by Mary toward their bedroom. As she was leaving the parlor, Jack spoke. "Mary, could you come back when you're done? I have something to say that will also involve you."

She nodded and disappeared down the hallway.

Grace sat stiff for a few moments more, then turned to Jack.

"I'm sorry. You don't deserve that kind of response. I'm so upset with myself. Here you're leaving on a dangerous journey, and I'm thinking about me."

Jack's scarred lips spread in a grin. "That makes two of us. I'm also thinking about you."

Her shoulders dropped, and her rigid frame became soft and compliant. "Oh, Jack. What is happening to us?"

At that moment, Mary walked back in, and Jack stood. She smiled at him and looked at her daughter, then snapped a second look at Jack. "Are you sure you want me here?"

Jack smiled at the older woman. "Please, Mary, join us. I have something to say to both of you."

He pulled out a document and a small book, holding them both up. "This is something I wanted to do before I leave." He handed the paper and book to Grace.

She opened it and stared at first the paper and then the book.

He had leaned back, smiling. She finally brought her green eyes up with disbelief. "Jack, this is a deposit book on our bank in our names." She passed it to her mother and continued, "It shows an account opened for us in the amount of fifty thousand dollars."

Mary had not gotten the book opened when Grace announced the amount and the account owners. She almost dropped the paper and book, caught them and fumbled to get the book open. "My good gracious sakes alive, Jack. What is this?"

"Believe it or not, in my travels I have made a couple of very successful investments." He laughed to himself. The gold mine had been no investment. He had happened across the vein when he was scrambling to save himself from a bunch of killers. "You folks were good enough to take me and Elijah in when the young fella really needed support, and I couldn't be there. This is just to smooth out some of the bumps you might face while I'm gone. There are no strings attached. You want to spend all of it on a trip around the world, have at it. It's yours, no ties, no commitments." With his last statement, he was looking directly at Grace.

There was an exquisite silence in the room. Finally, Grace spoke. "Jack, we can't accept this. People will talk."

Jack shook his head. "No one will know."

She shot back, "The bank will."

He smiled. "Yes, the bank will, but I have already taken care of that. I explained to Mr. Gleason, if there is a single breach of confidence, I will immediately move the remainder of my money and will let the world know of his inability to maintain confidentiality." He shook his head. "I don't think you have to worry about that."

Jack watched the women attempt to process their windfall, and remained silent.

Finally Mary, who had been staring at the account book, looked up, and in finality, said, "Jack, as wonderful a gesture as this is, we cannot accept it. We have our pride."

Jack leaned forward and gave Mary an understanding smile. "Yes, you do, Mary, but let me ask, how much food can you buy with that pride? When you need work done around your place, does the carpenter ask if you have sufficient pride to cover the bill? I know your pride is important to you, but I also know pride is a tool of the devil." Jack's mind thought of the many religious statements Mary had made. Maybe this argument would get through to her. "He doesn't want you to survive, not you, nor your family. He wants everyone in his control, and he often pulls pride from his toolkit. Are you really sure you don't want to accept a gift with absolutely no strings, that will provide for your entire family and your business?"

Mary sat back in her chair, contemplating Jack and his words.

He began again. "Let me just say, this money is only money. It is a tool. Yes, it is a gift, but it is given with no expectation of any return. I know what that little boy has gone through. It is impossible for me to give him my name and protect him, but I would if

I could. Knowing the two of you are offering him a refuge gives me comfort you will never know. Let me show my gratitude with something that means nothing to me. I use it as I need it and then very little. Please, Mary, take it. It will help you provide, maybe hire someone else who can give the two of you more time with the boys, but take it in the way it was given."

Mary's eyes had filled. "Oh, Jack. You are such a special man. You can be so violent on one hand, and so kind on the other. I'm sure I could never imagine, nor would I want to, what you have been through. Please accept my apology for even mentioning pride, and yes, I think I can speak for Grace, we accept with our deepest gratitude." With a handkerchief, she dabbed at the corner of each eye and stood. "I'm an old woman who needs her rest. I'll see you two in the morning."

Jack's eyes found Grace as Mary left the parlor. She sat gazing at him.

"You never cease to surprise me, you big, handsome, extraordinary, frightening man."

Jack was uncomfortable. He started to speak, but Grace stood, causing him to spring to his feet. She moved to him, and he wrapped his arms around her, finding her head turned up to him and her full mouth waiting. Lowering his head, he pressed his lips to hers, feeling the softness and warmth. They held the kiss, enjoying each other. At last, he raised his head. "Well, hello, Mrs. Blakely."

She smiled up at him. "I wish I had done that before you gave us this money. Will you ever believe me?" The two of them separated and sat facing each other on the couch.

"Grace, I'd believe anything you did or said. You have my complete trust."

"I'm sorry I got so testy, Jack. I have to warn you, I can be a handful."

He smiled. "I'll take that as a promise, but Grace, we don't have much time, and I'll be gone a long time on this assignment. Is there a chance we might pursue this relationship? I haven't asked another woman this question for almost twenty years."

She lowered her head much like a young girl. "Yes, Jack, I'd like that."

"It could be months before I return, even a year or more."

"I'll be here. You just make sure you come back."

"I'll be back. I promise, but right now, if they aren't asleep, I owe those boys a story."

"I like stories."

He stood and extended his hand. "Then come along. You might enjoy it."

THE RISING sun had burned the morning mist away when Jack strode out of Ma's place, feeling better than he had felt in many a year, dating all the way back to Algiers. There was a spring in his step that had been missing for a long time.

All of his goodbyes had been made. It was hard to say goodbye to the boys, especially Elijah, but he would be back, and then they would have all the time they needed. He could watch them grow into men. Mary was a sweet soul of kindness and gratitude, but it was Grace who held his heart and mind. She glowed with happiness, and he reveled in it, a lovely picture to carry with him.

Now his last appointment with the Claggs was next. Not the event he'd prefer to leave on, but at least the country would be safer with the extermination of this vermin.

Nearing Pauly's, he heard the stableman humming away from inside his barn. It was a beautiful winter day in Fort Smith. The sun was out, and it was unseasonably warm, which probably meant rain. "Pauly," he called, walking into the stable. The big man was busy mucking out Smokey's stall. His head appeared around the stall's corner, nodding to Jack's string. "There they are, Marshal. Ready to go."

Jack strode to his animals, all slick, fat, and rested, wearing new shoes, and clean. They hardly looked like the emaciated animals he had ridden in with two months ago. Smokey was saddled and occasionally stomped in anticipation. He slid the cleaned Winchester into its scabbard and tossed his saddlebags, bedroll, and slicker across the grulla's back, securing them.

"Where you heading this time, Marshal?"

Jack swung into the saddle. He had settled up with Pauly the day before and had found the time to whip up another batch of cookies, which hung off the saddle horn. "West, Pauly, a long way west. The judge wants me to stop in at the hanging on my way out of town, so I'll make a quick stop and then move out. You going to it?"

He leaned the pitchfork against the wall and shook his head. "Nope, don't find any joy in seeing another man die. I've seen too much of that in my lifetime." He gathered the lead ropes for Stonewall the mule, Jack's chestnut, Pepper, and the big gray, Thunder, and handed them to Jack. "It's been fine knowing you, Marshal. When you think you'll be returning?"

"Pauly, I don't rightly know. This one could lead me a long chase, or could be fast. My crystal ball just isn't working."

Pauly stepped back, giving Jack and his crew a clear shot at the door. "Well, good hunting, and I'll see you when I see you."

"Adios." Jack rode out the door feeling good. The exhilaration and anticipation were there. It felt right to be astride Smokey, his trusty grulla, who, along with Stonewall, had been with him since before Laredo.

He turned toward the gallows, which was positioned in front of the jail. It was a portable structure, built in such a way it could be assembled and disassembled in one day, and would hold up to five people. Any more and they would have to hang them in relays. A crowd had gathered as if it were a carnival. Barkers were among the crowd, selling their wares. It was not a sight Jack enjoyed, but this was what the judge wanted, and this was what he would get.

He pulled up in front of Marshal Berry's office. He could see a number of the people pointing at him and talking among themselves, again, what the judge wanted. He dismounted, tied his animals, and opened the office door. Buck was at the desk, his feet propped across it. Seeing Jack, he started to remove his feet, but Jack shook his head and grinned. "No sense you moving out of your regular deputy position."

Buck rolled his eyes.

"How long till the hanging?"

"Marshal Berry left a few minutes ago to get the Claggs. They should be walking out anytime."

Jack stepped inside, closing the door, and walked to the potbellied stove.

"You're awful duded up."

Jack shrugged. "The judge's orders. When was this coffee made?"

Buck thought on the question. "I think it was last night sometime."

Jack put away the idea of having a cup. As he turned to go back outside, he felt a premonition touch him. He always listened to his feelings. Those soft reminders or warnings had saved him on many occasions. He removed the leather loops securing his Smith & Wesson revolvers in their holsters and lifted each weapon an inch out of its holster to ensure it was comfortably loose.

Buck, alert to Jack's moves, removed his feet from the desk and sat up. "You see trouble?"

Jack shook his head. "No trouble, just a feeling."

Buck stood, turned to the gun case, and pulled out a shotgun. He opened the action, checked the loads, and clicked it shut, then gathered a handful of shells from the drawer, dropping them into two front pockets on his vest.

"Could be nothing, Buck."

The deputy shook his head. "I've learned to pay attention when you're edgy. You heading out?"

Jack nodded, his senses alert and ready. "Keep your eyes open. If something happens, let me make the first move, and try not to hit any bystanders with that thing. I'll step out for a bit before you come out."

"Yes, sir, Marshal."

Jack felt the old feeling, which dated back to when he was a boy. The excitement and apprehension mixed with a large measure of aggression. This was what he did. He wasn't proud of it, but he knew he was good at it. He opened the door and stepped onto the boardwalk.

The crowd had grown. He picked up movement to his left. It was Berry bringing out the Claggs. Milo led the group, followed by Flint and then Bo. Each stared at the crowd as if surprised at the large turnout.

Someone shouted, "You'll pay for your sins now, boys."

Flint immediately responded, "Not because of you, Johnson, you sniveling little coward."

There were no more shouts from the crowd.

Jack kept his eyes moving, surveying everything and everyone in the crowd. Nothing. Maybe he was mistaken. Disappointment momentarily touched him, but he thought, *I should be pleased. I have a family to think of now.*

The Claggs climbed the stairs, and the hangman positioned each man where he wanted him. He was about to pull the hood over their faces when Jack felt it and turned.

There he stood, grinning, Barrett Clagg. Unlike his usual appearance, Clagg was dirty and disheveled, but there was nothing disheveled about the Colt he wore on his right hip. He had come out of the second alley in the opposite direction from the gallows and stood no more than thirty yards from Jack.

"Kill him, Barrett," Flint screamed. "Blow his guts out. Show him what a Clagg can do."

Jack calmly faced the big man. "You're making a mistake, Clagg, I promise you. Drop the gunbelt. You don't have to hang like your brothers."

"Sage, you're the reason my brothers are dying. You killed young Joey and little Ben. You've destroyed my family. Did you think I'd let you get by with it? Here's where you end your killing. I'm gonna fill you full of holes."

"Did you kill Franklin, Barrett?"

"Of course I did. That whining excuse for a man. He said he wanted the boy, but all he wanted was to take his brother's kin and work him until he dropped. He was worthless. I did you a favor. You should thank me."

Jack almost felt like thanking him, for he knew he was right. If Franklin had left it alone, the judge would have awarded him Elijah, and the poor boy would have had to live a tortured life until he was eighteen. "Last chance, Clagg. Either drop your gun or make a move. I'm getting tired of waiting."

Flint shouted again, "Do it, Barrett, do it! You always was the fastest."

A cat raced across the dusty street with a mockingbird attacking him, dive after dive. The town clock chimed eight o'clock. Time for the hanging.

Barrett made his move. Jack's right hand slashed down to his revolver, and his hand melded with the Smith's butt. Like a single unit, his shoulder, arm, hand, and weapon moved as one. He had no thought of what his revolver was doing, for it was all muscle memory. As it was rising, the hammer was being pulled back by his thumb, and his wrist was rotating, his hand moving slightly forward and leveling the barrel.

Detached, Jack watched Barrett's Colt clear the holster even as he felt the Smith & Wesson buck in his hand. The thought raced through his mind, *I told you not to draw, Barrett. They never listen.*

Barrett's Colt fired into the ground and drooped lower.

Jack held his fire, his weapon still leveled. His bullet had struck a little left and high. Barrett might survive the shooting if he stopped now.

The crowd, after scattering, had halted and was silent. They had come to see three hangings, but they were getting a bonus, a real gunfight where one and maybe both men might die. They watched, eyes fastened on the dance of death.

Barrett, maybe because of his size or his determination or his luck, remained on his feet. His Colt slowly rose toward Jack.

"Drop your gun, Barrett. I don't want to kill you."

The man gasped out from some well of strength, "I wanta kill you," and continued lifting the weapon.

Flint shouted, "You can do it, Barrett. Kill him."

The sixgun wavered, swinging toward the crowd and back to Jack. He couldn't let Barrett kill some innocent civilian. He lifted the weapon and changed his stance into the one he had used on the range years ago. This time his arm was at eye level, the revolver pointed straight at Barrett Clagg.

Jack sighted along the barrel, concentrating on his target, and squeezed the light trigger. The sixgun bucked in his hand, and Clagg screamed.

The outlaw's weapon flew from his hand, propelled by the force of the .45-caliber slug. His trigger finger accompanied the sixgun. Barrett Clagg no longer had a usable right hand. Jack had elected to shoot the weapon from the man's hand. Clagg's right hand, what was left of it, would never draw another weapon.

Jack cleared the area, broke his sixgun open, removed the two empty cases, dropped two rounds from his gunbelt into the chambers, and snapped the revolver closed. He gave one more scan of the area. Deeming it safe, he dropped the revolver into its holster, then bent and pocketed his brass.

The street was filled with Barrett's screams. There was not a whisper from the crowd. Jack strode to Barrett, who was on his back, holding his right hand with his left. Reaching him, Jack knelt. Barrett's eyes had been clinched closed, but sensing Jack's presence, they jerked open, and he stared at the lawman. "Am I dying?"

Jack felt a hand on his shoulder and looked up to see the doc. "I don't know, Clagg. The doc here will be able to tell you." He moved back, allowing the doctor to move in.

He did a quick examination of the chest wound. "It looks like you were lucky, Barrett. Marshal Sage's bullet hit a little high. You could still die, but you have a chance."

Clagg shoved his mangled right hand in the doctor's face and gasped. "What about this?"

The doctor had waved several men up with a stretcher. "Take him to my office." He turned back to Clagg. "You won't be drawing any more guns with that hand, Barrett."

The man moaned and, through gritted teeth, said to the doctor, "Laudanum."

"I'll give you some when we get you to my office."

The doctor stood and allowed the men to load the wounded man onto the stretcher. He motioned toward his office.

The men started to move away, and Clagg whispered, "Stop." When they had halted, his eyes opened again, and finding Jack, his mouth pulled down in a sneer. "You're a dead man, Sage. I'll find you, and one of these days, I'll kill you."

"I did you a favor, Clagg. Don't waste it."

Before the last words were out of his mouth, the ragged bang of three trapdoors slamming open filled the square. Jack looked toward the gallows to see the three brothers swinging on their ropes. Clagg, his face pulled into a snarl and with all the hate a man could muster, whispered, "Kill you."

Following the doc, the men with the stretcher carried the wounded and bleeding Barrett Clagg, his eyes locked on his dead brothers.

Buck stood by Jack, his head going to the gallows and the three hanging men, and back to Barrett Clagg being carried to the doc's office. "I can't believe you missed, Jack."

"I didn't. I couldn't bring myself to kill the last member of the family. I may regret it."

Buck shook his head. "No maybe about it. I know them folks, and I can promise you, if he don't die, you will. When he gets out of prison, he'll come after you."

"He won't be the first. Luck to you." Jack headed to his string, anxious to be on his way. Reaching them, he untied the three, grabbed Smokey's reins, and started to swing into the saddle. He stopped when he smelled the familiar scent of fresh bread and roses. He felt her arms slip around his waist. Swinging around, he looked into the green eyes of the woman he loved. "I hope you didn't see that. It was brutal."

She nodded. "I did see it, Jack. You gave him a chance. I'm proud of you. Never fear, my big man, I love you."

"What about the crowd?"

For his answer, she pulled his head down and gave him a long passionate kiss. "Remember that."

Gripping her shoulders, he smiled down on her. "I love you too, Grace Kathryn Blakely. That kiss will keep me warm on a cold night, and I'll be back to collect more." He released her and swung into the saddle.

Jack laid his reins against Smokey's neck, turning him west.

In the distance lightning flashed, threatening another heavy rain.

* * *

Continue your adventures with Jack Sage as he searches for an accused killer.

Book 7:
JUSTICE OF THE STAR.

AUTHOR'S NOTE

I hope you've enjoyed reading *The Loyal Star,* the sixth book in the Jack Sage Western Series.

If you have any comments, what you like or what you don't, please let me know. You can email me at: Don@DonaldLRobertson.com, or fill in the contact form on my website.

www.DonaldLRobertson.com

I'm looking forward to hearing from you.

Reviews on Amazon are also appreciated.

I look forward to sharing Book 7 of the Jack Sage Western Series, Justice of the Star, with you in the near future.

Have a terrific day.

BOOKS

A Jack Sage Western Series

STRANGER WITH A STAR
WITHOUT THE STAR
RETURN OF THE STAR
THE HANGING STAR
FIVE WOMEN AND THE STAR
THE LOYAL STAR
JUSTICE OF THE STAR

Logan Mountain Man Series
(Prequel to Logan Family Series)

SOUL OF A MOUNTAIN MAN
TRIALS OF A MOUNTAIN MAN
METTLE OF A MOUNTAIN MAN

Logan Family Series

LOGAN'S WORD
THE SAVAGE VALLEY
CALLUM'S MISSION
FORGOTTEN SEASON
TROUBLED SEASON
TORTURED SEASON

Clay Barlow - Texas Ranger Justice Series

FORTY-FOUR CALIBER JUSTICE
LAW AND JUSTICE
LONESOME JUSTICE

NOVELLAS AND SHORT STORIES

RUSTLERS IN THE SAGE
BECAUSE OF A DOG
THE OLD RANGER

Printed in Great Britain
by Amazon